More Praise for *Thicker than Blood*

"With *Thicker than Blood*, C.J. Darlington proves she's a novelist for the long haul, a strong new voice in Christian fiction. This book speaks to the heart, from the heart, about the heart. Readers will not soon forget it."

SIBELLA GIORELLO, Christy Award–winning author of *The Rivers Run Dry*

"*Thicker than Blood* explores addiction, betrayal, and the common bond of family through the eyes of two sisters, both heartbroken, both longing for restoration. You'll cheer as the sisters discover each other's heart."

MARY E. DeMUTH, author of *Daisy Chain*

"Darlington provides a fascinating peek into the world of antiquarian books, as well as a riveting glimpse of a family undone and God's powerful reach in all their lives. *Thicker than Blood* will have you turning the pages, entranced with its beautiful prose and characters who won't let you go."

JENNY B. JONES, award-winning author of *Just Between You and Me* and A Charmed Life series

"C.J. Darlington explores the bonds between sisters and beautifully portrays the hope of redeeming a past full of regrets. A colorful cast of supporting characters rounds out a first-rate first novel. I look forward to more from this promising new writer."

DEBORAH RANEY, author of *Above All Things* and the Clayburn Novels series

THICKER *than* BLOOD

THICKER
than
BLOOD

— ❧ —

C.J. DARLINGTON

TYNDALE HOUSE PUBLISHERS, INC.
CAROL STREAM, ILLINOIS

Visit Tyndale's exciting Web site at www.tyndale.com.

Visit C.J. Darlington's Web site at www.cjdarlington.com.

TYNDALE and Tyndale's quill logo are registered trademarks of Tyndale House Publishers, Inc.

Thicker than Blood

Designed by Jennifer Ghionzoli

Edited by Lorie Popp

Library of Congress Cataloging-in-Publication Data

Darlington, C. J.
  Thicker than blood / C.J. Darlington.
    p. cm.
  ISBN 978-1-4143-3448-6 (pbk.)
  1. Sisters—Fiction. I. Title.
  PS3604.A747T47 2009
  813'.6—dc22   2009027310

Printed in the United States of America

15   14   13   12   11   10
 7   6   5   4   3   2

For Mom

My friend, encourager, and first editor.

I love you so much, squeeze, and I love you.

Acknowledgments

My deepest gratitude to God, my Savior, for making my dreams come true. You chose to place me in a family that nurtured my writing aspirations, and for that I'm eternally grateful.

Mom—what can I say? My characters would still be singing "How Great Thou Art" if it weren't for you! Your red pen has made this book ten times stronger. Thank you for helping me grow as a writer and a person.

Papa—for showing me that love truly is thicker than blood. I always look forward to giving you my stories to read. You have terrific insights, and I have many fun memories of you reading my stories out loud.

Tracy—my sister and best friend. I'm so glad our relationship is nothing like May and Christy's! Thanks for always being interested and letting me ramble on and on about my writing.

James Scott Bell—my writing mentor. Your encouragement and advice have meant so much to me. Thanks for giving so freely of your time to a newbie.

Jerry B. Jenkins—if it weren't for you and the Christian Writers Guild, *Thicker than Blood* would be sitting in a drawer. It means everything to me that you saw merit in this story.

The Christian Writers Guild staff—Andy Scheer, John Perrodin, Kerma Murray, Diana Holstine, Paul Finch, Janice Mitchell, Julie Adams, and Les Stobbe—your hard work and dedication have given so many writers hope and purpose. Me included.

Jan Stob—frankly, I don't know how you do it. Thanks for your tireless dedication to Christian fiction and to *Thicker than Blood*. I'm thrilled you're my editor.

Karen Watson—for such a warm welcome into the Tyndale family.

Lorie Popp—I truly appreciate your kind, thoughtful edits. You have made this experience painless, and this book is so much better because of you.

Jennifer Ghionzoli—for the coolest book cover ever!

The Tyndale marketing, sales, and publicity teams—thank you so much for everything you've done to spread the word about this novel.

Sibella Giorello—for encouraging me when I doubted my writing calling. I hope to write half as well as you someday.

Lori Fox—for screaming out loud at work when you heard I won Operation First Novel. You are true blue, dear friend. I am very glad to have you in my life.

Sergeant Kerry Nye of the Lititz Borough Police Department—for walking me through a DUI traffic stop. Any mistakes are mine.

Rel Mollet, Sheryl Root, Katie Hart, and Deena Peterson—for

reading and commenting on early chapters of *Thicker than Blood*. Thank you, ladies.

Jennifer Erin Valent—for traveling the road before me. Your spiritual support has challenged me at all the right times. Thanks for praying.

Travis Thrasher—for so graciously answering all my many publishing questions.

Baldwin's Book Barn in West Chester, Pennsylvania—for giving me my first book-scouting experiences. I based all the good parts of my fictional bookstore on your store.

Tom Doherty, manager of Baldwin's Book Barn—for teaching me the points of a first edition *For Whom the Bell Tolls* by Ernest Hemingway. Thank you for taking the time.

Erica Nantais—our childhood games inspired this story. I hope someday we'll meet again and that you'll get to read this book.

1

CHRISTY WILLIAMS DIDN'T see the cop until his red lights flashed in her rearview mirror. By then it was too late. He was tailing her, and she had no choice but to ease her Honda Accord onto the snowy shoulder of the freeway and let the cruiser slide in behind.

Jerking up the emergency brake, she threw herself back into her seat with a curse. She hadn't been speeding. She was sure of it. Christy forced herself to focus on the cruiser, squinting to see past its blinding headlights. She could barely make out the cop's silhouette behind the wheel. What was he doing?

At last the burly officer emerged from the patrol car, approaching slowly, his hand resting on his holster.

Christy put down her window, and a blast of frigid night air hit her face and rolled across her lap.

"Turn the car off, ma'am."

She did.

"I need your license, registration, and proof of insurance."

"What'd I do?" She fumbled for the items, then handed them to the cop. The name tag opposite his badge read *T. Jones*.

Jones glanced at them with a smirk. He gave one back. "License. Not grocery card."

Christy flushed as she flipped through her wallet again. *Real smooth.* She finally found her license and passed it to the cop. He took it with the other cards to his patrol car. What was this all about? Had she been swerving? She quickly crunched down on two fresh squares of peppermint Dentyne Ice. *Deep breath now. Chew. It's just a routine stop. My taillight's probably out. No need to panic. He doesn't know.*

Without the engine on, the car turned cold fast. Christy zipped up her fleece jacket and checked the cop again. After a minute his door opened, and her pulse kicked up a notch. *Please. Let this be nothing.* She couldn't face any more disappointment tonight.

Jones returned to her window. "Miss Williams, where you going?"

"Home."

"From where?"

"Just a late movie with some friends, Officer." She forced a smile, wishing it wasn't a lie. To celebrate with friends and family who loved her was the way it should be. But instead she'd spent her birthday alone as usual, longing for what could have been.

"How many drinks have you had?"

Adrenaline splashed across her chest, and she tried to relax her arms. *Don't look nervous. Don't look guilty.* "None."

"Know why I stopped you?"

"I wasn't speeding."

"You were doing 40 in a 65 zone."

"Just being careful. I don't like driving at night."

Jones rested a thick hand on her door. He looked at her with a slight grin like he'd heard it all before. "Please step out of the car."

Christy resisted the urge to glance at the passenger seat. Underneath it she'd carefully hidden her half-empty bottle of sherry. Knowing it would be useless to protest, she obeyed.

Outside, she shielded her eyes from the cruiser's spotlight. "Sir, I'm tired. It's my birthday. I just wanna get home."

"I need you to do some standard roadside maneuvers for

me." Jones gripped her left bicep, his fingers closing almost entirely around it, and led her to stand between the two cars.

She'd seen sobriety tests on *COPS* enough times. This was her chance to prove herself. Christy concentrated hard on the officer's instructions. She was gonna show this guy.

"You'll stand with your heels together and your arms at your sides," he said. "Then when I tell you, lift one foot about six inches off the ground and hold it there. Don't use your arms. And no hopping or swaying. You understand?"

"Yeah."

"Now at the same time, count aloud like this: one thousand and one, one thousand and two, one thousand and three. For thirty seconds, looking down at your foot."

Christy crossed her shaky arms, nodding. As much as she hated the embarrassment of being on display, she had to do it. If she refused, he'd arrest her for sure.

"I'll tell you when to put your foot down." Jones looked her right in the eyes, his breaths condensing and swirling around his head. "Understand exactly what I want here?"

"I got it."

He repeated the instructions, demonstrating the moves himself, and Christy assured him she knew what to do. If she passed this thing, would he let her go?

Jones stepped away from her. "You can start now."

She filled her lungs, then slowly let her breath out, willing herself to calm down. Uncrossing her arms, she squeezed them against her rib cage and lifted her right foot. Was that six inches? She raised it a little more. That seemed right. Her heart pounding, she made herself breathe, determined not to take her eyes off her foot. *Focus. Don't sway.* Then she remembered to count. She hadn't been counting. She risked a glance at the stoic cop. Had he noticed?

"One thousand and one. One thousand and two." Christy felt herself sway slightly. For a split second she tapped her toe to the ground just to right herself, but it was quick and then she was back to counting. "One thousand and three."

Half a minute. That's all we're talking about. Just to thirty.

"One thousand and four. One thousand and five."

I can do this.

"One thousand and six."

Keep my balance. Keep my cool.

"One thousand and seven."

Christy got to thirteen before she realized her arms had somehow lifted away from her body, like a trapeze artist walking the wire. She smacked them back down and kept counting. "One thousand and fourteen. One thousand and fifteen."

Her leg was made of lead. *Lift it up. A little higher.*

"One thousand and sixteen."

Quit shaking.

"One thousand seventeen."

Focus!

"One thousand eighteen."

"Okay, you can put your leg down."

She let out a burst of air. She must've been holding her breath. "How'd I do?"

Jones didn't answer, his face a mask of professionalism.

It was downhill from there. He put her through two more sobriety tests. She messed up four times walking that stupid line, and she had no idea what he was after when she followed his pen back and forth with her eyes.

Then the cop started grilling her again. "Honesty would go a long way here. Sure you didn't drink anything?"

That's when reality sank in. Christy knew better than to get behind the wheel, yet she'd risked innocent lives and driven anyway. The last thing she'd ever want to do was cause an accident, especially tonight.

"I . . . " She blinked back the tears that sprang to her eyes, desperate to keep from bawling in front of this cop who was only doing his job. After a late day at work, she'd spent the evening in her car parked by Union Reservoir, sipping sherry and reading Hercule Poirot mysteries by the dome light. All she'd wanted was to forget it was her birthday. Revel in the buzz that would abandon her by morning.

Christy let out a long breath. "There's a bottle of sherry under my seat."

Jones nodded, producing handcuffs from his belt. He pointed at the car. "Hands on the hood, please."

Christy rested her palms on the gritty, salt-stained metal, the front bumper jamming into her knees. She deserved to be locked up.

"Carryin' anything I should know about?"

"No."

After frisking her, he pulled each of her arms behind her back, clicking icy cuffs around her wrists. A semi zoomed past them, spraying cinder-filled slush against the cruiser door, and she imagined the trucker craning to see who the loser was this time.

Jones led her to the back door of the patrol car, opened it, and guided her head inside. She barely had time to glimpse a second cruiser pulling up before the door slammed shut behind her, as much like a cell door clanging as the one she knew waited for her at the police station.

Her shoulders went limp. Another truck sailed past, shaking the patrol car. The cop's garbled voice came from outside. She didn't try to comprehend what he was saying. No doubt he was reporting to his buddy about the drunk he'd caught.

Christy hung her head as the cuffs dug into her flesh. Thirty-three years old.

Happy birthday.

❧

Hours later Christy perched on the edge of the jail cell's plastic bed, her hands covering her face. The Breathalyzer test she'd taken a few minutes ago had confirmed to the cops what she already knew. Her blood alcohol level was well over the legal limit. And they'd booked her for it. Her mug shot and fingerprints were probably already scanned into some offender database, marking her for what she was—a criminal. They'd left her with nothing but her grubby jeans, sweatshirt, and sneakers. Not even one cigarette, which she'd do a lot for about now.

Her gaze wandered to the ceiling, where a video camera glared downward, scrutinizing her every move. They could probably hear her too.

Earlier, the cops had offered her the phone, but she didn't know who to call. The only lawyer she knew was Harvey Kurtz, but she hadn't talked to him in over two years.

She'd thought of Hunter Dawson, the owner's son and manager of Dawson's Book Barn, Longmont, Colorado's largest used bookstore and where she worked. Although she had a feeling he'd jump at the chance to help her, he was her boss, and she didn't want any problems there. Things were going so well. She'd finally found a job she loved, and she couldn't lose it now.

Christy rested her elbows on her knees. Who could she possibly call? Even if she did have friends, she'd be too ashamed to drag them into this. And family? They were hours away and probably wanted nothing to do with her. Not that she'd blame them. She was the one who broke the family ties and left without even a good-bye. What May must think of her after all these years . . .

That left Vince. She still flinched when she thought about him, but what other choice did she have? It was either him or spend the night in this creepy place where the stench of old urine hung in the air.

A few minutes later a balding cop with a gut hanging over his belt showed up to check on her, and she decided to make the call she dreaded.

When she was sitting in front of the phone, the cop picked up a pen. "Name?"

"Vince Dubois."

"Relation?"

Two weeks ago she would have responded *boyfriend*. Now she didn't know how to answer. "Coworker," she finally said, and it was the truth. Vince also worked at Dawson's Book Barn, overseeing online sales.

She held the receiver, the dial tone humming in her ear as she contemplated one last time what she was about to do. Then with a sigh she punched in his number.

It rang twice, and a deep male voice answered with a crisp "Hello?"

"It's me. Christy."

"A little late, isn't it?"

"I . . . need your help," she said, hating to admit it.

"So you're finally coming around."

"I'm in trouble."

The line was silent for a moment. "What kind of trouble?"

She told him what happened, lowering her voice. "I don't want to stay here."

"Give me thirty minutes," he said without hesitation. "And don't worry, darling. It'll be all right. I promise." It felt good to hear someone say it, even if it was Vince.

"He'll be here in half an hour," she told the cop.

And he was. When they released her into the waiting area, Vince stopped pacing, and his quick survey up and down her figure made her wish they'd let her clean up a little. She ran trembling fingers through her stringy blonde hair, regretting she hadn't taken the time this week to cover the dark roots. She must've looked as awful as she felt.

Vince, on the other hand, looked the same as always. Even at this hour he was meticulously dressed in crisp jeans and a ribbed gray sweater, his wavy black hair full of mousse.

She got back her purse and was given an arraignment date. She'd be in court for this at the end of the month.

"Let's get out of here," Vince said, wrapping an arm around her waist, shepherding her toward the parking lot. He kept his arm there until they got outside, then cloaked her shoulders with his leather jacket. A few wet snowflakes drifted from the sky as he helped her into his white Lexus. She breathed in the air, redolent with Vince's imported cigars.

"I'll pick up your car tomorrow," he said, buckling up and starting the engine.

Christy already had a Winston lit. She took several drags before speaking. "Thanks for coming."

"You don't belong in a place like that."

She pulled in another drag and exhaled, relief flowing through her limbs. Closing Vince's jacket tighter around herself, she sat silent, waiting for the heater to work.

"You did the right thing calling me."

"Please take me to my apartment."

The car's turn signal ticked off and on. Vince drove out of the parking lot in the wrong direction.

"My apartment."

"I heard you."

"I want to go home."

"Home?" He laughed and patted her leg. "Seems to me my place is your real home. Come on, Christy. Let me take care of you."

She was tempted to allow it. She didn't want to be alone,

but she'd be giving in by agreeing. She'd be going back to him. At least that's the way he would see it. "I don't wanna fight."

"Good."

When he got like this, it was like trying to have a conversation with an oncoming freight train. Jump out of the way or get flattened. She didn't have the will for either.

A few minutes later they pulled into the garage of the two-story country house Vince rented from his uncle.

Vince was immediately by her side to guide her to the door. "You're still unsteady."

"I'm fine." She tried to push his arm away.

But he held on. "I can see that."

At the door, she obediently slipped off her shoes, as Vince required of everyone, and he led her inside. The ubiquitous classical music station she remembered so well played faintly through the whole house over the speakers Vince had wired and installed himself.

Leaving the lights off except for the one over the kitchen sink, he pointed her to the living room and sat her on the pin-striped damask sofa. He knelt in front of her, holding her hands between his. "Hungry?"

"No."

"I can fix you something."

"I'm tired."

"Then let me get you a drink." Without waiting for a response, he rose and went to the bar in the corner of the dark room. A cabinet opened and glasses clinked. She could picture the scrupulously arranged rows of wineglasses, tumblers, and cordial glasses she'd watched him hand-buff countless times.

Vince returned with a tumbler half-full of sherry. "This'll calm you down."

Christy closed her eyes and sipped at the alcohol as Vince sidled next to her, drawing her into himself. His Siamese cat, Socrates, jumped up beside them, purring and butting his head into Vince's arm. Vince petted the animal, his arm still around Christy.

She stopped resisting. It wasn't important anymore that he'd hit her. That was only a distant memory. And she *had* provoked him. She hadn't been thinking of his side. As usual he'd vowed it would never happen again, and Christy believed him now. He'd come to her rescue tonight, something he would only have done if he truly loved her.

"You can rest now," Vince whispered, rubbing her back in comforting circular motions. "It's all over."

"I was . . . so scared. I didn't know what to do."

"Shh." He stroked her cheek with his fingertips. "You don't have to think about it anymore."

Christy rested her head on Vince's chest, his Polo Sport

cologne bringing back memories of other nights they'd shared together. It would be all right to fall asleep in his arms one more time.

2

Blood dripped down Beth Eckert's arm and fell off her elbow to the barn floor. May Williams stood poised beside her, ready to help as Beth sliced through the sedated but still-conscious and standing heifer's side.

With the practiced ease of a veterinarian twice her age, Beth quickly cut through the muscle and peritoneum with sterile scissors and plunged her bare, goose-bumped arms into the abdominal cavity. The scalpel was secured to her wrist to keep from losing it inside the animal. She would locate the uterus, cut through, and pull out the calf's back legs.

"Nice and warm now?" May joked. Beth had peeled down

to a T-shirt and lined vest, and in this frigid weather May didn't envy her.

"Oh, you bet," Beth grunted.

May chuckled, glancing at Ruth Santos standing on the other side of Beth. Her bony hands stroked the Hereford's neck.

"*Suave hija, está bien,*" Ruth whispered to the animal.

Nearly seventy, Ruth was May's partner in the Triple Cross Ranch. And even though May had twelve years of ranching under her belt, she still felt like a greenhorn next to Ruth, who'd lived on ranches since she was a kid. It was in times like these that Ruth's decades of experience made a difference. Ruth had woken the vet tonight. May would've held off and given the heifer more time in labor. In this case waiting could have meant the death of the calf, the mother, or maybe even both. Even now they could only pray the calf was still alive.

Beth slit the uterus and pulled out the calf's first hind foot. It hung from the surgical opening, part of the amniotic sac still wrapped around it. In seconds she'd located the other and withdrawn it as well. Ruth and May each grabbed a slimy leg. While Beth held the incision open with bloody hands, they lifted the brown and white calf from its mother's side and gently laid him in the straw. Steam rose from his motionless form.

Ruth was instantly on her knees beside the animal. "He's not breathing."

"Come on, boy." May tickled the calf's nose with a piece of straw.

Ruth toweled him down to increase circulation.

The animal's chest remained still.

"Does he have a heartbeat?" Beth asked.

May rested her fingers on the calf's left side, right below the rib cage. "Yeah, he's alive."

"Hold him upside down by the back legs. He probably has fluid in his air passages."

Together May and Ruth did as they were told, the limp calf dangling in the air between them. May was holding most of the weight and felt the muscles in her back and shoulders flex. Even though she was five feet eight and strong from years of working outside, holding up an eighty-pound calf took some brawn.

After thirty seconds they lowered him to the ground. This time May used the towel, and Ruth coaxed the calf to sneeze with a piece of straw.

Suddenly the calf coughed, phlegm spurting from his nose and mouth all over her boot.

"There you go, boy. There you go." May rubbed more furiously, and Ruth cleared away the mucus with her fingers.

The calf sneezed, then coughed again, his eyes cracking

open. May never tired of watching an animal see the world for the first time.

"He's gonna make it." She let out a sigh of relief, cleaning him off with the towel like his mother would've done with her tongue had she been birthing him out in the field.

In a few moments the calf was breathing normally.

"No way she could've had him on her own," Beth said, sewing up the uterus. "Wouldn't have made it past her hips."

When she finished, May helped load Beth's instruments into her truck. "How much?" she asked.

Beth shut the tailgate and walked around the truck to the driver's door. She opened it, and the cab light blinked on, illuminating her face. Her raven hair was pulled back into a ponytail, and dried cow's blood smudged her cheek. She pulled her down parka off the front seat and quickly slipped it on. "We'll deal with that later. You've got enough going on."

"I'd rather settle it now, if you don't mind. We don't need any more debts hanging around." May tried to laugh about it, even though there was no money. They really couldn't afford this. But if the bill wasn't paid now, it probably never would be, and May wasn't going to owe money to her best friend. Something else would have to give instead.

"May, let's—"

"How much?"

Beth was about to protest further, but May stopped her with an upraised hand. Her friend mumbled a figure. It was much lower than May knew it should've been.

May scribbled out a check and handed it to Beth. "Stay for coffee?"

"Thanks," Beth said, climbing into her truck. "But I'm gonna go for some sleep. You could get a couple hours yourself before sunrise."

"We'll see."

Beth started the truck. "Try and take care of yourself."

"You got it." She waved good-bye and started for the small house she and Ruth shared.

Ruth was already inside. Their only ranch hand was taking the next shift checking the expectant cows so they could both go back to bed. They checked the herd every three hours during calving season to catch any difficulties a cow might experience, like what happened tonight. It was always a long, grueling two months.

Ruth poured two mugs of coffee and brought them to the kitchen table as May fell into a chair. Unlike Ruth, she usually couldn't drink coffee and go straight to bed. But tonight May knew she couldn't sleep anyway, so the caffeine wouldn't matter.

They sat across from each other, silent and staring at the

worn table surface. May guessed they were thinking about the same thing.

"Can't we do something?" She could almost repeat verbatim the bank's demand letter they'd received two days ago by certified mail, even with all the legalese. She'd read it over and over, searching for a loophole and hoping somehow she'd misunderstood.

"Not without $250,000."

This wasn't the first time the ranch had experienced financial trouble. Back when May first started working here for Ruth, things had been tight, but the insurance money May saved from her parents' death was enough to get the bank off their backs for a little while and buy her partnership into the ranch.

"They know we can't come up with it." May closed her eyes as emotion rose in her throat.

Cattle prices last fall weren't what they'd expected, and the ranch didn't break even. No matter how hard they'd scraped, they hadn't made the full mortgage payments for over six months. Now the bank was calling the whole debt.

"God'll take care of us," Ruth said.

"If we lose the ranch, I don't know what I'll do. I can't do anything else."

"You could, *chica*." Ruth rested her calloused hand on May's. "I'm the one who's too old to change."

"Don't say that."

"You're young. You could start again."

May leaned forward, squeezing Ruth's fingers. "You *can't* lose this place. Not after the years you and Luis put into it."

"Somehow the Lord will take care of us. We have to trust Him."

"I don't know if I can."

The older woman stood stiffly and patted May's shoulder. "Some sleep might help."

May tried to smile, but she knew any chance of her sleeping again was long gone.

After Ruth went to bed, May dug out the bank's letter. How could they come up with this kind of money? She snatched the calendar off the wall, the one Walker's Feed Store gave out every year with the American landscape scenes. She set it on the table in front of her. They couldn't. There was no way.

Tapping her finger on yesterday's date, she was about to start counting forward to the bank's deadline sixty days from now when she read her own scrawled words: *C's birthday*.

May rubbed her temples at the reminder. Every year she hoped Christy would find some way to contact her, some way to let her know she was safe. But for the past fifteen there had been nothing but silence, and she'd just about given up hope of ever seeing her sister again. Was Christy even still alive?

She slid her chair back across the worn linoleum and knelt beside it. The floor felt hard and cold against her knees. Tears filled her eyes, and she buried her head in her arms on the seat of the chair. How could she trust the Lord when her dreams were crumbling before her eyes?

In the silence of a house that soon might not be hers, May prayed for a long time.

❧

This time it was a rare copy of *Huckleberry Finn* that was missing from Dawson's Book Barn. Hunter Dawson tried not to think about it as he perused Ted's cartons of books to see what the store could use, but it gnawed at him anyway. It had vanished right out of a display case, unlike the other two this month that were swiped off the shelves. The thief was getting bolder, and this one made it close to a grand sucked down the drain.

Hunter barely glanced at the hopeful twentysomething scout's last box of pocket paperbacks. The store didn't buy many of them, and he gestured toward the two stacks of books he had chosen to purchase. Piled with the rest of the yet-to-be-priced recent acquisitions on the antique table in the middle of the Barn's packed entrance room, he wondered if one of them would be the thief's next target. "Afraid this'll be all today," he said to Ted, who hovered near his shoulder. "I can give you forty-five for them."

He'd limited his selection to hardcover copies. General fare mostly. A few popular novels, a scattering of juvenile series books like the Hardy Boys, two cookbooks, an Andrew Wyeth art title, and a few others.

With one finger Ted nudged his glasses up from the tip of his nose. "Nothing real valuable?"

Hunter skimmed the books. Ted was just starting out. It was the second time he'd brought books into the store, and Hunter always tried to offer helpful advice to new scouts. They were an important asset to any used bookstore. They came to you, bringing books from wherever they could get them for cheap. When they got good and picked books specifically with your store in mind, they were invaluable.

"I'm probably giving you the most for this one here." Hunter picked up the art title. "The rest are bread and butter. Good to have around but not rare."

Ted stacked up the rejected boxes to take back to his car.

"Check'll be waiting," Hunter said.

A lady patron appeared, a tower of books sandwiched between her chin and arms. "I can never leave empty-handed," she said, dropping the books in front of the register with a huff.

"That's the way we plan it," Hunter said, leaving the

pricing table to ring up her purchases. He'd been handling the register besides his managerial duties this morning without too much trouble. But he wished he knew where Christy was. This was her job, and she should have been in hours ago.

When the customer and Ted were gone, Hunter reached for the phone to try Christy again, but his father walked into the room before he could dial. Hunter quickly replaced the receiver. "Hey, Pop."

Robert Dawson set a tweed touring cap on his white head. "I'll be out till four. Think you can hold down the fort?"

"Sure thing."

By now Pop trusted Hunter enough to let him oversee most of the Barn's sales and book buying, but Pop still had the final say in everything, including employees. That's why Hunter didn't mention Christy's tardiness. She had too much potential to let a few late days get in the way. The love of books was ingrained in her heart, the same way it was in Hunter's. And it wasn't just the enjoyment of reading. That was part of it, but he'd gotten to the point where the musty smell of old pages thrilled him. Cradling a two-hundred-year-old leather volume gave him a rush like a drug.

Some people thought he was odd. Even Pop made fun of him once in a while, but Christy understood. That's one of the reasons he'd hired her four years ago. And it was also why he was grooming her for book buying. Up until now Hunter and Pop had been the only ones with that responsibility, and it hadn't been easy convincing Pop that Christy could handle it.

Pop had been buying estates since he'd acquired and renovated the century-old dairy barn thirty-six years ago. And even though people sold their old books on eBay and other online selling sites much more now, the Barn still got calls to make offers on entire libraries. Hunter used to go to them by himself, but in the last few months he'd been taking Christy. He always enjoyed it when they had a job together, and he found himself looking forward to each one. She'd learned quickly, and he knew she was ready to tackle an appointment by herself.

Her first was scheduled in a week. She'd be evaluating the books, making an offer, and if it was accepted, packing them out. All without him. He hadn't seen this library, but he trusted Christy's judgment.

Hunter waited for Pop to leave before trying her number again. The answering machine picked up. He didn't bother leaving another message.

"Busy morning?" Vince's voice boomed from the storeroom doorway behind him.

Hunter ignored him as long as he could and returned to the pricing table. "Not too bad."

Vince came and stood beside him. "Your dad still here?"

"Just left," Hunter said without looking up.

"When you see him, let him know I want to talk to him."

"He'll be out till four."

"Whenever."

Hunter picked up the Wyeth book he'd purchased from Ted. Vince always made it a point to discredit his authority by going directly to Pop. Maybe he still thought of Hunter as the owner's son or his old girlfriend Abby's kid brother. Anything but his boss.

"Make sure those books from the Thornton estate get online," Hunter called as Vince walked away.

"Don't worry."

"They've been sitting up there for a month."

Off-limits to the public, half of the second floor of the Barn was devoted to the online department, and all quality volumes were cataloged there first before making it to the shelves. The goal was to keep the charisma of antiquity while staying with the digital times, so all computers were kept hidden as much as possible.

"Got it," Vince said with a dismissive wave of his hand.

Hunter removed a sharpened pencil from his back pocket and neatly wrote a price of forty dollars on the flyleaf of the Wyeth. "Make sure of it."

Vince swung around to face him again in Columbo-like fashion. "By the way, Christy won't be in today."

Hunter met the man's granite eyes. "Why not?"

"That flu thing's been getting around. She wasn't feeling well." Vince paused, then added, "She was still sound asleep when I left."

Knowing that last statement was meant to surprise him, Hunter didn't give Vince the satisfaction of a reaction. He lifted the nearest book, a red spiral-bound *Betty Crocker's Cookbook*, like he didn't care.

But he did. When Vince disappeared into the bowels of the store, Hunter whacked the cookbook onto the table. He thought Christy had left Vince weeks ago.

❧

May pushed her key into the lock of Great-aunt Edna's front door, and a frenzy of barking exploded from inside. Peering through the door's textured glass, she could barely make out Scribbles, Auntie's black and white terrier mix, jumping at her. May opened the door, stepped inside, and stooped to pet the twirling dog. He rolled onto his back at her touch. "Miss me, boy? Where's Auntie?"

The tiny old woman appeared at the top of the staircase in polyester pants and a sequined sweatshirt. When she saw May, every line in her face turned up, and she let out a cute squeak as she slowly started down.

May stood and gave her a big hug as soon as she reached

the bottom. She breathed in the old woman's familiar scent of Downy fabric softener and facial cream, glad Ruth had encouraged her to take the morning off for this visit. Just seeing Aunt Edna made her feel better. And the two-hour drive up to Monument had provided plenty of thinking time.

"What a wonderful surprise!" Auntie said, cupping May's chin in her hands. "But is everything all right? You look troubled."

May cracked a smile. "I never could hide anything from you."

Auntie glanced down at Scribbles.

Laughing, May scratched the dog again. She'd surprised Auntie with Scribbles three Christmases ago. At least she thought she did. Later she found out Auntie's Bible study leader volunteered at the animal shelter and had accidentally revealed her secret.

Aunt Edna's voice turned serious. "It's the ranch, isn't it?"

"Yeah. And Chris. I wanted to talk to you about her."

May wrapped her arm across Auntie's bony shoulders, and together they walked into the kitchen, where a teakettle was just starting to sing on the stove. This house had been her home for years after her parents died and Auntie took her in. More than one person called the woman crazy for opening her house to an angry teenager, but May thanked God she had. She wouldn't be where she was today if it weren't for the kindness of Aunt Edna.

"I love being here, Auntie. At least this place—and you—will stay the same even if nothing else does."

"You're always welcome," Auntie said, shuffling toward the stove.

May quickly stopped her. "Let me do that." She drew a box of Bigelow English Breakfast tea bags from the cabinet above the stove. Dried sachets of basil hung from the knobs, compliments of the greenhouse window. Auntie always did have a green thumb, keeping potted ficus and Christmas cacti in almost every room.

Aunt Edna eased into a kitchen chair. "Christy's been on my heart too."

"Hard to believe I have a sister out there somewhere."

"I so wish I could've had you both here with me."

What would *that* have been like? To graduate from high school with her sister there to hoot and holler when they called her name. To have had Chris at her baptism. May still remembered looking out at the crowd that day, her heart aching to fill the hole only her sister could.

May took out two mugs, placed a tea bag in each, then poured the boiling water on top. She cracked the door of the fridge plastered with Aunt Edna's collection of dog breed magnets and pulled out the 2 percent milk. "I want to find her," she said, dribbling some milk in her tea and giving Auntie's a pinch of sugar. She brought both cups over to the table. "But I'm scared of being hurt all over again."

Aunt Edna's hand trembled slightly as she lifted her cup. "I'm not making excuses for her, but we don't know what she was going through. It was a very difficult time in both of your lives, and she was older than you, experiencing it all differently."

"We both lost the same parents. We were both alone." Missing Mom and Dad had been bad enough, but to be ditched afterward by her only sister had made the whole thing unbearable. "I did forgive her. But lately I've been thinking about her so much."

Aunt Edna gave her a knowing look. "Sometimes it's the Lord who brings someone to our minds like that."

"You think God wants me to find her?"

"Maybe."

May reached for her cup and took a gulp of tea. "What am I supposed to do? Rent a billboard? Post an ad saying: 'Lost: one sister, brown hair, green eyes, comes to the name of Chris'? And what if I do find her? I'm not even sure she wants to know me again."

"One thing I've learned." Aunt Edna smiled over her teacup. "The Lord doesn't make mistakes."

"So you *do* think it's God."

"I think she's your sister, dear. And you're not the only

one who's had a burden for her." Aunt Edna sighed. "Every night I pray."

"But I don't even know where to begin."

"The Lord knows exactly where she is, honey. He'll help you if you ask."

If God knew where Chris was, then why hadn't He brought her back a long time ago?

"What if she's dead?" The thought sank like a stone in May's stomach.

Aunt Edna's eyes met hers. "She's not."

"How can we know that?"

"I don't think the Lord would have me pray if she was gone."

May took another sip of her tea, then set the cup aside. Even after all this time she still asked herself why. Why did her sister leave? What had she done to push her away? One minute Chris was with her at Mom and Dad's funeral, then poof. She was gone. Taking part of May's heart with her.

3

The late afternoon sunlight woke Christy. Brightness poured over her face, and she groggily sat up in the king-size bed as objects came into focus. Socrates sleeping on the pillow beside her. Vince's carved oak dresser that stretched almost to the ceiling. The matching armoire. The carved pineapple bedposts. She closed her eyes again for a moment and rubbed her skull with her fingertips. This should never have happened.

When she finally tossed off the down comforter, her head still throbbed. Shuffling to the bedroom door, she cracked it, listening. Soft strains of a Mozart symphony met her ears as Socrates' furry body rubbed against her ankles.

"Vince?" She stepped out into the hall and hung over the balcony railing.

All was quiet.

"Vince?"

No answer. Good.

Checking the whole house, she finally relaxed when she knew he was gone. It was four in the afternoon. He would be at the Barn for at least another hour and had promised to tell Hunter she was sick. Christy hated lying to him, but there was no way she could've come in today feeling like this.

After a steaming shower, she scrounged in the dresser drawers and found a pair of sweatpants she'd left behind. It was wonderful to slip into the clean, soft fabric. In the kitchen she swung open Vince's well-stocked double-door fridge and discovered half a turkey sandwich behind the soy milk and lettuce.

She brought it into the study. The largest room in the house, it took up half the first floor. And though the remodeling was finished before she'd ever lived here, she knew exactly how many walls had been knocked out and every dollar spent in creating it. She could almost see Vince and the dramatic arm flourishes he'd used to show it to her the first time. The cherry floor-to-ceiling bookshelves; the massive stone fireplace; the hidden, fireproof safe.

But it was the massive painting of the bear hunt that

overwhelmed the room. Hanging over the mantel, the original Victorian-era oil pictured the last grotesque moments of a lone bear, bleeding and fighting for survival while twenty snarling dogs lunged at it from every side. It had always given her the creeps. Vince prized it.

This was where he spent most of his time. Christy lounged in one of the two matching white leather chairs and slowly ate her sandwich. Socrates poised on the other chair, tracking her every move with his startling blue eyes. Many an evening she'd spent in here reading while Vince worked at his computer in the corner. Besides his work at the Barn, he maintained a small private inventory he sold online. It was less than a thousand books, but most were rare and expensive. Half of the shelves in here housed them; the other half held Vince's personal collection of philosophy titles. All the tomes were carefully placed so their spines lined up exactly with the shelf's edge.

Once in a while when she'd first moved in, she'd helped him package a few of the volumes he sold. He'd at least made an effort to include her in the beginning, but over the last few months he'd grown more secretive about his books. She even suspected he kept some locked in the attic. And if she ever dared to question him about where he got them, even out of simple curiosity, he'd put her off with hostile verbal attacks.

The books were why he'd hit her last time. She'd been

glancing over his shelves one night, wondering as usual where Vince was getting all of his rarities. She erred in asking about them. When he tried to shrug off the question, she pressed him for a real answer.

"It's none of your business," Vince said.

Christy thought it was. "What are you hiding from me?"

In an instant, he'd sprung from his chair and slapped her. "I said it's none of your business."

She had pressed her hand to her stinging cheek and let the subject drop. But the next day when he left for the post office, she'd rushed about gathering her stuff and was gone before he returned. It wasn't just that he'd hit her. He'd done that before. It was the look on his face—a look she'd never seen before. Like he'd checked out. Like if she pushed him too far, he'd be unable to stop.

Besides, his house had never been her home. Everything was his. When she'd surprised him with a new recliner, he returned it. Vince had never allowed her to add her own touch or change a single thing. She'd always felt like a guest.

Christy gave Socrates the last bite of her sandwich and set down her plate, wishing she could have a smoke. But that was another thing prohibited in Vince's home, though of course he was allowed his cigars. She almost lit one anyway. *Take that, Vince.* But she didn't. The sting of his palm was still too fresh in her memory, and a feeling of suffocation welled up inside her.

Why hadn't she remembered any of this last night? Because of him, she'd even lost all her savings, small as it was. When she moved in, Vince persuaded her to move her money into a joint checking account so he could manage it for her. The day she left, Christy drove straight to the bank to withdraw her money, but Vince had already closed the account. The price of her freedom.

That was two weeks ago. Coming back was a mistake. Seeing the comfort he lived in only angered her. Her downtown apartment offered none of this security. A guy was shot just last week in the street right beneath her window. Mice roamed the halls. But it was all she'd been able to afford. Her salary at the Barn was never enough. Vince lived like a king compared to her.

Christy gazed at the shelves just inside the study door where her own book collection used to sit. Made up mostly of first-edition mysteries, it included her prized copy of Agatha Christie's *Murder on the Orient Express*. A rare U.K. edition, it didn't even have a dust jacket, but it had been the first collectible book she'd ever bought. Later the mystery was released in the United States under the title *Murder in the Calais Coach*, and she hoped someday to have a first-edition copy of that as well.

As a girl she'd first been drawn to the author because Agatha's surname was the same as her first, but after reading that one book she was quickly won over by Agatha's engaging writing style, and the book became a favorite. Any day now she'd have to sell it to survive.

Her collection was the first thing she'd packed when she left. Now the three shelves were full again. She left the chair and knelt in front of them. Vince hadn't wasted any time. She browsed the spines, shaking her head. More rare books, mostly collectible hypermoderns, books published within the last ten years or so. One book in particular caught her eye. *Shadowmancer* by G. P. Taylor. She slipped the softcover from the shelf.

Amazing. The print run for this originally self-published title was small, only twenty-five hundred, making first-edition copies of the now-famous author's first book all the more collectible. Recently Christy heard of one selling for nearly twelve hundred dollars. It wasn't an easy find. Yet Vince had it.

If he ever found her snooping like this . . . She listened for him, then chuckled at her stupid nervousness. *Relax. I'm alone. No need to get jumpy. I'll be gone before he gets back.*

Vince didn't go to many public book sales. He despised waiting in line, boastful small talk, and networking with other book dealers and collectors. They were amateurs as far as he was concerned.

She sat at his desk and jiggled the computer mouse to wake up the monitor. So where was Vince getting the books? He didn't do garage sales, which took time and patience, and how many auctions did he attend?

A car door shutting outside made her jump, and she walked into the living room to make sure Vince wasn't back. He wasn't, but she noticed her Honda parked in the driveway, apparently retrieved from the police station as Vince promised.

Christy returned to the study and the computer. Most of the programs required passwords, but perhaps she'd still be able to access the book database. What if she looked around a little? Her fingers hesitated over the keyboard. Would he know she'd been on the computer? Shrugging off her worries, she double-clicked the database icon.

She'd just started scrolling through the titles when she noticed a book beside the monitor. *The Martian Chronicles* by Ray Bradbury. Vince wouldn't be *reading* science fiction. She pulled it closer. He went for the dull Descartes and Spinoza stuff, always turning his nose up at her chick lit and mysteries. Hadn't she seen this book somewhere recently?

Christy scooted the office chair closer to the table and hit something under the desk with her foot. A cardboard box. She slid it out. Inside were more books: *Animal Farm*, *East of Eden*, and *Tales of the South Pacific*. Nothing noteworthy about the titles alone. They were all classics in their own right and easily purchased used and new. But these copies were all firsts.

In fact, the whole box contained first editions from the forties and fifties, many highly collectible, and once again vaguely familiar. She pulled out a Faulkner title, *The Town*, holding it like it was made of glass. The dust jacket was pristine. Not a tear, chip, or stain.

The Thornton estate.

Setting the book down, she ran her fingers through her hair, her heart thumping faster. It clicked. Four weeks ago she and Hunter had gone to the late Irwin Thornton's home to evaluate his library. She remembered the guy's son haggling with Hunter about a final price, but eventually they reached an agreement and Hunter and Christy packed the books together. A former book reviewer, Thornton's collection consisted of the finest first editions she'd ever seen, all immaculate with dust jackets, most having been read only once to review. She'd had so much fun drooling over them with Hunter.

That's why she recognized them. She'd packed them herself.

It was all coming back. She'd carefully stowed the books flat on their sides to eliminate stress during the van ride, packing unused newsprint in the cracks. Just like the paper here. Christy yanked the box closer. Vince knew how valuable these books were. And he was one of the few who would have access to them before they were put on the shelves. Most would have been brought upstairs to be entered into the Barn's Internet database first, one of Vince's responsibilities.

She swore under her breath. He'd stolen them from the Barn. Even after he promised her this would never happen again. And she'd believed him. Believed him like a fool.

It was one book two years ago. *A Is for Alibi* by Sue Grafton. A first edition worth hundreds. She found it in this same study on Vince's desk. When she confronted him, he admitted he'd taken it from the store but assured her it was the first and last time.

What an idiot she'd been for not catching on sooner. Christy sat cross-legged on the carpet, staring at the box. The signs were obvious now. Where else would he be getting books of this quality? Why else the secrecy? It explained everything, even his violent reaction to curb her questions. Only her moving out had relaxed him enough to leave this box out in the open.

"I'm sorry, Hunter," she said when she thought of the money the Barn had lost to Vince. "You didn't deserve this."

She should've known Vince's word was mud. It disgusted her that she'd come back last night, letting him hold her like nothing had changed between them.

She opened the Faulkner book again, flipping through the pages and stopping on some of the passages she knew. So this was how Vince could afford to lease that Lexus. What other books here belonged to the Barn?

For a moment the mechanical grinding sound didn't register. She'd heard it so many times before. Realization came with a twist of her stomach.

Garage door opening.

Vince. And this box was out in plain view! Christy jumped to her feet and shoved the box back underneath the desk. What would she say? He would know she'd moved something. Hadn't he fired the cleaning lady for daring to dust this room?

The grinding ceased, and Socrates leaped off the chair for the kitchen and his master. The Lexus would be inside now. Then the grinding again, the door closing.

Dashing into the living room, she nabbed her purse from the sofa. Now that her mind was clear, she wouldn't be able to spend another minute with him. If he'd lied about this, what else was a lie? She burrowed for her keys. Where were they? Only then did she remember. The cops had confiscated them last night. They would've released the keys to Vince this morning when he picked up the car, but no way would he have left them out for her.

Her mind whirled. She had to escape without him hearing. If she didn't, Vince would surely manipulate her into staying. Or worse. What would he do to her if she confronted him this time?

Whistling. A door slammed.

The key peg! Christy raced into the kitchen and flung open the spice cabinet to see the row of pegs where Vince kept extra sets of all his keys labeled with string and colored tags. Gold keys. Silver keys. Round. Square. Antique. Was her extra set still here?

Something thumped to the floor. Probably Vince's briefcase.

Yes! She spotted the two silver keys to her Honda and went for them. But she grabbed too quickly, and the whole rack clattered to the counter.

"Christy?" Vince's muffled call came from the garage.

With clumsy fingers she rooted through the tangled mound of metal and string. *Where'd it go? Come on!*

Footsteps tapped on concrete. "Christy?"

Read the blasted tags! Lexus . . . toolshed . . . post office box . . . Finally she spotted the one labeled *Christy's car*. Hooking it with her finger, she ran, making it to the front door as she heard Vince enter the kitchen.

"Where are you, darling?"

Her car. She had to get to the car.

"Christy!"

"I've gotta go," she called back.

"Why? What's the matter?"

Down the steps. Across the yard. The car seemed miles away yet right in front of her at the same time. She forced the key into the lock, scratching the paint around it.

Vince stuck his head out the front door. When he saw her, he sprinted. "Just wait a minute!"

She vaulted into the car, slamming and locking the door. She revved her engine to life.

Vince's contorted face was against her window, the veins on his neck bulging. He pulled on the door, rocking the car. "I deserve an explanation!"

Christy swerved into the street, forcing Vince to jump out of the way. She left him standing in the middle of the road.

4

MAY STOPPED AT the corral fence and leaned her arms on a post. Covered in snow, the fields were dotted with cattle chomping on hay cut last summer. Each snort or bellow from the animals sent plumes of condensation into the chilly air.

It was all hers—four thousand acres stretching toward the Spanish Peaks, or what many locals called the Wahatoya Mountains. From here she could even see several of the over four hundred huge dike walls that radiated out from West Peak like spokes on a wheel. The magnificence of this landscape had penetrated her heart as soon as she started working here. She couldn't have dreamed of ever owning the ranch with Ruth. She was just a girl in love with horses and the outdoors. Now this ranch was as much a part of her as her skin.

May took it all in. This morning the normal chores—throwing hay from the back of the pickup and chopping up the ice over the water hole—seemed different. She was conscious of every act, wondering if it would be the last spring she performed them. Her land. What would they do with it? Would a bulldozer tear it to pieces so cookie-cutter houses could take over?

Tires crunched on snow, and she ripped herself from the fence to see Beth's Blazer drive into the yard. It wasn't unusual for neighbors or friends to show up without calling around here. And she'd known Beth for years, before vet school and before she joined her father's veterinary practice. May had watched Beth struggle to gain the respect a male vet would automatically have. They'd journeyed into womanhood together, and now they were both working hard in places few women did.

Beth got out and pulled on Gore-Tex work gloves. "Was in the area and thought I'd check on that heifer." The nippy air brought a flush to her cheeks. She didn't need makeup. May had always thought Beth had her dad's joker personality, but she'd definitely inherited her mom's Navajo features. "Mercers lost five calves to scours yesterday," Beth said.

May grimaced for her neighbors. Scours, or diarrhea, could kill a calf within twenty-four hours, and she was glad their ranch hadn't dealt with it much this year. Everyone hated losing a calf. An innocent life didn't get the chance to live, and it hurt the bottom line, too. By the time sale date rolled around, each calf was worth hundreds.

May took the lead to the calving shed. It was a smaller building beside the barn that had once been a toolshed. They used it this time of year to bring in cows that might need assistance or, if the weather was bad, those they knew were ready to drop. Most of the births happened in the field, but there were still times like last night when a natural birth was impossible.

Inside the shed May flicked on the lights, barely aware of the smells—a mix of soap, iodine, and Hereford. She gestured toward the second pen on the right. Ruth and Luis had refurbished the shed to hold six cows, three to each side. "Mama's right over here."

Beth stepped in with the cow, slowly approaching her. Even from here May could see the animal's puffy incision and stitches.

"Little swelling," Beth said. "But nothing to be concerned about."

May picked up a broom and swept the aisle as Beth continued her examination. Animals never worried. They were oblivious to everything but eating and breathing. Whether horses, cattle, or barn cats, life in their world was simple and perfect. Like this heifer's calf. All he knew was safety. He was sheltered and protected, with no worries of losing everything he'd ever worked for.

May turned away from Beth to hide the tears she was fighting. How on God's green earth would they get the money they owed? Her credit rating, as well as Ruth's, was pathetic. There would be no more robbing Peter to pay Paul.

The weight of it all was suffocating. She wanted to scream so loudly that cattle miles away would lift their heads at the sound. A tear managed to escape and trickle down her cheek. May wiped it away with her glove.

"God's bigger than this," Beth said. "He's gonna take care of you."

It took all her resolve to keep from totally losing it. Beth wouldn't mind, but keeping herself under control made her feel stronger. She was glad Beth didn't try to fill the silence with meaningless chatter. Just the fact that her friend was here was solace in and of itself.

"I haven't talked much about my sister, have I?" May said, changing the subject. Beth knew the basics, but May wanted to share more. Now was a good time. Beth was always a good listener, and it would help May forget the bank for a little while.

"I thought you didn't want to. But I've sometimes wondered."

They walked out of the shed toward the house, both silent for a few steps.

"I actually don't know much about her anymore," May said. "I mean, you've been more of a sister to me than she ever was."

Beth stuffed her hands in her coat pockets. "You've never heard anything from her?"

May shook her head. "Aunt Edna got a postcard a few days after she disappeared that said not to look for her. Other than that it's been fifteen years of wondering."

"So you weren't very close."

May thought about that for a moment. They hadn't been best buds or anything, but they'd shared a room when they were little, and May still remembered those silly whispered conversations they'd had when they should've been sleeping.

"Our beds were across from each other, and we had this code we'd use at night," May said, smiling. "If either of us heard Mom or Dad coming down the hall, we'd whisper, 'PYA.'"

"Which stood for . . ."

"Pretend You're Asleep."

Beth laughed.

"And I used to be scared of the dark. We had this long hall in our house to get to the bathroom. In the middle of the night I'd wake Chris and beg her to stand in the doorway as I ran down the hall. She always did. Never gave me a hard time."

May took in a long breath and glanced up at the gray sky. "We were different. She stayed inside and read a lot. I spent as much time as I could outdoors. I hated school; she got A's. But I looked up to her more than I think she knew."

They were walking slowly, and May kicked at a clump of snow. It disappeared in an explosion of crystals. "When we were older, I remember talking to her about Mom and Dad's drinking. We both hated it. I was probably too young to understand everything, but I think she did. Chris would get into awful arguments with them, everyone yelling. They'd end lots of times with her storming out of the house. I'd wait and wait, but sometimes she never came home."

"Wow. That's tough."

"It was. About as hard as not knowing where she is now."

"What's she look like, anyway? You?"

"Wanna see a photo?"

In the house, May led Beth to the extra bedroom at the end of the hall, where she and Ruth kept their desks. There wasn't space for much else. She opened the bottom drawer of her desk and pulled out a framed picture. "I never put this one out because it hurt every time I saw it."

She handed it to Beth. "We weren't much of a picture-taking family, and I didn't have the sense to keep more of that kind of stuff when Mom and Dad died. This one's from a family vacation to Yellowstone."

Her parents stood holding hands in front of the RV they'd rented for the trip. She and Chris posed in front of them, Chris's fingers making ears behind May's head. May was six, which would have made Chris nine.

"They weren't drinking much back then. I remember falling into the lake and Dad had to fish me out."

Beth tapped the glass. "She looks like your mom. Same nose and eyes. Pretty."

"I heard that a lot." May handed a second photo to Beth. "Aunt Edna gave me this one yesterday. It's Chris's tenth-grade class picture."

Beth compared the two photographs side by side. "Big difference. She looks a lot tougher in this one."

May couldn't disagree. Chris's expression was sullen, the playful kid long gone. That time period would have been just after Dad lost his job. Right when the serious drinking started.

She set both photos on her desk in plain view, where they belonged. "Beth, how am I gonna find her?"

❧

Christy smashed her fifth cigarette butt into the wooden ash-tray that had been her father's. Probably the only thing of his she had. She could still picture Dad in his favorite recliner, reading his *Post*, scotch in hand, the ashtray full of Camel butts. Sometimes as a little girl she'd snuggled up beside him and pretended she was reading the paper too.

All morning as she prepared for work, she'd debated whether to expose what Vince was doing. Hunter deserved to know. The books she found were worth several grand. At her core she knew she should. But this wasn't just any employee she'd be snitching on. She'd seen what happened when she made Vince angry.

The phone rang, and Christy knew who it was even with-out the caller ID. Vince had already left several messages she'd ignored last night. Now that he'd had time to cool, she might as well get this conversation over with.

She scooped up the cordless.

"Why'd you run off like that?" There was an edge in his voice. Not a good sign.

"You honestly thought I'd stay?"

"Maybe I thought you'd finally come to your senses."

Christy waited for him to go on. He was the one calling; let him talk.

"I took you in. Even after you dumped me. Don't I deserve some thanks?"

"Thanks."

"That's nice."

She felt a twinge of guilt at her coldness but quickly reassured herself there was no reason for it. She was in the right. She wouldn't let him intimidate her.

"I don't understand."

Christy slouched back into her lumpy sofa, coffee cup in hand. "You knew I couldn't stay."

Vince exhaled into the phone. "Look, I've put up with a lot from you. But I'm willing to overlook this little game of yours because of how much I love you. Only I don't think it's fair for you to treat me like this."

"Oh, give me a break."

"I deserve better."

"For what? Lying to me?"

Silence.

"How 'bout *A Is for Alibi*? You promised me that would never happen again." She knew she'd gotten him.

"Your point?" Vince said.

"Those books in your study—you stole them, too, didn't you?" Christy paused long enough to set down her cup and light a cigarette while cradling the phone in her neck.

His silence confirmed everything. "You would never

understand," he finally said, which surprised her. He wasn't denying her accusation.

"I'm not stupid."

"I didn't tell you because I knew it would upset you."

"How could you do this to them? They're your friends."

"Wrong!"

She flinched at his sharpness.

"We *were* friends," Vince said a little softer. "But Rob's so stuck-up these days he completely ignores the people and talent who got him where he is. Without me his precious Book Barn would've gone the way of the abacus. He wouldn't even know how to turn on a computer. I've brought the whole business into the twenty-first century single-handedly. But what thanks have I gotten? How am I better off today than when I started? Rob's raking it in at my expense. He owes me. Big-time."

Christy's stomach tightened with each word he spoke. She took a long drag from her cigarette. Did she have the courage to speak her mind? "That doesn't justify what you're doing."

"They'll never know a book or two is missing. And since when did you become Little Miss Righteous?"

"At least I have a conscience," she said, knowing before she finished the sentence that he would never let her get away with that one.

"Really?"

"Yes, I—"

"Aren't you the one who cheated your wonderful buddy Hunter out of those choice estates?"

"That was years ago," Christy said in a lowered voice.

But she still couldn't deny what happened. Four years prior she was a callow cashier at the Barn, barely making enough to pay her rent. Back then more of the store's books came from estate sales. Mr. Dawson had a deal with a local lawyer who would give him the pick of the estates with books. Everyone knew about the arrangement. Dawson's Book Barn was the lion of the estate world and usually took everything, much to their competitors' dismay.

When Mark Fletcher, the owner of the Barn's biggest competitor, a store half its size two miles down the road, offered Christy three hundred dollars every time she informed him about the estate sales the Barn was privy to, it was an offer she couldn't refuse. Because of her, Fletcher had been able to beat the Barn to the best books several times. She fed him the information for six months before calling off the deal when she got to know Hunter better. Another secret she'd been trying to forget. No one knew about it except Vince.

"And what about the workdays you've squandered away on your little benders?"

She watched the ash at the end of her cigarette lengthen. Vince's jabs always met their marks. "Getting pleasure out of this?"

"Let's not forget the problem with the cops. I wouldn't want Mr. Dawson or Hunter to know about your DUI, either."

"I'm not proud of my mistakes."

"But don't you think Hunter deserves to know his pet is really a low-life boozer who's responsible for cheating him out of who knows how many thousands?" Vince laughed. "Not fun to think about, is it? Sometimes it amazes me how you've deceived him. Hunter trusts you. He actually thinks you care about his store. Little does he know you'd sell him out as fast as I would."

Christy pounded her cigarette into the tray until it was nothing more than a deformed filter. There wasn't a thing she could say.

"I don't know. . . ." Vince's voice was taking on an odd casual tone. She pictured his feet propped up on his desk as he leaned backward, puffing on a cigar. "I have a conscience too, believe it or not. I think Hunter should know the truth. We could go in together and tell him, if you'd like. Or I could do it for you."

Was he implying what she thought he was implying? "Just cut the bull, okay?"

"I need you to work with me."

She almost threw the phone at the wall.

"You need your job. You wouldn't risk losing it."

Her stomach twisted tighter.

"Actually I'm glad you found those books."

"What are you—?"

"Because I need your help."

"If you think I'm—"

"Wait to hear my idea before you refuse."

Christy stood. "I don't care about your stupid idea!"

"Your first estate's on Monday, right?"

"Are you even listening to me?"

"I want first pick."

She clenched her fist, unable to respond.

"I understand if you need time to think it over. You're obviously worked up."

"Forget it! I'm not doing it again."

"Darling," Vince said, then went quiet. She could hear him breathing. "I'm counting on you."

Christy realized what he was saying, and his threat hit her like a gunshot. She switched the phone to her other ear. Her darkest secrets, the ones she'd shared with him out of what she thought was trust and love, were his bullets. "How can you do this to me?"

"I wasn't the one sticking my nose in other people's affairs."

"You dirty son of a—"

"Go ahead. Curse me if you like. But I expect you to—"

She hung up.

5

MAY OPENED THE squeaky barn door and stepped into the darkness, the sweet smell of horseflesh and saddle soap teasing her nose. She left the lights off and flicked on her flashlight. She'd just finished her shift checking the herd, and thankfully there were no problems. Life went on as usual. But so did death.

Exhausted, she slumped onto a hay bale and let her tears fall. When Aunt Edna's attorney Harvey Kurtz called her this evening right as she was about to sit down to dinner, his voice betrayed him. She'd instantly known something was wrong. But she'd never guessed it would be Aunt Edna.

May pulled in a jerky breath, clutching the Bible Auntie had given her when she was baptized at eighteen. The black leather was ragged and soiled now, and a few pages were almost pulled free, but it was what reminded her of the woman more than anything else. She lived her life by this book and had taught May to do the same.

"I'm trying, Auntie," May whispered. "I'm trying so hard."

She didn't know how long she sat there, but all at once the door screeched and the barn lights came on. Squinting against the sudden brightness, she looked up to see Jim Parker, their ranch hand, walking through the doorway. He was dressed against the cold like she was, a frayed jean jacket and a stained down vest worn over his coveralls.

He stopped when he saw her. "Oh. Sorry. Didn't know you were in here. I'll just get what I need and leave you alone."

She wiped at her cheeks with the back of her gloved hand. What time *was* it? "It's all right."

Jim walked past her to the adjoining tack room and returned with a halter and braided lead.

May sniffed, trying to hold back more tears. Jim was a good guy. He wouldn't make her uncomfortable, but she still didn't want to blubber in front of him. They'd hired him six years ago when they bought the stock of a retiring rancher friend and increased the Triple Cross's herd to two hundred head.

In the beginning it felt weird to be anyone's boss, especially a guy like Jim, who was in his midforties and knew more about ranching than she did. But Jim had always respected her, and she'd appreciated that, making sure she never barked orders at him or took him for granted.

May ran her hand across the Bible's front cover. "I can't believe she's gone."

Jim hesitated beside her, like he was trying to decide if she wanted to be alone or not, then dragged another hay bale next to hers. He sat down, the halter dangling from his fingers. "She was a good lady."

Aunt Edna always visited the ranch for Thanksgiving and Christmas, and May was glad Jim and Ruth had gotten a chance to know her. Between Ruth's flair for Hispanic cuisine and Auntie's German, the holidays were all about food, laughter, and love. They'd even managed to get Aunt Edna on a horse a few times.

"She gave me love when I felt abandoned," May said, unable to keep her tears at bay. They dripped down her face, and she didn't bother wiping them away. She knew Auntie wouldn't have wanted her to grieve, but sorrow overpowered her. "She encouraged my dreams when everyone else told me they could never happen. Even this ranch. When I told her I was gonna ask Ruth for a job, she never once discouraged me."

As a kid, every time May passed a corral full of horses, saw grazing cows, or caught glimpses of men working cattle, something in her heart stirred. When all the other girls in high school wanted to become doctors, lawyers, and mothers, May said she wanted to be a cowgirl. Didn't know a lick about being one, but Auntie said God wouldn't have given her the desire if He didn't have a way to fulfill it.

"Always did have a good word for everybody." Jim smiled through his handlebar mustache. "Even me."

"She kept me from feeling like the orphan I really was. Even when I moved out here, her advice was always just a phone call away. You know the way she was, with that calm, reassuring voice of reason. I'm—" May bit her lip—"never gonna hear it again."

Jim slowly pulled the braided lead between his fingers, then lifted his eyes to hers. "You will, May. She's not gone forever. She's *in* forever now. No more cryin'. No more pain."

"That's the only thing that makes this halfway bearable." May leaned her head against the barn wall, and it thudded against the wood. Auntie was truly happy. She was with her beloved Savior. Forever. But May longed to be held by her one last time.

"I wonder if Chris'll be at the funeral. Because it sounds to me like Harvey is in contact with her." May stood and Jim did the same. "I asked him if he knew where she was, but he wouldn't answer me. Which makes me think he does know. I don't get that at all. I mean, for crying out loud, she's my sister. He knows how much I've missed her. I was just over there for New Year's."

Jim gave her a sideways hug, and she returned it. "You'll find her when the time's right."

May followed him out of the barn. A few stray flurries wafted down from the sky. What would she be feeling without friends like Jim and Ruth? They were her support now, and they would keep her steady. But what about Chris? Did she have friends? Was she happy?

With the Bible held close to her chest, May whispered a prayer for her sister as she walked toward the house. Chris was the only family she had left.

In Christy's dream the infant was always crying. Clasping him to her chest, she'd console him by rocking back and forth. Back and forth. Slowly and gently. But his cry only grew louder. Louder until it became an inconsolable wail. She didn't understand. She was trying everything, stroking his forehead, wiping his silky hair, and kissing him, but none of it helped.

Darkness encompassed her, and she could no longer see him, though she could still feel his warm body against her as he kicked and wriggled in her arms. But his wailing didn't ease.

Suddenly someone grabbed his feet and yanked . . . trying to wrench him from her grasp. She pulled back, but the other hands were stronger. They gripped the child with no pity. He screamed in Christy's arms. She frantically squeezed him, but he was sliding from her anyway, his cries now shrieks of pain.

In one movement he was gone. Torn from her. She desperately reached into the darkness, searching to pull him back, but her hands groped in emptiness. She couldn't move.

Then came a shriek unlike any human sound she'd ever heard.

No.

Christy struggled to get up, but invisible bonds held her.

No!

She knew what was happening. She didn't have to see to know they were torturing him, cutting him, slicing off first a finger, then a hand, axing off an arm . . . his feet. Then silence.

"Stop!" Christy shot bolt upright in the bed, the shrill cries echoing in her ears. "Please stop!"

There was no answer, and she sobbed into her hands. Falling back into her pillows, she closed her eyes again, longing for a clean mind. Somehow, maybe this time, she could return to sleep. Just this once. But even as she yearned for it, she knew it wouldn't happen. The vicious dream always held on and so did the guilt.

She got out of bed and stood at her third-story window. Cracking it, the bitter wind blew over her sweat-drenched T-shirt. Guilt was always her companion at night. There were times she'd stayed up until morning drinking and watching the late, late shows rather than face her nightmares.

All she wanted was one night of peace. One night of sleeping till morning. Christy dropped to her knees, her fingernails digging into the paint of the windowsill. One night without regret. "I don't wanna live like this, God," she whispered.

It was a futile attempt at prayer. What right did she have to call on God? He had enough decent people to watch out for. He didn't need to listen to a shameful woman like her. She wasn't worth His time.

Christy knew just one way to escape, and she hurried to the kitchen cabinet to find it. Leaving all the lights off, she brought the bottle of vodka to the sofa without bothering to bring a cup.

It would take only a few minutes before her nightmare would fade.

❧

Harvey said it was important they talk in person, but Christy still wasn't sure why she'd agreed to meet him for dinner.

What was she thinking? She hadn't seen him since her parents' funeral, and they'd only talked a few times on the phone after that.

When she skipped town after Mom and Dad died, her intention was to lose contact with everyone, including Harvey. He'd been her father's friend since high school, and they'd served in the Marines together. When Mom and Dad died, he sold the house, paid the debts, and gave Christy and May the gift of not having to worry about any of the financial details. An estate attorney, he'd managed to track her down and cut her a deal. If she would keep in contact with him, he would promise to keep her whereabouts confidential for as long as she wanted. She'd gone along with it. After collecting the life insurance money, she'd kept the calls few and far between. And she'd become adept at evading most of his questions and keeping their conversations brief and superficial.

Christy pulled into the parking lot of the Olive Garden and switched off her engine. What could be so important that he couldn't tell her on the phone? Even when she tried to milk it out of him, Harvey had insisted he needed to speak to her face-to-face. Curiosity got the better of her, and here she was.

She smiled as she got out of her car. Little weasel.

Harvey was waiting for her in the lobby. Bespectacled and

over six feet tall with a receding hairline, he looked the same as she remembered. When he saw her, he beamed. "How are you, honey? I wasn't sure if you'd show."

Before Christy could answer, she was enveloped in a hug—that same warm, fatherly embrace she knew as a child. She would play the part of the confident woman who couldn't be better or happier to see him. "You piqued my interest. How could I resist?"

Harvey held her at arm's length for a second, but his gaze wasn't critical. He gave her forehead a quick peck. "It's so good to see you."

He already had a table and led her to it. When they were seated, a waiter took their drink orders.

"A glass of the house Merlot, please," Christy said without looking at Harvey, who ordered a Coke. She made small talk until the drinks came and the waiter brought salad and hot breadsticks.

Harvey tossed the lettuce in the serving bowl and reached for Christy's plate. "All the hot peppers, right?"

She laughed that he remembered she hated spicy food.

Once they were eating, Harvey took on a serious tone. "Unfortunately, I have some bad news."

Christy paused with her wineglass to her lips, her fingers tightening around it. She took a long swallow of the Merlot as a sudden dread filled her veins. "Is May all right?"

"Yes, she's fine. But do you remember your great-aunt Edna?"

Christy nodded, then set down her glass, the wine sloshing up its sides. Of course she did. May was sent to live with her.

"Edna . . . she died two days ago. I'm her executor. I know you weren't close, but I still wanted to tell you in person. And I needed to give you this." Harvey reached inside his coat and handed her a sealed envelope. "We found it on Edna's desk."

She took the envelope from him. It was thin and letter-size, addressed to her in wobbly handwriting.

"It seems she penned it the day she died." Harvey set down his fork and folded his hands in front of his plate. "You may not know that you and May are her sole beneficiaries."

Christy didn't attempt to hide her shock. She looked at him with the letter still in her hand. "No, I didn't." If she'd ever been in Aunt Edna's will, she would've expected to be written out by now. Tact kept her from asking how much the woman was worth.

Not sure what to expect, Christy opened the letter.

Dearest Christy,
I don't know how to start, but I have prayed the words
will come. It won't be long before I'm gone. The Lord

has revealed this much to me. Knowing that, somehow
I wanted to express some things and let you know that
I've never forgotten you. Years and distance may have
separated us, but many times I have been on my knees
asking that the Lord be with you. I've wanted so many
times to hold you close and show you my love.

May hasn't forgotten you either. She desires so
much to see you again. She loves you too, dear; you
must know this. And though I don't know where
you are, I can only hope that this letter will reach you.
I understand that the passing time will make my request
all the more difficult, but you and May need each
other. This is what is on my heart. My very last wish
on this earth is to see you and May together again as
God intended.

I love you.
Great-aunt Edna

Christy let Harvey read the letter and took another swallow of her wine. Touching. There wasn't a hint of the condemnation Aunt Edna could have rightfully felt toward her. An honorable request, too. The sweet, dying aunt wishing her great-nieces together again, hoping for a storybook finish. But this was real life, and she wasn't sure if she was ready to see her sister.

Not that she didn't want to. So many times over the years she'd been within moments of digging out the phone book and calling May. What path had she chosen for her life? Was she happy? But if Christy was truly honest with herself, she was afraid to have a relationship with May again. Because she knew if May got to know her now, she would be incredibly disappointed in her big sister. May had looked up to her, and she'd shattered that trust.

"I spoke with May. She wants to talk to you." Harvey leaned on his elbows. "She asked me directly if I knew where you were. I managed to avoid the question for the time being, but I thought after we talked, you might release me from my promise."

Christy returned the letter to its envelope. Apparently he wanted them to reunite just like Aunt Edna did, but it looked like she was going to let them both down. She picked up her menu. "The manicotti sounds good."

Harvey cleared his throat. "Think about it. I know this isn't easy for you, but I just keep picturing you two as little kids and the fun you had together. Remember those Monopoly tournaments?"

Christy managed to smile. Lemonade stands and Monopoly. That's what summers had been about for her and May. They'd set the game up on the big round marble coffee table in the living room and kept it out for days at a time.

"Even roped me in a few times."

"And beat your socks off."

Harvey laughed. "How come you always managed to own Park Place *and* Boardwalk?"

"I looked good in blue."

"Wasn't May's favorite game piece the man on the horse?"

She nodded. Second choice was always the dog.

"Can I ask you something?" Harvey fingered the edge of his napkin and didn't wait for her to answer. "Why don't you want to see her?"

Christy didn't respond for a moment and sipped at her Merlot. That was what it must look like. "It's not that," she finally said.

"Then what is it? How can I help?"

"I just need time." She spotted their waiter two tables down and lifted her hand so he'd see they were ready to order.

"Christy, this isn't right anymore. You can't expect me to keep this up."

When the waiter appeared, Christy welcomed the diversion. What must Harvey be thinking of her? Could he ever understand she hadn't meant to hurt May like she knew she had?

Harvey went for linguine Alfredo. She played it safe with pasta and marinara sauce. But after the waiter left, she found herself in the same awkward spot of not knowing what to say.

"She lives about three and a half hours from here in Elk Valley on a cattle ranch," Harvey said, continuing on like everything was perfectly normal. "Co-owns it. Did I tell you that?"

Christy shook her head, hoping he'd elaborate but not daring to ask. It wasn't hard to picture May living on a ranch. She'd dreamed of owning a horse since she could walk, and Christy always seemed to be bandaging up some part of her sister. Like that time May scraped her entire shin, from ankle to knee, box sliding with the boy next door. Or when she'd tumbled off her bike into the creek and had to get twelve stitches in her arm.

"The funeral's this weekend."

She saw where he was going with this and smiled at him. "Work's been very busy. I'm not sure I'll be able to make it."

"I understand." Harvey pushed aside his plate and removed a folder from his briefcase. "Now, to business. Edna requested her estate be split evenly between you and May. I don't have the exact figures yet, but roughly it's worth about a quarter million."

Christy felt disbelief spread across her face. A quarter *million*?

"She also had a few personal items she specifically stated would go to each of you. She left her books to you."

It took her a moment to recover. She drank from her

wineglass, then wiped her lips with her napkin. "Wow. This is . . . unexpected to say the least."

He smiled. "I know. She loved you both very much."

"And her books too?"

"Several hundred."

She remembered Aunt Edna's library. Each of the few times her family visited the old woman, Christy always managed to wander into the room lined with bookshelves. She could still hear Aunt Edna encouraging her to touch and read anything she liked, a wonderful privilege. Mom and Dad didn't keep many books at home. Aunt Edna remembered her love of books after all these years?

"Things'll be in probate for a little while," Harvey said. "But I don't see any reason why you can't take the books now. I have a big basement. You can keep them at my house if you want. I'm already taking care of Edna's dog for May till she can come get him."

Christy might have taken him up on it if he hadn't brought May into the picture. She wouldn't put it past him to ambush her by inviting May over at the same time without telling her, and she wasn't willing to risk a chance meeting with her sister. If they were to see each other again, it would have to be planned, so she could prepare for it.

"I appreciate the offer. But I don't want to burden you, and I'd like to keep them with me anyway." She'd have to stack them in her already-cramped apartment until she could afford storage.

Harvey was quiet for a moment. She had a feeling she'd disappointed him. "You really don't want to see her, do you?"

"It's complicated, Harv."

"You'd like her."

"I'm sure I would." Christy laughed and tried to make light of the subject, wondering if Harvey saw through it.

"What should I say to her? You're leaving me in the middle here."

She pulled a pack of Winstons from her purse, not sure how to answer. This had nothing to do with not wanting to see May. Hearing the tidbits from Harvey actually made her yearn to see what her little sister had grown up to be. What she didn't want was for May to see *her*.

6

May usually enjoyed the days she ran errands in Elk Valley. Picking up an order at Walker's Feed Store, making a bank withdrawal, even grocery shopping at Safeway was a nice change from her ranch chores. But today she just wanted to finish them as fast as she could and get back home. While it still was her home.

She parked her pickup at the curb of The Perfect Blend coffee shop. She'd stop for a quick bagel and coffee, then head over to the post office. The bell above the door jingled as she entered, and she waved to the owner, Stan Barlowe, busy at the espresso machine.

"Hi, May. What can I get ya?" Stan gave her a big smile. He'd opened the shop a year ago, and with more tourists visiting Elk Valley these days, business had been brisk. The Spanish Peaks and the nearby Sangre de Cristo Mountains were always a draw to campers and RVers in the summer and fall, but even at this time of year there were still some enthusiasts staying at the newly reopened Cuchara Mountain Ski Resort.

"Medium coffee and egg bagel," she said.

"Cream cheese?"

"Sure."

May ate the bagel at one of the tables by a window, then took her coffee with her as she walked to the post office. She loved how the cool, invigorating air brushed her face this time of year. She always had. Being outside in the open made her feel free. Like a wild horse. It's why as a kid she'd walked to school rather than take the bus.

That one year when she was twelve and three blizzards blew into town just about drove her crazy. Staying cooped up in the house while the snow swirled and the wind howled was like corralling a starving filly next to a field of lush alfalfa. She'd never understood how Chris could actually enjoy the time inside.

A lump rose in May's throat, and she swallowed more coffee to keep it down. It bothered her to no end that Harvey wouldn't answer her questions about where Chris was living. The niggling feeling that he knew but wasn't telling her messed with her brain. Why would Harvey do that? Tonight she planned to find out. She was going to visit Harvey and his wife, Betty. They still had her over for dinner every couple months, and since she needed to pick up Scribbles, they'd invited her to stay for Betty's signature roast beef.

At the post office May pulled out the letter she'd been carrying in her coat pocket, and with a deep breath, she stepped into the line of waiting patrons. The inheritance money she'd be getting from Aunt Edna wasn't even close to what they owed, but maybe the bank would accept it as a partial payment and work out a plan with them for the difference. It had taken an hour for her and Ruth to find just the right words for the letter.

When her turn came at the counter, she paid to send it certified with delivery confirmation and watched the teller drop it into the mailbag. Time for the waiting game.

"Here's our number." Hunter held out a yellow three-by-six-inch card to Christy. The number 156 was handwritten on it in black marker, and *Perlman Auctions* was printed beneath that.

Christy looked at the card, wondering why he was giving it to her. "But you're doing the bidding."

"Nope." Hunter shook his head, grinning. "You are."

They were standing in the small foyer of the auction house, and nervousness seeped through her body. She'd been to only a handful of book auctions with Hunter, and she'd never done the bidding.

"Come on. I'll be right beside you." Hunter guided her into the great room, where the auction was held. Ten rows of folding metal chairs were set up in front of the auctioneer's podium, and dozens of tables full of books and ephemera to be auctioned lined the perimeter of the room. In the back on the floor were the box lots.

People swarmed around the tables, the hum of their voices like the drone of a thousand bees' wings. Book auctions were a dying breed, and Perlman Auctions was the last of its kind in the area. It was hard to make money as a specialist any-more, so most auction houses supplemented with antiques or household goods. But Don Perlman was determined to keep his dream alive, though he feared each auction would be his last.

Christy followed Hunter to the first of the tables where they could study the offerings. It was still preview time, when people could see and handle all the books, plan their maxi-mum bids, and otherwise mingle. And while most everyone knew each other, competitiveness laced the air as it always did when you got a group of book dealers together. Most were middle-aged men who loved to boast about their past glories, but Christy found even that was somewhat of a stereotype. There was a whole new wave of twentysomethings cropping up and listing their books exclusively online, and she was starting to recognize a whole family or two that showed up at the auctions and book sales.

When Hunter wasn't looking, Christy took a moment to study him. He didn't fit the mold either. Thirty-five and wearing his usual jeans, hiking boots, and chamois shirt, she often thought he appeared more like a mountain guide than a bookstore manager.

"Look at these," Hunter said, flipping through the auction's seventy-five-page catalog. He pointed at lot 56, a six-volume set called *The History of the Indian Tribes of the United States* by Henry R. Schoolcraft. Most of the lots contained one book each and were labeled with strips of paper sticking out of the books, but several were multivolume sets or a collection of books on a related topic.

Christy lifted one of the heavy volumes in lot 56. Five hundred plus pages. Published by Historical American Indian Press. Brown boards. Unobtrusive. She leaned toward Hunter. "How much is this worth?"

He lowered his voice. "We could get at least eight hundred."

According to the catalog the set was actually a facsimile of the original books published in the 1850s. Christy thumbed through the pages. Illustrated with engravings and color plates, a set like this would be invaluable to anyone studying American Indians.

They went through the rest of the tables, and Hunter pointed out other lots he wanted her to bid on. Many of the books would be general stock, but there were still several, including the Schoolcraft set, that Hunter knew he had a buyer for. With the Barn's reputation, many individual collectors had standing orders with the store to purchase books in their area of interest. And Hunter's memory was amazing. He could remember titles people had years ago told him they wanted, which served him well when buying for the collectors.

Ten minutes before the auction started, Christy found them seats in the back row. It was better to sit where she could see who was bidding. Hunter had taught her that at their first auction a couple months ago when she tried to sit in the front row.

Hunter handed her the catalog with a smile. "Not too nervous now, are you?"

She returned the smile, not wanting him to doubt her abilities. Most of her four years at the Barn had been spent at the register ringing up purchases and directing customers to their subjects of interest. She always tried to take notice of what was sold and for how much. And Hunter always answered her questions, often enthusiastically elaborating on the history of certain books and what points made them valuable or not.

Over the last year her hunger to learn had grown, and Hunter had started teaching her the fine details of acquiring and pricing. It was why she'd gone with him to the Thornton home—preparation for the new responsibility of going to estates solo, which she considered her redemption. A chance to secretly make up for cheating Hunter and his father and to show she was an asset to them. She wanted them to see she wasn't in it temporarily like many of the college students the Barn hired and assigned to packing and shipping or shelf stocking and maintenance.

She wanted to be someone they could trust, someone they could promote. And she enjoyed nothing more than being surrounded by books all day. It was the only part of her life that brought her any pleasure at all.

"I still get nervous," Hunter said.

"Sure you don't want to do this yourself?"

"Yep. You'll do fine."

She turned to the first page of the catalog, noting Hunter's penciled maximum bids. They wouldn't start bidding until lot 12, which contained three coffee table art titles. He was willing to go up to thirty on this one.

"Hey, Hunter. Christy."

Christy turned around at the New York accent to see Mark Fletcher standing behind them. In his fifties with a bushy, graying beard, he tucked his dog-eared catalog under one arm, extending his hand to Hunter.

"How are things?" Fletcher said, grinning.

This was not what she needed.

"Fine, fine," Hunter said. "You?"

"Still kicking." Fletcher turned his attention to Christy. "He showing you the ropes today?"

Christy tried to smile, desperate to keep Fletcher from seeing how uncomfortable she was. He wouldn't bring anything up in front of Hunter, would he? "There's some great stuff here," she managed.

"Oh, I know."

"Anything in particular you're looking at?" Hunter chimed in.

Fletcher rolled up his catalog and stuffed it into the pocket of his wrinkled sport coat. He wagged a finger at Hunter. "Just have to wait and see now."

Thankfully, Fletcher left them to find a seat somewhere else. In fact, everyone was now finding their seats.

A hush came over the room as Don Perlman strode toward the podium. He was probably only sixty, but his white hair made him look older, and she didn't know a time when she'd ever seen him clean-shaven. He picked up the ancient corded microphone, tapped it a few times, then began. "Thanks for comin' out today. We've got some fine books here, and I hope you buy a ton." He took a deep breath and they were off.

Don's nephew, a gangly teen in a T-shirt and jeans, brought the first book. His shoulders drooped, giving away his boredom as he stood in front of the podium holding it while the bidding started.

"Who'll give me five, five dollars. To start things out. Five dollars." Don's words came out fast and furious, typical auctioneer style.

Christy glanced at the catalog. *The Book of the American West*. Edited by Jay Monaghan, Bonanza Books reprint of 1963 edition, 608 pages. It was a common book, and she was surprised they were offering it.

Don nodded at a bidder. "Five dollars. Who'll give me ten?"

No one did.

"Sold to bidder #43 for five dollars."

Who was #43? Christy scanned the room but couldn't tell. She hadn't seen anyone lift their hand. Which of course was typical. If the auctioneer knew a bidder, sometimes all that was necessary to bid was a nod.

"It was Jack Mason," Hunter said. "See him sitting up there in the front?"

All she saw was the bald head of an elderly man leaning on a cane.

"He's a collector. Buys all the Americana he can. And the thing about collectors is they'll pay much more than a dealer can. A dealer's gotta make a profit, but a collector can pay retail if he wants. Whenever I see old Jack walk in a room, I know I'm beat on the Americana."

"Will he want the Indian tribe set?"

"Not sure."

Lot 12 came all too fast, and Christy readied her number.

"Okay, folks. Got a nice selection of art books here. Rockwell, Remington, and William Matthews. Who'll give me fifteen?"

"Just wait till he drops the price," Hunter said. "He'll start high and then go down if no one bids."

"Fifteen. Fifteen. Do I have any bidders? Ten. Let's start it at ten. Who'll give me ten? Ten dollars."

Christy raised her number.

Don saw it and pointed in her direction. "I have ten. Who'll give me twelve?"

Her cheeks were suddenly hot. It was one thing to watch Hunter do the bidding. It was a whole different ball game to be doing it herself.

A hand went up across the room. She didn't recognize the bidder, an older woman with shoe-polish brown hair. Was she another collector?

Don glanced at Christy. "Fifteen dollars. Fifteen."

She kept her number in the air. She wasn't chancing him missing any gestures.

"Twenty? Who'll give me twenty?"

The gray-haired lady lowered her number.

"Seventeen? Seventeen?"

No hands.

"Sold to #156 in the back row."

Christy tried to keep from smiling at her success as the kid brought her the books and Don noted the bid in his ledger. He still went the old-fashioned route, swearing he'd never use a computer.

Hunter elbowed her. "Good job."

There was no time to bask in the excitement as the bidding continued at breakneck speed. Hunter also wanted the next four lots, more art titles, which sold well at the Barn. Things went the same as before. The gray-haired lady bid once or twice, then gave up, and Christy got the lots for less than Hunter's maximums.

"I'd really like to get 55 and 56," Hunter said, tapping the listings in the catalog.

"Tom Swift?"

Number 55 was a box lot containing twenty original Tom Swift Sr. books in the illustrated mustard-colored cloth, many with their dust jackets, something she didn't usually see on that series.

"Got a guy who's starting a collection. Maximum we'll go—" Hunter lowered his voice—"ten apiece. We can turn them fast for twenty; otherwise, we normally don't buy for half retail."

Christy liked the way he used "we" instead of "I." She shifted in her chair, readying herself for bidding again. It wasn't as hard as she thought it would be, and Hunter's quiet confidence in her skill was helping.

"All right folks, lot 55." Don tilted his head to read from his own copy of the catalog. "Tom Swift. Gotta love that guy. Okay . . . let's start bidding at twenty." His voice ratcheted back up to full speed. "Twenty dollars. Start 'er up. Give me twenty, twenty."

Christy began to raise her number, but Don caught sight of someone on the other side. He pointed at the man, and Christy realized it was Fletcher. She clenched her jaw. This was bound to happen sometime, her bidding against Fletcher. Out of the corner of her eye, she watched Hunter. Calm and confident. Hopefully she could draw from some of his reserve.

"Twenty-five. Twenty-five."

Her hand went up.

Don nodded at her. "Got twenty-five. Give me thirty. Who'll—?"

Another bidder jumped in.

She leaped back into the fray, bidding the lot up to fifty. Tom Swift was hot.

Don stopped his singsonging and just pointed from bidder to bidder.

Fletcher. "Sixty."

Jack Mason. "Seventy."

Christy. "Eighty."

Fletcher. "Ninety."

Christy. "One hundred."

She kept her arm raised and glanced over at where she'd seen Fletcher. He did the same in her direction, giving her a toothy grin. She quickly looked away, focusing on Don.

Back and forth. In all of ten seconds she was bidding two hundred. *Come on, Fletcher. You don't need this stuff.*

"Two hundred fifty." The New York accent boomed, and she shot another glance at Fletcher. Did he have a buyer? Last time she checked, Fletcher's store specialized in technical subjects, not children's.

"Anyone make it two sixty?" Don paused.

Christy dropped her hand to her lap, swearing under her breath.

"Sold to bidder #27."

"Don't let him bother you," Hunter said, resting his hand on hers for a brief, reassuring moment, then returning it to his own lap.

Then it was on to the Indian tribe set. Christy revved herself up again, card hand at the ready.

"Lot 56. We're gonna start bidding at fifty for this landmark work."

A card went up in the front row. Jack Mason.

Hunter sighed. "You know what to do. Let's just hope his pocketbook's tight today."

"Seventy-five. Who'll give me eighty—?"

Christy got her bid in before he could finish.

Don acknowledged it with a nod. He glanced at Jack Mason, and the old man nodded back. *Here we go.*

"Eighty-five. Eighty-five. I've got eighty-five. Who'll give me a hundred?"

Jack kept nodding.

She lifted her hand a little higher.

"One hundred fifty."

Some guy two seats over with long hair and a scruffy face added his bid. Who was he? She recognized him from the last auction, but she would have to ask Hunter later.

The bidding danced across the room. One second she was the high bidder; the next she was on the outskirts of the frenzy, trying to jump back in. Her heart pounded. They were nearing her maximum of three hundred. If she couldn't get the Tom Swifts, she at least wanted to get this one for Hunter.

"Two seventy-five." She could barely understand Don's auction voice, but she could catch the numbers.

Don glanced at her, and she waved her number. Perfect.

"Two seventy-five. I've got two seventy-five. Anyone for three hundred? Three hundred?"

Yes! She was gonna get it.

Don's gaze shot to the side. "Three hundred. Who'll give me three twenty-five? Beautiful set here. Worth every penny."

An arm popped up to her right, and she realized Fletcher was the bidder. Without thinking, Christy lifted her card. She couldn't lose another lot to him.

Don was back to her. "Three twenty-five. Three twenty-five."

Fletcher. "Three fifty."

Christy. "Three seventy-five."

Fletcher. "Four hundred."

Hunter reached for her arm and gently pulled it down. "Christy."

She shook her head. "He doesn't need that set!"

"Well, he's got it."

"Sold to #27. Thank you, sir."

Just like that it was over.

Excusing herself to buy a bottle of water, Christy walked to the snack bar Don's wife ran in the back of the room. How could she have lost her cool like that right in front of Hunter? What could he be thinking of her abilities now?

She took the water outside and lit up a cigarette, inhaling a long drag. She was positive Fletcher didn't really want that set. He wanted to beat her. And now Hunter was losing to Fletcher all over again.

7

MAY PULLED HER truck into Harvey's driveway. His home in Woodmoor was at the edge of a suburban development of oversize houses in undersize lots. She took her time walking to the door of his three-story house. Little electric candles shone in each window, and two spotlights set back in the snow illuminated the front of the house like it was a museum exhibit. When she pressed the doorbell, Scribbles's bark detonated. Had it been only four days since she'd been standing on Aunt Edna's porch just like this?

The door opened and Scribbles jumped at her. She dropped to her knees on the welcome mat and opened her arms to the dog, vaguely aware of Harvey's presence. Scribbles's rough tongue bathed her face, and she cuddled him. In a moment he was licking tears from her cheeks.

"I think he misses Edna too," Harvey said softly.

May stood and hugged him. She was suddenly a child in need of comfort, and Harvey's arms offered that to her. It felt good to be held.

After a moment Harvey closed the door against the cold. A sweet smell hovered in the air, and she guessed Betty was baking something for dessert.

"I'm very sorry to see you under these circumstances," Harvey said, taking her coat. He was dressed in slacks and a brown cardigan. A leather eyeglass case stuck up from his shirt pocket.

"Thanks for taking care of him." She pointed at Scribbles, purposely changing the subject. If she dwelled on her loss, she'd be crying again.

"Is that May?" Betty's voice called from the other room, and the plump, rosy-cheeked woman rounded the corner, wiping her stubby fingers on a dish towel.

"It's me," May said, smiling.

Betty enveloped her in a loving, motherly embrace. May let herself remain in the woman's arms, as she had in Harvey's, and it hit once more that she would never hug Aunt Edna again. That pleasant Downy fabric softener smell in her clothes was only a memory. There would be no more midnight calls for advice and prayer. Tears came again, and May tightened her hug around Betty.

"It's okay," Betty said, patting her back.

"I'm sorry." She let Betty go and wiped her eyes. "I thought I'd be all right."

"I'll get you something warm to drink."

May nodded appreciatively as Betty disappeared into the kitchen. She followed with Harvey. "What a rough week," she muttered.

He squeezed her shoulder. "I'm glad you're here."

In the kitchen, Betty handed her a mug of steaming herbal tea that smelled like berries. "Work on that. It'll help."

May thanked her and sipped it, but the liquid was too hot to take a full swallow. She cradled the warm mug with both hands, trying to get her thoughts together. She'd only hinted at the ranch's money problems with Harvey on the phone. Now she needed to tell both of them the whole story. She might as well just come out with it. "They want to foreclose on the ranch."

Betty pivoted away from the oven, hot pad still in hand. "Oh, honey, I'm sorry."

Setting the mug on the kitchen table, May went to the silverware drawer beside the fridge. It would be better to keep her hands busy, and she didn't want Betty doing all the work.

"Is there anything I can do?" Harvey asked.

"We've missed so many payments," May said. "I just kept hoping something would change and we'd be able to work it out. But they sent us notice on Saturday. If we don't come up with the whole deal . . ."

"Forgive me for asking, but your inheritance—that doesn't help?"

"It's barely half."

She picked out three forks, spoons, and knives. Harvey and Betty still used their wedding silver for everyday use, and the letter *K* of *Kurtz* was engraved on each piece in flowery script.

Harvey rubbed his chin thoughtfully. "Why don't you tell me exactly what's happened to this point."

As she set the dining room table and Harvey got out the candles, May relayed how late they were, what they owed, and the letters sent back and forth.

"I'm assuming neither of your credit allows you to take out a second mortgage?"

She shook her head.

"You do know I wish I could lend you the money myself."

"I would never—"

He raised his hand, and the chandelier lights caught his Marine Corps ring. Her father had worn a similar ring, and May wished he'd lived long enough to see her grow up.

Would Dad have been proud of the woman she'd become? Or would he have been disappointed she didn't pursue loftier dreams?

"If it weren't for Tom and Emily . . . ," Harvey said. "I owe it to them to—"

"I know. Your children have to come first. I wouldn't want it any other way."

Dishes clinked, and Betty brought plates and salad bowls to the table. "Do you have any friends or acquaintances who'd consider buying in?"

May shook her head again. Jim had already tried to take out a loan for the ranch, but they'd refused him too. She'd just found out about it a few days ago and been touched by his selflessness. She knew Beth would jump to help, but May could never bring herself to ask.

"I'll be happy to call the bank for you," Harvey said. "And see if there's anything we can do."

"Is there even a chance?"

Betty handed her a plate. "There's always a chance."

"But, really? Am I fooling myself here?"

"Let me call," Harvey repeated. "Then we'll go from there. But I won't lie to you. Getting their money is really all that matters to them. If they can't get that, getting your land is the next best thing."

Twenty minutes later, they were eating Betty's signature

roast beef, creamed spinach, Yorkshire pudding, and roasted potatoes. May tried to keep the conversation light for as long as she could, but she knew she'd have to broach the subject that had plagued her sooner or later.

"Okay, guys," May said, taking a deep breath, "I need some honest answers from you."

Looks passed between husband and wife sitting at either end of the table.

"The other day on the phone, Harv, I asked you about Chris. You very expertly dodged my question."

He popped a chunk of roast beef into his mouth, not looking her in the eye.

"I think you know how much I want to talk to her."

A nod.

"And you know where she is, don't you?"

Harvey's forehead crinkled at the question, and there was the same hesitation she'd picked up on before. But this time, after a few seconds he gave in and said, "Yes, I do."

Her heart leaped. "Where?"

"I'm not free to tell you right now."

"What?" May couldn't hide her shock. "Why in the world not?"

Harvey sighed and looked at Betty, who set down her fork and wiped her mouth with her napkin. "We don't know why she's doing this," she said.

Harvey's eyes finally met hers, and they were full of sadness. "I gave a promise to your sister years ago that I wouldn't tell anyone where she was unless she said I could. I was trying to prevent her from cutting all of us off, to somehow stay in enough contact with her to know where she was. I didn't know she'd want me to keep it up. I wish she didn't, but I can't go against my word."

"Didn't you explain I wanted to see her?"

"Yes, but—"

"And she still wouldn't let you tell me?"

He shook his head. "Try to understand my position here. This isn't the way we want it either, believe me. We'd like nothing better than to see you two together again."

May tried to digest what he was saying, but it felt like a rock in her stomach. They were doing their best to soften the devastating blow they were delivering, but it wasn't working. She'd suspected this but hadn't wanted it to be true, hoping things might have changed. Over the years she'd consoled herself by giving Chris excuses. Her sister ran away because she was confused, immature, just reacting to their parents' sudden death. Maybe she hadn't meant to hurt her. But with this news all May's hopes were dying fast. Chris didn't want to see her.

"For crying out loud, this is my only sister." Fresh tears came to her eyes. "What did I ever do to her?"

"Nothing," Harvey said. "I've spoken with her only a handful of times over the years myself. And never much more than pleasantries."

May stared at the half-eaten food on her plate, a scene of long ago flashing through her mind. After Mom and Dad's funeral, Chris drove May to Aunt Edna's, where the few family friends were gathering. They'd pulled up to the street in Chris's old car, and they both sat still for a minute, like it was just hitting them what had really happened. Mom and Dad were gone. All they had was each other now.

"You go on ahead," Chris said.

May bit her lip, reaching for the door. She started to open it, then stopped, looking back at her sister. "It's gonna be okay, right?"

Chris didn't answer the question. With her face turned away from May, she whispered, "Just go in the house."

And May did, wobbling a little on the borrowed dress pumps that pinched her toes.

It was the last time she'd ever seen Chris.

"Harv, if you talk to her, can you tell her something for me?"

He smiled. "Sure."

"Tell her I miss her. Tell her I want my sister back."

❧

"Slow going?" Hunter stepped into the Barn's front room, and Christy smiled at him from behind the counter. They'd finished at the auction and made it back to the store by four. Now it was almost closing time. He hadn't brought up her blunder once all day, and she wished she could thank him for it.

Hunter knelt in front of the potbellied stove in the corner of the room. Sparks shot out as he fed it a log. He took pride in starting it every morning and babysitting it throughout the day. Even chopped all the wood on the weekends.

"Only two customers," she said.

Hunter brushed his palms on his jeans, just watching her for a second with one of his silly half smiles. She felt warmth creep up her neck and busied herself needlessly straightening the pens, bookmarks, and business cards behind the counter.

"You've got to see something." Hunter disappeared into the storeroom and returned holding a book. He gave it to her.

She cradled the copy of *For Whom the Bell Tolls,* careful not to open the boards too far and possibly weaken the binding. She instinctively flipped to the copyright page. There was the seal of the publisher, Charles Scribner's Sons, and the letter *A* right above it that had to be there for the book to be a first.

Christy turned the book over to see the photograph of Hemingway at his typewriter on the back of the dust jacket. An important point in this book was whether or not the photographer was credited beneath the portrait. If he wasn't, the dust jacket was in its first state, the most desirable. There was no credit on this copy, which made it worth several hundred. "Not bad."

"You missed something," Hunter said with a grin. "Check the title page."

When she saw Hemingway's signature, she returned Hunter's smile.

"It's authentic," he said.

"Where'd you get this?" A signature shot the book's value up into the thousands.

"Right before closing two days ago a very old man brought in a box of books. He told me his wife had recently died, and he was moving into a retirement home. They were her books. I could tell he needed the money, but as I went through the box, I was trying to figure out how to nicely say we couldn't use Reader's Digest Condensed novels. Then I spotted this." Hunter held up the Hemingway. "At first glance I wrote it off as a book club edition, not at all expecting it to be a first. Should've seen the look on that guy's face when I offered him seven hundred. A fifth or sixth its value, I'd say. I love making someone's day like that."

She loved it too, and after Hunter left for his office at the other end of the Barn, she kept thinking about his honesty. He could have ripped that old fogy off. The guy hadn't known what he had. But Hunter did the right thing regardless. It wasn't an option for him to act any other way. Would she have done the same thing?

Christy sat down behind the counter. Vince wouldn't have. She could see him offering the man twenty bucks, acting like he was doing him a favor by taking it off his hands for so much. His ignorance would be Vince's gain. "What you don't know won't hurt you, but it won't help you either," was his favorite coined saying.

Behind her the storeroom door squeaked, and footsteps padded toward her. Fabric rustled with each step, pant legs rubbing together. She caught a whiff of his cologne.

Vince came and sat on the edge of the counter, resting his hand on hers. "I was thinking about when we first met. Remember?"

She did. Very well. On her first day of work, Vince was the one who charmed her and made her feel comfortable at the strange new job. Their conversations that day and the days after had been intellectually stimulating. Vince knew all she wanted to know. That's what attracted her to him most.

She'd loved what she thought he was: a cultured, knowledge-able gentleman, someone to be emulated.

"I loved those grand chats before opening when we'd sit by the stove and talk about books." Vince waved an arm toward the cane-backed chairs scooted close to the stove. Weary patrons loved to rest in them while paging through their treasures, especially during the winter.

"How about it?" Vince said. "Let's sit together for a while."

"Not happening."

"We need to talk."

"We've already talked."

"Then we need to talk again."

Christy tried to pull her hand out from under his, but he held it down. He leaned toward her. "About our agreement."

"I never agreed to anything, and get your hand off me."

Vince let her go with a chuckle.

"You think it's funny?"

"I need an answer, you know."

She rubbed her knuckle. "You're serious about this, aren't you?"

"If you'd quit being so paranoid, you'd see the fun we could have together. Just think of the treasures waiting to be discovered."

"I can't do it. I told you that."

"But you will."

Christy walked away from him, scooping a stack of colorful Easton Press leather editions off the pricing table and marching toward the display case by the door. If she ignored him, maybe he'd go away.

But Vince followed her, a wolf trailing his weakening quarry. "I'm trying to be patient."

She set the stack on the floor by her feet and consolidated the books already on the shelves to make room. Tears gathered in her eyes, but she blinked them away. She would not cry.

Vince's breath tickled her ear. "You aren't making this easy."

Christy shelved first one book, a red one, then the next, a blue.

"Don't ignore me."

She whirled toward him. A book thudded to the floor. "I trusted you! How can you do this to me?"

That same wide-eyed, glaring expression she'd seen when he'd hit her in the study rushed to his face. She shrank from it.

Vince grabbed her arm, the blue vein on his temple pulsing. "Let's not talk about trust. Because I trusted *you*. I opened my home to you, and you violated my trust."

"They were right out in the open. I—"

"What were you doing at my computer?"

"I was just . . ."

"Snooping?"

"Checking my e-mail."

"You don't get it, do you?"

"Please let me go."

"I'm giving you another chance."

"I don't want—"

His fingers tightened. "I love you. I *need* you."

Christy held her eyes shut, not from the pain of his fingers pinching her skin but because she knew the only answer she could give.

"A team. That's what we can be."

He didn't leave her a choice. Hunter and Mr. Dawson couldn't know about her dealings with Fletcher. Vince knew she'd worked at too many fast-food joints to risk losing her job at the Barn. Even Aunt Edna's money couldn't bail her out because she had no idea how long it would take Harvey to get the money to her. She had to keep from being fired.

Vince caressed her neck with his free hand. "Give me another chance, darling. Give *us* another chance."

Nodding, she opened her eyes, unable to keep a tear from escaping. She felt it slide down her cheek.

He let her arm go. "It'll be the best thing that's ever happened to us. You'll see. Everything'll be all right."

When he finally left her alone, she found refuge amid the Priority Mail boxes and bubble wrap in the storeroom. In the shadows she cursed herself. Vince might be wrong about everything else, but he was right about one thing. She *was* a lowlife.

❧

Saturday morning Christy pulled into the driveway of Aunt Edna's home in the van she'd borrowed from the Barn. Two pine trees towered over the house, their fat roots cracking the cement. She sat for a minute staring at the house, an unwanted memory materializing. The last time she'd seen May was right here. After Mom and Dad's funeral.

Christy got out, slamming the van's door. Funny how it was another funeral, Aunt Edna's own, that brought her back. It was scheduled for later today in this very town, and she still hadn't decided if she was attending.

As she unlocked the heavy front door with the key Harvey had given her, a burst of wind sent the wind chime hanging from the gutter into a clanging flurry. She pushed the door shut and, standing in the silent foyer, breathed in the stale air that hadn't escaped for days.

The few other memories she had of this place were filled with laughter and music. She remembered the time Aunt Edna invited her and May to spend the night and be her special guests. They'd nibbled on fancy petits fours while pretending they were royalty, baked cookies, and stayed up eating them, watching old Disney movies as they huddled together on the sofa.

Christy kept her jacket on and went to the library door, through the living room on her right, pausing in front of it. How selfish she was. She hadn't cared enough to visit when Aunt Edna was alive. Only because there was something in it for her had she come today.

She entered the room and stared at the beautiful sight. It was just like she remembered. The whole length of the wall facing her was lined with white, built-in shelves, crowded with books. Stepping up to them, she gently fingered the spine of the nearest. It didn't seem right to take these precious volumes from where they'd been lovingly displayed for so many years.

Easing into a creaky rocker in the corner where she imagined Aunt Edna liked to relax and read, Christy tried to make sense of her thoughts. Regardless of her timeworn memories, she was a stranger in this place, and more than that, she would have been a stranger to Aunt Edna. Why had this pure old woman given her these books? Was it simply because she remembered the passion for reading Christy showed the few times they'd spent together?

She rocked slowly in the chair. It pained her to think they might have had more in common than she'd ever realized, because now they would never have the opportunity to share their mutual passion for books and reading. All because of her.

Originally, the plan had been for her to live with Aunt Edna too. That's what everyone assumed would happen, including May. Christy told no one of her intention to run away to Kansas with her boyfriend. She didn't doubt she'd shocked and hurt both of her relatives by her disappearing act. The only contact she ever had with them was a postcard to let Aunt Edna know she hadn't been abducted, and that was just because she didn't want the cops on her trail. She'd moved back into the state five years ago, and she'd been careful to keep an unlisted phone number.

Christy scanned the bookcase. Was this last loving gesture of Aunt Edna's an attempt to reach out to her even after her death? Was the gift of these books supposed to, in a way, be Aunt Edna telling her she was forgiven? She wanted to believe that. For it was clear this library was a gift from one book lover to another.

How ironic. Aunt Edna gave her the books she'd honestly accumulated over a lifetime, right when Christy was about to filch books right out from under her employer.

"I would be an awful disappointment to you, Aunt Edna," Christy said. "I wish you could know how much I don't want to do it. I don't want to do wrong. I don't want to steal from

Hunter." Then she glanced up at the ceiling and raised her voice. "But what choice do I have?"

She pulled Aunt Edna's now-wrinkled letter from her jacket and reread the scrawl. Somehow she'd known she was going to die. Why had she chosen her last moments to write this? Why was it so important to Aunt Edna that Christy reconcile with May?

The funeral was at three. Six hours from now. May would be there.

Christy stuffed the letter back in her pocket and tried to stuff away her thoughts as well. She retrieved several boxes from the van and started taking books from the shelves. She would absorb herself in packing. So much could be learned about someone from what they read, and she suddenly wanted to know more about Aunt Edna.

There was a section of classic children's books like *The Adventures of Tom Sawyer*, *Winnie-the-Pooh*, *The Wind in the Willows*, and *Little Women*, many in beautiful antique bindings. Almost all of them Christy remembered checking out from the library as a girl. She held *Little Women* a bit longer than the rest, realizing for the first time that it was here in Aunt Edna's library room where she'd first dreamed of building castles in the air with Jo March.

On one of the lower shelves she found a whole set of Nancy Drew books, several of the thick blue type, most with their dust jackets. She pulled out number five in the series, *The Secret at Shadow Ranch*, and before she knew it, she'd read the first three chapters. She'd had a copy herself as a girl. The illustration on the cover pictured Nancy on a horse riding as expertly as everything else she did in her stories. This was one of the few books May borrowed from her more than once when they were growing up.

Christy placed the set in two boxes all their own, thrilled to have them. She wondered how much time May had spent in this room when she lived with Aunt Edna. How many of these books had she read?

By ten o'clock Christy had filled only eleven boxes and was in the middle of the twelfth. She couldn't bring herself to go any faster. Some of the books had Aunt Edna's handwritten notes, and she couldn't resist reading them. She started on a new shelf and reached for the next book, a thick and heavy Bible concordance. They got them at the Barn once in a while, and she knew they weren't cheap. She would probably sell this one. Flipping through the pages, she stopped at the gift inscription on the flyleaf: *Aunt Edna, I hope this will be a blessing to you as you study God's Word. Love, May.*

Christy slowly packed the volume in her box. May gave it to her? She went for the next book, something called *The Message*. It also had an inscription from May. *Auntie, this paraphrase really made the Bible come alive for me. Try reading your favorite Scriptures in it. Sometimes it can be a real eye-opener! Love in Him, May.*

She packed the book, digesting the meaning of the words. May was religious?

When she'd considered the many ways May could have changed, she never factored that possibility into the equation. If May was into religion, it would give her all the more reason to be disgusted with Christy. Religious people had morals and rules. She'd broken every one.

The entire next shelf contained more religious books—Bibles, study guides, devotionals. They took up several boxes, and many of them had May's notes written inside. Apparently she'd never had a shortage of gift ideas.

By the time Christy finished, the van was loaded with twenty-five boxes. With a sigh of relief and exhaustion, she locked Aunt Edna's door and stared at the van. She couldn't avoid thinking about it any longer. She had to decide. The funeral started in an hour. She could get to the church on the other side of town in ten minutes or she could go home. It would be so easy to chicken out.

Maybe it was the letter or perhaps her growing curiosity about her sister. Maybe it would be her way to thank Aunt Edna for caring about her even when she was so undeserving, but Christy snatched her dress and heels from the front seat and ran back into the house to change.

8

CHRISTY SLOWLY CRUISED past the church to scope it out.
Was that Harvey's Park Avenue? She wasn't sure. After several
laps around the block, she mustered the courage to park at
the edge of the lot beside another car. She'd keep the Barn's
van as inconspicuous as possible.

Thirty minutes to go.

She would wait. After this thing started, she'd find a seat
in the very back, honor Aunt Edna, then get out. In the
meantime, she lit a cigarette with the van's dashboard lighter.
She wore her best outfit—a dark blue velvet dress and a comfortable yet dressy pair of black mules.

As the parking lot filled, Christy tried to picture what kind of car May would be driving. She studied each vehicle, expecting her sister to be behind the wheel. What was she going to do when she saw her? It was nerve-racking to think how close they were to meeting. All these years she'd wondered what it would be like to see May again. Now that the experience was upon her, she found herself struggling with two entirely different emotions. One minute she wanted to flee like an unarmed soldier from enemy fire, and the next she longed to see May's face.

But this religion thing was a concern. How much had her sister changed? The fact that May owned a ranch gave Christy some comfort. If that cowgirl dream was still a part of May's life, maybe there was hope she hadn't become a religious fanatic.

She sucked her cigarette down to the filter, jammed it into the ashtray, then lit another. Two cars with old couples parked beside her on the right. Then came a minivan. Almost before it stopped, the sliding door opened and three kids, no older than ten, jumped from the running board. They latched onto their slower parents' hands and disappeared through the church doors.

How well did all these people know Aunt Edna? Were they casual acquaintances who said hi every now and then, or did they know her on a deeper level, like Christy wished she had?

Twenty minutes.

She ran a finger over the grimy furrows of the steering wheel horn. Why was she doing this? Aunt Edna was dead and gone. So she wanted her to contact May. Big deal. She'd never know if her wish was fulfilled. Christy could ignore it. No one was making her do this.

She almost drove off right then, but a turn of her head brought her face-to-face with the overflowing boxes from Aunt Edna's library. She leaned back in her seat. She did owe Aunt Edna something.

If only she had a drink. That would calm her right down. She should've stopped for one before coming here. Maybe after this was over she would reward herself with a visit to the White Horse, her favorite bar. Home was ninety miles away. If she planned it right, she could have a drink in hand within three hours.

She almost missed the Dodge Ram. A man with a black cowboy hat was driving, and two women sat beside him. When she saw the woman in the middle, Christy straightened in her seat.

Was that May?

Despite her desire to keep a low profile, she craned to see better. She had to make sure. First the man at the wheel got out, a tall guy, probably in his forties, with a handlebar mustache. And then the woman in the middle slid across the bench seat after him. Christy could barely see her face, but something about the way she moved instantly told her it was May. Christy sucked at her cigarette without breaking her stare. It was actually happening. She was seeing her little sister after all these years.

May turned away and started toward the church. The other lady with her, an older Hispanic woman with a long, salt-and-pepper braid, fell in step beside May, resting a hand on her shoulder. The cowboy-hat guy did the same on the other side. Was he May's boyfriend? husband?

She watched the back of the threesome the whole way, her pulse pounding in her ears. May had on a winter coat with a jagged tear in the elbow. A piece of white stuffing hung out of it, and Christy wondered if May knew the hole was there. No one noticed Christy until right before they disappeared into the building, and then it was only the man. As he opened the door for the ladies, he turned in her direction and looked directly at the van. Did he see her?

Her gaze dropped to the floor, hoping he hadn't. By the time she looked up again, they were gone. So much time had passed, but May still looked so much like that fifteen-year-old Christy remembered. That same dirty blonde hair, same lanky frame.

Ten minutes.

Christy spent the last moments before the service touching

up her makeup. Only when it was five after the hour and the cars stopped arriving did she get out and walk inside toward the faint strains of organ music. Showtime. If she did meet May today, she wanted to come across confident and success-ful, a woman who had her life together.

❧

May stared at the cheap pine casket. There was no viewing. Aunt Edna hadn't wanted anything elaborate, just a simple service with her pastor sharing. But that hadn't kept people from sending flowers. The sprays covered the altar and cof-fin with reds, greens, and yellows, a brilliant display of how much Aunt Edna meant to so many.

May sat in the front row, flanked by Jim and Ruth. She knew everyone was watching her. They would be checking to see how she was taking her aunt's death, most of them truly concerned. It was nice to know people cared, but it didn't make getting up in front of them any easier. She'd never given any kind of speech before, not even in school.

Clutching her Bible, she whispered to the Lord for strength. This was the church she'd attended with Auntie before she moved to the ranch. Some of these folks had even been witnesses at her baptism. She knew the fluttering in her chest wasn't necessary. These people loved her, and they all missed Aunt Edna as much as she did.

Only when she peeked at the crowd behind her to check how many people were here did she recognize the face of the woman sitting in the last row.

❦

There was no going back now. Christy slouched in the hard pew, already regretting her madness. Some hymn belched from the organ, and she pretended to sing along, repeating what words she could decipher in a quiet alto. At least her mouth was moving. No one would know she hadn't set foot in a church for the past fifteen years.

She searched the room for May and caught sight of her in the front row with the man and woman who'd come in with her. From this angle Christy couldn't see any of their faces. When the hymn ended, the people sat down as a reverend took the stage. His muttonchop sideburns ran all the way down to his chin like some Dickens character.

Christy shifted in her seat, not really listening to him. This was a stupid idea. She should've abandoned it when she had the chance. The family ties had finally been broken, and she was a fool to pick them up again. The door was only a few feet away. . . .

"No one knew Edna like her great-niece May," the reverend said, and she homed in on her sister's name. "She wants to share a few words with you."

Christy couldn't move and gripped the armrest at the end of the pew with a sweaty hand. Fine. She would stay long enough to hear what her sister had to say.

May went up to the podium and stood next to the reverend, who hugged her and stepped back. From May's vantage point she would see Christy's row clearly. Would her sister even recognize her?

"I planned to talk about many things," May said in a voice that was deeper as an adult. "I was going to tell you about Aunt Edna's volunteer work and her faithfulness to this church, but as I was sitting down there—" she pointed to the front row—"I decided I wanted to share how she affected my life."

May was definitely taller, and even at this time of year, her face was tan. But it was her expression that intrigued Christy. She couldn't place exactly what made it different. She could tell May was doing her best to keep from crying by the way her lip twitched and by the long breaks between sentences, just like she used to do as a kid. But oddly there was no grief on her face. She was smiling as she wept.

This service wasn't anything like their parents' funeral, where the heaviness of gloom was a vulture hanging over everyone.

"I was fifteen when my parents were killed in a car wreck," May said. "From that day, Aunt Edna took me into her home and treated me like her own daughter. In the beginning I had my days of hostility and anger, and I sometimes took it out on her, but it didn't take long for Auntie's gentleness and love to win me over." She paused. "There were so many fun times."

Christy felt guilt's cold hand on her shoulder. May didn't mention why she'd been alone or angry. She didn't say it was because her sister deserted her without even a good-bye, vanishing out of her life, as far as May knew, never to return again. Why should May want to see her now?

"But the greatest gift my aunt gave me," May continued, "was God's love. She lived it out for me and helped me see Him for who He is, a Father who cares and loves all of us. I had some trouble grasping that because most of my life I'd experienced an earthly father who didn't know how to give that to me or my sister." May's gaze landed on Christy.

Christy wanted to melt into the floor.

"Aunt Edna showed me that God hadn't taken my parents, like I once believed, either. That just happened because of choices they made and because this is an evil world. Once I understood that, it helped me to accept God and His Son, Jesus. He used Aunt Edna to reach me in that hurting time." May sniffed and looked around the room. "I'm joyful today that she's with the Lord. We certainly don't need to weep for her." Then with a grin she added, "Can you picture her now? Strolling down those streets of gold, finally home? Oh, people, when your loved one dies and they know the Lord, it's not good-bye forever. We're gonna see Auntie again."

As May took her seat, the people sang some upbeat song about heaven. This time Christy didn't try to sing along. Not only had she left her sister when she needed her most, but by leaving, she'd driven May off the deep end.

The moment the service ended, Christy bolted, making it to the lobby before the crowd stood. She was leaning into the exit door's crash bar when someone called, "Chris! Chris, wait!"

She stopped. It had been years since anyone called her by that shortened version of her name. She revved herself again to leave, trying to ignore the voice, but she knew who was calling. Christy spun around to see May racing down the aisle, pushing past people and waving her arm. "Chris, please wait!"

She froze, still poised at the door. Great.

May made it to the lobby and ran over to her, grabbing her in a hug before she could react. Christy politely returned the greeting.

"I am so glad to see you," May muttered into her shoulder.

When she finally let Christy go, they stood staring at each other, Christy looking up at May, who was taller by a few inches.

May dabbed at her eyes with her fingertips. "I don't know what to say. I just can't believe you're here. I didn't think you'd make it."

"I almost didn't."

A smile stretched across May's face as if she truly was glad, and small wrinkles appeared on her cheeks. It was strange to see them. The picture Christy had in her mind of May was still that of a teenager.

"I'm sorry about Aunt Edna," Christy said.

"Thanks," May said, then looked like she was groping for words. "Can we sit and talk or something?"

Before Christy could hatch a response that would say no without hurting her sister, an official-looking woman in a business suit approached May. "Excuse me. I'm sorry to butt in like this, but we need you in the receiving line." The woman, perhaps the funeral director, latched on to May's arm to guide her back into the sanctuary.

May glanced helplessly toward Christy. "Will you wait?"

She hesitated. If she responded in any affirmative way, she knew it would be a lie, and for some reason she was having trouble bringing herself to lie to May. "I'll try" was what came out as May was sucked back into the sanctuary, leaving Christy standing alone.

Back in the van she felt safe enough to sit for a minute. It would be a while before May came looking. She kicked off her mules and stuck on her sneakers. She'd seen May. She'd fulfilled Aunt Edna's wish. So why was she regretting leaving?

Because she knew she hadn't fulfilled Aunt Edna's wish at all. She was trying to justify disappearing from May's life. Again. Aunt Edna didn't just want them to see each other's faces; she wanted them to have a relationship.

Who was she kidding? If all she'd really wanted was to know May was all right, she would've been content with her conversation with Harvey. But she hadn't been, and that's why she'd come. She'd hoped attending the funeral would be a salve to her conscience, enough of a sacrifice to rationalize getting on with her life without more guilt about May. But as she sat in the van with the heater blasting in her face, Christy longed for more. She didn't want to leave, and it caught her off guard to feel that way. There was no denying May was a part of her and always would be. May's blood ran through her veins too.

Christy lit a cigarette with the dashboard lighter. She had to get over this. She wouldn't let herself entertain hopes of May accepting her back, of having a sister again.

Tap. Tap. Tap.

She reflexively jumped at the rapping on her window. The cowboy-hat guy who'd been with May was standing outside her door. Christy lowered the glass halfway.

"Sorry to startle you. My name's Jim. I'm a friend of May's." He handed her a small piece of paper folded in fourths. "It's the ranch address and phone number, in case you didn't have it."

Christy released her emergency brake, unsure what to say. "Thanks."

Jim stepped back from the van to let her pass, then took one step toward her again as if he was about to say something more. Christy didn't give him the chance and drove away.

❧

As soon as she could, May burst back into the foyer, hating that she'd kept Chris waiting. She searched the room, but she quickly realized none of the people loitering there was her sister.

She smacked a hand to her forehead. She'd been an idiot to leave her. After feeling the hesitation in Chris's hug and knowing what Harvey had said, she should have guessed Chris wouldn't wait. It all happened too fast. If only she'd said something. Done something.

Acting on one last impulse, May ran out the door, only to be met by Jim. She raced past him. Chris had to be here. Maybe she was waiting somewhere in the parking lot.

"She's gone, May."

Stopping in midstep, her determined shoulders fell. She went back to Jim. "You sure?"

"As soon as you told me she was here, I went to find her and keep her busy. But by the time I did, she was practically driving away."

"You're kidding." May shook her head. "I don't believe this. She's doing it to me again."

"I gave her your address and phone number."

"You talked to her?"

"Barely even had time to hand her the paper."

May watched the traffic barrel down the street in front of the church. She wished, though she knew it was futile, that she would see Chris driving back.

"She could be going to the cemetery."

The cold wind whipped May's dress against her legs, and she held her arms around her ribs, hesitant to voice her fears.

Ruth came up behind her. "Where's your sister?"

"She . . . left."

The three of them headed for the truck as the funeral director placed magnetic flags on the hoods of all the cars, readying them for the procession. May slipped into her truck, the cloud of regret thickening around her heart. She could've just missed her only chance to talk to Chris.

And there was something else lurking at the edge of her thoughts. An apprehension. Renewed worry over what her sister had become. For when they'd been close enough for

May to smell the cigarette smoke in her sister's bleached blonde hair, the face staring at her wasn't the one of beauty and youth she'd idolized as a girl. Even caked with makeup, there was no hiding the hollow look on Chris's face. Her eyes, once clear and bright, were now hard, dull, and blood-shot. They were an old woman's features on her thirty-three-year-old sister.

May's throat tightened at the question bubbling up inside. What had happened to Chris?

9

CHRISTY PARKED THE Barn's van behind the silver Escalade and checked out the country manor in front of her. Nestled in a stand of pines, it had a clear view of Boulder Mountain and not a neighbor within a mile. A six-bed, five-bath kind of place. Hopefully the guy who'd died had as much good taste in books as he did in homes.

She let out a long breath and undid her seat belt. She should be excited. Today she could finally prove herself to Hunter and Mr. Dawson by pulling this thing off. What an opportunity.

Stepping out of the van, Christy walked up the flagstone path to the huge, leaded-glass front door with brass fixtures, trying to appear relaxed, like she did this all the time. But if she bought these books today, Vince expected her to bring them to him first. He'd even left a message giving her a meeting time: today at two, his place. He'd make her a gourmet lunch to celebrate.

She rang the doorbell, and a decked-out woman with a cell phone to her ear answered. "Yes?"

"I'm Christy Williams from Dawson's Book Barn. I have a nine o'clock appointment with Ann."

The woman spoke into the phone. "That book person's here. I'll call you back." Snapping it shut, she extended a hand toward Christy. "I'm Ann." Her grip was dry and all business, like the gray pantsuit she wore.

"Nice to meet you," Christy said and walked inside to the smell of fresh paint.

"Glad you came today," Ann said. "We're having the shelves taken out tomorrow and our entertainment center delivered the day after. Gotta get rid of those books."

Christy followed her through several rooms furnished with sofas, lamps, and chairs that could have been shipped directly from an Eddie Bauer Home catalog.

"Should've seen this place before," Ann said over her shoulder, her heels leaving small dents in the carpet. "Michael's father hadn't bought a new piece of anything for thirty years!" She held open a door at the back of the house. "In here."

Christy found herself in a room coated with burgeoning bookshelves, works of art themselves. A Greek mythology theme with gods and horses and sword-wielding men was intricately carved in the woodwork up by the ceiling. A fireplace with a marble mantel lay cold against the right wall, but the room still had the faint odor of smoke, like the Barn did in the summer when the stove was dormant. Immediately Christy knew this guy had been a book lover. All the dust jackets were protected with clear plastic covers, and the books were neatly arranged by size.

"We're getting a plasma TV to go right here," Ann said, holding her arms out in front of the left wall of shelves. "Satellite too. You just can't pick up any good stations out here."

Christy pretended to share in Ann's delight by smiling as if she understood. But that wasn't easy. Selling the books themselves was one thing. Keeping her father-in-law's library would be like Ann having to wear his shoes. They might fit him wonderfully and be worn to the point of perfect comfort, but they would never fit her. Even so, tearing out the shelves altogether seemed cruel. Surely there must be somewhere else in this huge place for a TV.

"If I could look these over," she said, "I'll be able to make you an offer in a few minutes."

"Take your time, but I need to leave by twelve," Ann said, then left her alone.

Christy took a step back and inspected the books, trying to reassure herself by pretending Hunter stood beside her. Bad idea. It only reminded her of the crime she was about to commit against him.

She removed *Richard Carvel* by Winston Churchill, wondering if Ann's father-in-law had thought, like so many others before him, that the novel was written by the former prime minister of England. It wasn't. An American novelist of the same name had penned this historical novel of the Revolution as well as several other works. Eventually the prime minister wrote the American novelist suggesting one of them change his name to help the confused public. Mr. Prime Minister started signing his name with the middle initial *S.*

Christy returned *Richard Carvel* to the shelf. When she'd discovered those stolen books in Vince's study, she'd despised him for what he did. What made her any better? Now she was doing it for him.

Plucking the books off the shelves and examining them, Christy calculated in her head how much she could offer. What were one or two books when the Barn was getting hundreds? No one would ever notice. Not even Hunter. She was the first and only person to lay eyes on this library. And yet Hunter trusted her enough to pre-sign a check for her to use in the purchase. He had confidence in her integrity and in her ability to do this. It had been a long time since anyone had confidence in either. Letting him down had become a ball in the pit of her stomach. Hunter was starting to matter to her in a way she didn't fully understand.

She remembered his pride when he showed her *For Whom the Bell Tolls* and the boyish delight in his eyes. She shared that delight. Could that be why he was giving her the chance to make something of herself?

Christy continued going over the books, her trained eye looking for anything interesting. She didn't have time to examine every individual title, but the skill came in guessing their average value and making an offer that benefitted the Barn while pleasing the client. In this collection she found a large selection of military history titles like *History of United States Naval Operations in World War II*, a popular set history buffs and veterans alike snatched up every time. The Barn would be pleased to have it.

So would Vince.

She squatted to check the bottom shelves. He'd promised to limit his selections to one or two choice titles each time, but she knew it wouldn't stay that way. He'd push for more, like he did with everything else.

Christy was having trouble concentrating. If Ann accepted her offer, what she decided to do with these books today could change her life forever. There was still time to back out of Vince's scheme. But if she did, she was almost positive

Vince's threat to tell all to Hunter had been real. Maybe it was a bluff, but could she risk the chance it wasn't and lose the best job she'd ever had?

With only minutes remaining before she'd need to make her offer in order to have time to pack up the books, she had to hurry her examination of the library. Say she lost her job. What would she do? There was Aunt Edna's inheritance. That money would be more than enough to keep her afloat while she shopped for another job. But she had no idea when it would come. Maybe she could wait until she got the money to do the right thing. . . .

One last shelf to go. She removed a copy of *The Call of the Wild* by Jack London. It still had its dust jacket. She expected it to be a reprint like all the other copies she'd seen. Instead, the copyright page read beneath the publisher's name, *Set up and electrotyped. Published July, 1903.*

Christy stared at the page. She was sure the first printing was in July. Carefully, she checked under the dust jacket to see the boards beneath. They were vertically ribbed, with thin, upraised lines in the cloth running from top to bottom. The points of a first edition. All of London's firsts were collectible, and usually a first edition of *The Call of the Wild* would run around five hundred. But it was the dust jacket that made this copy worth thousands. In the strange world of rare books, dust jackets were often worth more than the book itself. Especially true with this title, because so many of the original owners had discarded the dust jackets.

She paged further to the title page and the wonderful glossy frontispiece on the opposite page by Philip R. Goodwin. No hints of foxing, the brown stains often found in older books, could be seen on any of the illustrative plates. Hunter would die when he saw this.

The ball in her stomach tightened. Out of all these books, this one took the prize. Vince would want it.

Steps came briskly to the door, and Christy realized her time was gone. She placed the book back on the shelf, trying hard to keep her thoughts from spinning out of control. She forced herself to center on the task at hand. Hunter taught her to play fair in making offers, and she intended to put that into practice.

Ann accepted her first offer of eighteen hundred dollars for the whole lot with a suppressed grin. Although Christy would have been willing to negotiate, Ann obviously hadn't expected that much. Filling in the amount on the check, Christy knew she'd done well. For approximately three hundred books it was a good price, both ways. This wasn't junk from the attic like they so often saw. Almost everything would be sellable. She'd allowed around three dollars per hardcover, less for the softcovers, more for the set and a few other juicy titles. Eight hundred dollars went toward *The Call of the Wild*.

A wearying two hours later, Christy heaved the last box into the van and slammed the door with finality. She lit a cigarette and admired her handiwork. Success! She'd acquired a clean, sellable collection for the Barn without a hitch.

She leaned against the van's door, letting her body finally rest. Vince would be expecting her soon. She smiled to herself as a spark of determination grew into a flame within her chest. Vince didn't deserve these books.

Climbing into the van, she knew what she had to do, and shoving aside her fears, she started the engine. For once in her life she would take the high road. Make Aunt Edna proud. With her spirits high, she blasted her favorite classic rock station and pointed the van toward Dawson's Book Barn.

It was later on the freeway, when she neared the exit that would have taken her to Vince's, that her determination wavered. What would she say to him? What would he do?

She turned up Yes's "Owner of a Lonely Heart," blew past the exit, and sang along at the top of her lungs.

❧

The view from Squatter's Mountain always took May's breath away. But today, standing with her gelding, Spirit, at her side, it did more than that. It tore open her heart.

This was her special place to get away from everyone when she needed it. The ranch's buildings were out of sight, two miles away as the crow flies. But the Spanish Peaks remained, their serrated tops slicing the blue sky. Only two trails accessed this summit. The one visible when approaching the peak was the shorter cattle trail. It was too dangerous to attempt on horseback in the snow, though it made a great hike in warmer weather. The roundabout path she'd used today was longer and clearly the safer route for riding. Worn wide from years of use, it wound up the back of the mountain and offered relatively secure footing for Spirit as it twisted through the firs.

Nothing had changed in the eleven years she'd been coming here. But today the mountains chided her; the trees whispered that in a few months they would belong to someone else. The bank's response had come today. Another certified letter. It was a page full of their legal explanation, but it could all be summed up in one word: *no*.

She tightened her hat's stampede string beneath her chin as the wind gusted. What would she do without this ranch? Hire herself out to another outfit and start over? That's what Jim would do. He was good enough for any foreman to want him, but she wasn't. And what about Ruth? There was no doubt that she had the experience and knowledge, but May knew Ruth considered herself too old to begin again.

May followed a red-tailed hawk as it glided across the sky, level with her vision. Besides her horse she was utterly alone, and that's the way she wanted it. Ruth had never thought of herself. She'd always been so grateful to have May on board. Training her to eventually take over completely had been Ruth's only goal, so her beloved ranch would remain long after she was gone. Would they both be forced to move to town? Could she survive a nine-to-five job?

"I can't stand the thought of losing this place, Lord."

Her only answer was a snort from Spirit.

Reaching into her saddlebag, May removed the ratty paperback Bible she always carried there. Sometimes on long rides home when Spirit was more than willing to have a free rein, she'd read from the saddle, one hand on the horn, the other holding the book.

She turned to the Psalms. "'The righteous cry out,'" she read out loud, "'and the Lord hears them; he delivers them from all their troubles. The Lord is close to the brokenhearted and saves those who are crushed in spirit.'"

Keeping her finger in the pages, May lifted her face to the sky. That was her. Brokenhearted. In trouble with no way out. Holding the book to her chest, she knelt on the ground, not caring if her knees got wet in the snow.

Spirit nuzzled her shoulder as if sensing her distress, and May stroked his velvety nose. Losing the ranch wasn't the only thing bothering her. Just like she'd suspected, Chris hadn't been at the cemetery, and May's old teenage feelings of blaming herself resurfaced. Why did Chris leave all those years ago? Somehow she must have done something to drive her away, right? If she'd only been the good kid she was supposed to be, maybe Chris would actually want something to do with her now.

May returned the Bible to her saddlebag and mounted Spirit. With a click of her tongue, she urged him back down the mountain. She was losing everything she cared about these days.

&

At 10 p.m. Christy's phone rang. She'd just poured herself a glass of sherry to celebrate her day. She'd had a wonderful time showing her catch to Hunter at the Barn, and he'd been as pleased with the books—and with her—as she'd hoped.

The display lit up and revealed Vince's cell phone number. She picked up the cordless and sank into her sofa. He needed to know where she stood. "Please don't grill me."

"Of course not." His tone was kind. Maybe this would go better than she thought.

"You've got to understand, my life with you is over," Christy said. "I'm not coming back."

"Not even after all we've been through together?"

"I've made up my mind, the same way I have about the books. I couldn't go through with it."

"I noticed."

She tensed at his response, wishing he would leave it at that.

"I'm up for trying again," Vince said. "You'll have plenty more opportunities. If you did as well as I imagine, Hunter will assign you more."

Christy took a gulp of sherry. She'd need the boldness it would bring if she was to get her point across. "No, I'm done. *We're* done."

"You're not looking at this right. It's not about the books. I want us to be together. A team. Like we used to be."

"We were never a team, and you know it. You had your way no matter what I thought."

"I can change that."

"What did you think I was? Some kind of idiot?"

"That's not . . . that's not it at all. I can't live without you. I . . ." His voice cracked. "I can't."

She squeezed the bridge of her nose and closed her eyes. He was making promises again, weaving a seductive web to catch her. But this time she knew his words were vacuous. As soon as she gave in, it would be back to what it had always been. Domination. Complete control over everything she did. Toward the end he was making her check with him before even going to the grocery store. "It's over."

"Christy . . ."

"No. I'm not arguing."

"Then don't."

"Can't you just accept that I don't want to be with you anymore?" She took another sip of sherry.

"What did I do wrong?" Vince asked. "I gave you my home, my love . . . everything."

"Don't even talk about love."

"But I still love you. You're the only woman I've ever loved. We could—"

"You love yourself. No one but yourself."

"If you'll give me a chance, I can—"

"What? Change me? 'Cause that's all you've ever tried to do."

He let out a long breath. "Is it the money? We can share our profits. We both know what's valuable, and Hunter's too dull to catch on."

"Always have to malign him, don't you?"

"I wonder why that bothers you so much."

"He's my friend."

"Is that all he is?"

Christy threw back the last of her sherry, then filled the glass again. "What's that supposed to mean?"

"You're drinking, aren't you?" Vince sighed into the phone. "Don't you see what you've become? You're a drunk."

He was doing it again—snapping from charming to cruel

in one breath—and Christy was glad they were having this conversation over the phone.

"I thought you were smarter than this," Vince said. "Don't you realize I can get you out of that dump you call an apartment?"

She hesitated, which bothered her. "Our relationship's over. Right now. If you don't get that . . ."

"Come back to me. We need each other."

"I don't need you."

A moment of silence. All she heard was his breathing. "This is your choice," he whispered. "Remember that."

There was something about the way he said it. What happened to the man she'd fallen for? She used to feel safe with Vince. Just his presence would set her at ease. But now he was scaring her.

"Darling, you really should close your shades at night."

Christy turned around. The shade was open.

"If some weirdo saw you all alone up there, he might get some nasty ideas."

"Just leave me alone, okay?" Her gaze fell to the street. A white car sat at the curb, engine running, headlights on.

"Have a good sleep," Vince hissed in her ear, then hung up.

The car pulled away. A Lexus.

Christy wrenched down the shade and tried to breathe evenly.

10

NOT AGAIN.

Hunter flattened his palms on the glass display case next to the register, his eyes locked on the empty right-hand corner. The case was like a jeweler's, lined with green velvet and lit with a small aquarium lamp, and it was where the Barn kept their unique and rare finds to be examined by customers only upon request.

The Hemingway was gone.

He scrambled behind the counter. Last night he'd locked this case himself, and only full-time employees knew where to find the keys. Rooting through the books and papers on the counter, he hoped someone had carelessly left the title out in the open after showing it to a customer.

It was nowhere.

"Hunter." His father's bark came from across the room.

He looked up, hoping desperation wasn't written all over his face.

"I need you in my office."

"Can it wait? I'm really busy."

"My office now, please."

Hunter started to fire back another protest but decided against it. Whatever it was, he'd be better served to avoid an argument. At least hear what Pop had to say. After that they could disagree as usual.

He followed Pop through the door that opened into the Barn's addition on the north side. Employees were the only ones allowed in here. The first floor contained a small kitchen along with Pop's and Hunter's offices. Above, on the second floor, was a three-room apartment. When he was young, it was rented out, but now Hunter lived there. Pop and his stepmother resided in the stone farmhouse elsewhere on the property, out of sight from the Barn.

Hunter followed Pop to his office. A lone Tiffany lamp shone from Pop's desk, leaving much of the room in shadows. Vince sat in front of the desk puffing on a cigar. No surprise there. Vince and Pop often hung out together, sometimes at the country club golfing or at the tavern, doing the things Pop wished Hunter enjoyed. And even though smoking was prohibited in the Barn, Pop always made an exception for Vince's cigars.

Vince didn't stand when they entered. The only sound was the chair creaking as he uncrossed his leg and recrossed with the other.

Hunter waited for an explanation.

"Tell him," Pop said.

"I have some information about Christy. Remember when Fletcher kept beating you to estates?"

He gave Vince a small nod. For years Pop had an arrangement with a friend from college who was now an estate attorney. Pop's friend assured the Barn first pick at estate sales, and in return for the favor, Pop promised to give his friend, also an amateur book collector of science fiction, all the books he wanted in that genre. Then Fletcher started beating them to estates. He'd managed to finagle his way to the books by contacting the families directly, bypassing the attorney altogether. By the time the Barn got there, the best books were already sitting in Fletcher's store.

"Christy was responsible for that," Vince said.

Hunter shot a glance at Pop, but he just stared at him.

"She informed Fletcher each time she found out about an upcoming sale," Vince said. "Then Fletcher would beat you to it."

"Where'd you hear this?"

"She told me."

Hunter tried to keep his reaction even, but if this was true . . . "Explain."

Vince released a small cloud of cigar smoke. "He paid her for each legitimate tip. I don't know how much. I was shocked when she told me, and I still can't believe she did it."

"She wouldn't," Hunter said, wishing he felt as confident as he sounded. Or would she? She'd only been a cashier back then, making close to minimum wage. An offer of a couple hundred dollars as a finder's fee would tempt a lot of people.

Vince leaned forward. "Christy wouldn't lie to me."

Hunter smirked. Leave it to Vince to betray a confidence. "If you knew about this, why are you just now telling us?"

Pop said, "Apparently informing Fletcher is just the tip of the iceberg."

"I had to be sure," Vince said. "I love her, and I certainly didn't want to wrongfully accuse her. But the third time I saw her slipping a book out to her car, I had to speak up."

Hunter felt his insides jolt. "Wait a minute. I don't believe this." He wanted to sit down, but Vince had the only chair.

"I wouldn't have either if I hadn't seen it with my own eyes," Vince said.

Hunter glared at Vince. The snake sure didn't seem upset.

And he supposedly cared about Christy? He almost seemed to be enjoying himself. "What proof do you have?"

Pop sat down behind his desk and folded his hands in front of himself. "Hunter."

"I'm only trying to help here," Vince said, giving Pop a look Hunter had seen all too often. If he'd rolled his eyes, it would've had the same effect.

"Pop, could we talk alone?"

His father sighed and looked at Vince. "If you don't mind . . ."

"Not at all," Vince said, smiling at Hunter as he left.

Hunter closed the door and sat down in front of the desk where Vince had just been. The seat was still warm. Pop's shoe tapped on the floor as Hunter struggled with what to say next.

Pop didn't wait. "What do you think?"

"I'm not surprised you believe him. You always do."

"And you never do."

Hunter closed his eyes briefly. *Here we go again. Another lap around the same old track, Pop defending Vince.* "I don't trust him."

"This is not about Vince."

"Isn't it?"

"No. And I think the sooner you get over your dislike of him the better."

"That's all you think this is about? Me not liking him?" Hunter laughed in total frustration. No matter what he said, Pop never changed, and Hunter knew why. Maybe Pop would never say it to his face, but his father's disappointment in him was obvious. He'd never been the kind of son Pop wanted. Pop wished he were more refined and ambitious like Vince, who was more interested in the money books brought in than the books themselves.

Even when he was a kid, Pop had tried to mold him into a man he could never be, someone who shared his interests in sports and hunting. Pop never understood how any boy would rather be reading instead of tagging along with his dad on the golf course or watching the Super Bowl with the other guys Pop invited over every January. It wasn't that Hunter didn't try. He probably tried too hard to please Pop, and as he got older, Hunter finally realized it would never happen. Enter Vince. Hunter's older sister, Abby, had started dating him in college when Hunter was fourteen, and Pop and Vince immediately connected. Within months Pop offered Vince a job, and the rest was history. Abby finally got tired of being slapped around and she and Vince eventually broke up, but by then Vince could do no wrong in Pop's eyes. He never even noticed how abusive Vince had been to his own daughter.

It was nothing new to be arguing over Vince with Pop, but this time there was more at stake than a simple business venture Vince wanted to follow that Hunter didn't agree with. This was about Christy. Hunter was the one who'd pushed to have her hired. Over the years he'd stuck up for her more than once to Pop. Perhaps in the beginning he did it for his own reputation, but now he did it for something more. Christy was the only person, besides Abby and his late mother, who seemed to understand him. And when she'd fallen for Vince, he'd kicked himself for not speaking up right away and telling her what kind of guy Vince was. Because of that, he was now watching his sister's nightmare played out again. Only this time Christy was the girl Vince was manipulating. If Hunter could do something to make up for that, he would.

"Ever considered he might be lying?" Hunter said.

"He has no reason to."

Hunter stood and paced the room. "You want me to like him. I want you to open your eyes. Christy lived with the guy; now she moved out. Have you seen them interact? She's terrified of him. Don't you think he could be doing this simply out of spite toward her for leaving him?"

"We're talking about some very serious accusations. If she did anything close to what Vince is saying, we have a problem."

"I realize that, but you're making assumptions without hearing her side."

Pop took a stack of papers out of a drawer and set them on the desk. He picked up a ballpoint and looked at Hunter. "You know I would have let her go before this. She isn't reliable. Not even you can deny that."

"I still can't believe she's our problem," Hunter said, but his voice didn't hold the confidence he wanted. He also couldn't deny the missed days of work and the excuses she'd given that he knew weren't true.

"I suggest you find out," Pop said.

❧

"Everything okay?" Christy said to Hunter, pushing a box of books away from the back door. She'd been clearing space in the storeroom for new inventory all morning, and she'd just noticed Hunter watching her from the doorway. He didn't look happy.

"Actually, no." He said it without a smile or any other hint he was kidding around.

She stopped, wiped her dirty hands together, and walked over to him. Something was definitely up.

"I really don't know how to talk to you about this," Hunter said. "I just got through meeting with my dad and Vince. I'll be honest with you. Vince accused you of some things I hope aren't true."

"Like . . . what?"

He scratched his head. "Remember when Fletcher kept beating us to the estate sales?"

As soon as he asked the question, Christy knew what was coming. It was as if she were suddenly in the path of a swooping fighter jet loaded with bombs. Running wouldn't help her. Ducking was useless. She could only watch and wait for the moment of doom. "Yes," was all she could say.

"He's telling us that was your doing. I don't want him to be right, but I have to know from you. Were you informing Fletcher about the sales?"

Her first instinct was to deny it all. Let him have Vince's word only; that might keep him at bay for a little while, but she knew sooner or later he'd find the truth.

Christy couldn't look at him as she acknowledged the question; she turned her face away and nodded. "I wish I'd never done it. You don't know how much. But everything was completely new, and I needed the money. I know that doesn't make it right. I was the one who called it off after I got to know you and realized, truly realized, how it was hurting the store."

She went on apologizing, dredging up excuses for herself, somehow explaining, but Hunter's expression cut those words short. Or more accurately, his lack of expression. Only the muscle in his jaw twitched once. It was sign enough that his trust in her was shattered.

"I'm so sorry," she said.

"That I found out?"

Christy didn't blame him for asking, but the question still sliced. "That I did it."

"I am too."

They stood three feet from each other, neither moving. Christy turned away from his wounded eyes, disgusted with herself. How could she have risked losing this friendship for money?

Mixed emotions kept her from speaking. She'd dreaded Hunter knowing her past. Yet a part of her was deeply relieved it was over. Everything was finally out in the open. She had nothing more to hide. And one thing Vince didn't realize was that by trying to hurt her in this way he'd freed her to finally speak up about what he was doing to the Barn.

"Come with me," Hunter said before she had a chance to tell him anything.

It was a command. Christy followed him into the entrance room, where he positioned himself in front of the display case and gestured for her to stand beside him. He pointed at the case. "What's wrong with this picture?"

"What do you mean?"

Hunter tapped the glass over the top right corner. "Something's missing."

Then she realized what. She herself had been the one to

display *For Whom the Bell Tolls* only two days earlier. "Did we sell it?"

"No."

"I leave it out or something?"

"It's gone."

She knew what he meant, and her moment came. "I think I know where it is."

"Do you?" Vince said from behind them.

Hunter grimaced.

"I think so." Christy whipped around to face Vince, but it would have been so much easier to tell Hunter when they were alone.

Vince threw her a hostile smile.

It was time to play her ace. "Vince needs to tell you," she said to Hunter while boring holes through Vince so he would get the message she wasn't backing down.

"He already has," Hunter said.

She turned around. Vince confessed?

"Why do you think I'm asking you about the Hemingway?"

Christy stared at him, confused.

Hunter went on. "Vince told us something even more disturbing than Fletcher. He says he's seen you remove books from the shelves and hide them in your car."

"What?"

"You expected me to stay silent forever?" Vince said.

She felt like she'd been slugged. "I didn't take anything from this place!"

"It's hard for me to believe you would," Hunter said. "But—"

"I swear it's a lie. He's lying!"

"Christy," Vince said in that patronizing tone she hated, "how can we believe what you say after what's happened before?"

She whirled at him and poked a finger at his chest. "You're the thief. You've been stealing from this store for years!"

"That's enough, you two." Hunter moved to stand between them. "Christy, I know it's your word against his. But think about this. Vince wasn't lying about the estates." He sighed and looked back and forth between her and Vince. "Frankly, I don't know what to think. But I do know we're going to have to sort things out before I can have you working here again."

"You're firing me?"

Hunter hesitated too long before answering. "I have to figure this out before Pop will let you come back."

Countless responses came to her, but she couldn't speak. Vince was right. They'd never believe her now about the stealing. How convenient. Hunter would think she was smearing Vince to save her own hide. She looked at Vince with tears in her eyes. "How can you do this to me?"

His response came back a whisper. "Darling, you did it to yourself."

It took all the strength Christy had to walk normally from the room. There was nothing she could say. The decision was made. Hunter believed Vince. Could she blame him after what she'd done? She gathered her jacket and purse in a daze.

Hunter caught up with her at the back door. "I'll walk you to your car."

It had started snowing again. Neither of them spoke as they walked. Everything in her wanted to fight this and convince Hunter of the truth about Vince. But no matter what she said, he wouldn't trust her now. He couldn't.

At her car Hunter said, "Can you understand where I'm coming from? I trusted you. When I think of what you did behind my back . . ."

Christy's ire rose at his words, but she quieted it. She couldn't let herself blame him for anything. All of this was her fault. Whether Vince betrayed her or not, the fact still remained, she stole from Hunter. She deserved what was happening. "You have every right to do this."

"Why couldn't you have told me about Fletcher yourself?"

She let out a laugh, glanced at the sky, then back at him. "Because I wanted to bury that stupid deal and forget it ever happened."

The sadness in his eyes was unbearable. Christy unlocked her car and got inside. "Guess this is good-bye."

"Something might work out."

She smiled at the words, amazed Hunter could bring himself to speak them after what he'd just learned. "I admit I was dishonest before. But please know I had nothing to do with the stolen books. If you believe anything, believe that."

He looked at her, and there was still kindness on his disappointed face. "I wouldn't put much past Vince."

"I'd do anything to go back and erase what I did."

"I know you would."

Closing her door, she put down the window to apologize again, but Hunter wasn't focused on her anymore. He was staring at something in the back of the car. "What is it?"

He touched her shoulder. "Where'd you get that?"

"What?"

"That book." He motioned toward the seat behind her.

Christy twisted around as he opened the door and reached for whatever it was. Her car was often littered with books, but they were usually cheap paperbacks she could abuse without care. "I'm always reading something."

"I didn't know you liked Hemingway." Hunter lifted a hardcover book from the seat and turned it around so she could see the title. *For Whom the Bell Tolls.*

"I didn't take that!" She jumped out of the car and pounced for the book.

But he swung it out of her reach. Only after he paged through it did he hand it to her with a snort of disgust. "See for yourself."

Christy immediately saw the flyleaf. There were Hunter's neat penciled words: *First edition, first issue dust jacket, signed,* and on the title page was Hemingway's valuable signature.

The missing book.

She gave it back to him. "I can't expect you to trust me, but I didn't do this. I don't know how that book got in my car."

Hunter looked from the book to her.

"It's the truth," she said. "Vince is trying to frame me."

He held the bridge of his nose between his fingers, his eyes closing for a moment.

"You don't believe me."

Hunter shook his head. "Thanks for finding it." Then without another word he walked back into the store. The door closed behind him, the Authorized Personnel sign jeering that she wasn't welcome to follow.

All Christy could do was drive away. As she did, she glanced back, trying to imprint Dawson's Book Barn in her memory, as if she might never see it again. The smoke curling to the sky, the colorful art books on display in the window.

She'd looked forward to seeing these familiar sights every morning for the past four years.

Now they pushed her away.

Christy waited for the traffic to let her out on the road and looked back once more. Vince leaned against the side of the building with a cigar dangling from his fingers.

He waved.

11

From a dark booth in the White Horse bar, Christy ordered another martini. She nursed it like she had the last one, enjoying the alcohol's warmth gliding down her throat. As she took a drag from her Winston, the two sensations combined to bring the bliss she depended on.

She rubbed her thumb up and down the glass. But not even a martini could make her forget there was no rising early for work tomorrow. Her life was crumbling. That was a fact getting drunk wouldn't change.

Balls cracked at the pool table, and Christy tried to tune out the blaring football game on the TV. She pulled out her cell phone and contemplated calling it off. She'd been the one who instigated it half an hour ago when she rang Vince and asked him to come down. She could cancel. But no. She returned the cell to her purse. This time, she *wanted* to meet with Vince.

Two minutes early he walked through the bar's front door, scanning the smoky room. When his gaze lit on her, his lips curled up into that movie star smile she used to find so charming. Christy took another swallow of her drink and watched Vince swagger toward her. Always on time. No doubt he thought she'd called this meeting to grovel at his feet and beg for forgiveness. Stirring her martini, she chuckled, watching the olive spin round and round on the bottom.

Vince slipped into the bench across from her. "Hi."

She just smiled. It would be fun to see how he reacted to her silence.

"You wanted to talk?"

Stonewalling him for as long as she could, Christy bumped out another cigarette. "Sure, let's chat. Just like old times."

"About today. I—"

"Not like anything's happened between us."

Vince unzipped his leather coat, shrugging out of it. He scowled at her glass. "How much have you had?"

"I wanna thank you." She flicked her Bic lighter and held it on for a second, watching the flame dance before her face.

Lifting her eyes to Vince's, she removed her thumb, and the flame disappeared. "For screwing up my life."

He leaned his elbows on the table. "You're smashed."

She flicked the lighter again, this time touching it to the end of her Winston.

"You can't even think straight," Vince said.

"I'm thinking perfectly straight."

"Christy . . ." Vince reached for her hand, but she grabbed her martini and leaned back into the bench, keeping herself out of his reach.

"Bet you think I'm angry." Blowing out a long stream of smoke, she let the words hang in the air. "But you know what?"

Vince steepled his fingers into an I'm-still-in-control gesture, shooting her an amused smile.

"I'm celebratin'."

A young waitress materialized at their table. Vince started to wave her away, but Christy caught the girl's arm. "Hey, how ya doin'? Mr. Excitement here'll have a scotch on the rocks."

Vince's lips pursed. "Make it a 7UP."

The waitress hesitated, looking to Christy. They'd always been friendly to each other.

Christy shrugged. "Get the man what he wants. And I'll have another one of these." She tapped the half-empty martini glass with her fingernail.

Leaning against the wall, Christy slipped off her sneakers and pulled both legs onto the bench. She loved the way alcohol emboldened her. She was no longer the spineless woman who wouldn't stand up for herself. "Welcome to my party, Vince."

"You're making absolutely no sense. Listen. My car's right outside. Let me take you home, and together we can get you sobered up."

"Oh, and thanks for the Hemingway. But I already have a copy."

"You need help."

"I don't need anyone's help. Especially not yours."

"But you do." Vince raised his hands, palms up, to indicate the whole room. "Look around you. Is this what you want for your life?"

That hit a nerve. "How dare you insult me after what you did today."

"You chose that deal with Fletcher knowing full well what you were doing. But you didn't care, did you? What did he pay? A hundred bucks? The truth is, what happened today was your own fault. And it could've been prevented, by the way."

"*You* put that book in my car!"

"You gave me no other choice."

Christy pulled a drag from her Winston. "Oh, please."

"You didn't keep your end of the bargain."

"And if you happen to ruin someone's career along the way, no problem, right?"

"All I'm saying . . ." His voice trailed off when the waitress returned to their table.

She set down their drinks. "Here you go."

Neither of them thanked her.

"All I'm saying," Vince said, lowering his voice, "is that you'll never amount to anything by yourself. But with me you could be someone. Success, Christy. Don't you want that?"

"Just shut up." She hammered the remains of her cigarette into the table's brown plastic ashtray, lighting up another without missing a beat. "All you did today was set me free."

"You're not listening to me."

Christy wrapped her fingers around her glass. "Why should I? I gave you everything. And what did you do? Threw it in my face."

"It doesn't have to be this way. We can talk to Rob together and work something out. He'll listen to me."

She laughed, hot anger flaring in her veins. "It was a stupid move too. Hunter already suspected you. Now you've freed me to tell him all about your schemes."

"He won't believe you."

"Sure about that?"

"This is getting us nowhere. If you'll just—"

"I'm gonna destroy you. Like you destroyed me."

Vince shoved his drink aside, 7UP splashing on the table. "Don't threaten me."

"Doesn't feel so good, does it?"

"You're making a huge mistake."

"What? By sticking up for myself? I'm not a rug."

"I'm serious."

"So am I." Christy held up her cell phone for Vince to see. "We could tell him together if you want, or I could do it for you." She was mocking him now, and she felt no fear.

The vein on Vince's temple bulged, a sure sign she'd punched a button. But she didn't care. Not tonight. Vince was smaller than he'd ever been, and she reveled in her new-found independence. She didn't need anyone. Not Vince, not Hunter, not the Book Barn. She was in charge of her own life. No one was going to tell her how to run it anymore.

"Speed dial 3, I believe," she said.

"I'm giving you one last chance." Vince emphasized each word, his bushy eyebrows dipping. "Even now I'll forget about everything, and we can start over. Just put the phone away, and let me help you to the car."

Finishing her martini with one last gulp, Christy dropped the cell phone back into her purse. "Shook up now, aren't we?"

Vince's eyes narrowed, the corner of his mouth pulling into a smile that was anything but jovial. "Think you're clever?"

"No, I think I'm done with you."

He looked away for a second, then quickly looked back to her. "I love you. Doesn't that mean anything?"

"If this is love . . ." Christy tapped ash off her cigarette, then met his eyes. "You know, I used to love you too. When we met, I thought maybe I'd finally found someone who loved me for me. But you don't love me."

Vince stood and sat down beside her. He reached around her shoulders, rubbing her arm with his warm fingers.

She tensed, and he felt it.

"Just relax. We can stay here for a little bit if you want. I do love you."

Even through the alcohol's haze, she wasn't fooled, and she wouldn't let Vince manipulate her again.

"We're meant to be together."

"No, Vince." She tried to push him away with her elbow.

He leaned his clean-shaven face closer to hers, his voice tender. "Don't. I won't let you go."

A sudden ferocity filled her limbs. She carefully set down her drink, then shoved Vince away with both hands. His face had just enough time to register surprise before he tumbled over the edge of the bench and onto the floor.

Three hefty guys in baseball caps at the nearest table turned toward her. Someone laughed.

Vince scrambled to his feet, a reckless shaft of hair falling into his eyes. "What are you doing?"

Another laugh, this time from one of the baseball hat guys. "Guess she don't want you, dude."

Swearing at the guy, Vince grabbed his jacket and towered over her. His starched gray oxford was half-untucked. "Think you can just throw me away like a piece of trash?"

She laughed too and started in on the third martini. It was ecstasy to be the one in control. Out of the corner of her eye she saw two of the men at the table stand up.

Vince pointed at her. "Well, you can't."

"How 'bout you just get lost, 'kay? I'm enjoying myself here."

One of the guys at the table stepped closer. "There a problem?"

"Yeah. This man is harassing me."

Without another word Vince stormed away and out the door.

Finishing her drink and pack of Winstons, Christy relished every second. She was finally free.

When the bar closed at two, the middle-aged bartender with glossy red lipstick reminded Christy it was time to leave. "Party's over, hon." She walked Christy to the door and gave her a light push into the night. By the time Christy turned around, the door had locked behind her, and the neon Budweiser and Coors signs flashing from the window were the only lights on.

She stumbled to her Honda at the edge of the parking lot and practically fell into the driver's seat. She wouldn't be stupid. She'd wait it out a bit. Let the alcohol wear off before driving home.

By the time she came to, the sky was turning predawn gray. She blew on her hands to thaw out her fingers and peered through the car's foggy windows. If she could just make it home, then she could zonk out and warm up. It was only two miles away.

Turning down her street, Christy faced two empty police cruisers, lights flashing. A drug bust was her first thought, but then she saw the fire engine and neighbors from all over her complex huddled at the curb. Some wore jackets over their pajamas; a few only had bathrobes that flapped in the chilling breeze. Her landlady, Mrs. Mendoza, stood in the middle of the crowd, curlers still stuck in her frosted hair. When she saw Christy drive up, she pointed at her, and the rest of the neighbors stared.

Christy's stomach lurched as she saw the blown-out windows and soot-drenched bricks of the third floor.

Her floor.

Jumping from the car, she forced her legs to hold her and ran toward the cluster in the street. "What happened?"

Mrs. Mendoza broke away from the others. "Where were you?"

"My apartment. Is it okay?"

"It's bad," the landlady said with a shake of her head.

Christy felt herself reel.

Mrs. Mendoza caught her arm. "We're lucky someone smelled the smoke. The whole building could've gone up."

"But how?" She looked up at the windows again. "I'm so careful about turning stuff off."

"They're telling me," Mrs. Mendoza said, waving toward the firemen, "it could be arson, and it started in your apartment."

"What?"

"Found a can of kerosene, I think. I'm sure they'll want to talk to you about it."

Christy spent the next half hour being questioned by firemen and police. "When did you leave? Did you lock the door? Did you have any arguments with anyone? Who else has a key? How long have you lived here?"

At some point a news van arrived, launching its satellite pole high into the air. The reporter got wind of the arson theory and demanded an interview. Christy refused, and Mrs. Mendoza eagerly took her place in front of the camera.

Christy left the crowd to their own devices and stood by herself on the sidewalk facing the apartments. She covered her eyes with her hand. How could this be happening?

She had to get in. See what was left. Knowing the firemen probably wouldn't let her inside alone, she made sure no one was watching before rushing up the steps into the building. She didn't care if she was allowed. If someone tried to stop her, they'd have to drag her away kicking and screaming.

Christy reached the third floor with heaving sides. Fumes scratched at her eyes and throat, and even when she held her sleeve over her face, she could barely breathe. She hesitated, then forced herself forward. She had to face this.

Her door hung crookedly on one hinge, chopped and splintered where the doorknob once was. The firemen's entry route.

Plink. Plink. Plink.

Water dripped from the ceiling, and even though she'd braced herself, she wasn't prepared for the destruction and foul smell. She strained to recognize what was supposed to be her home. The carpet was a swollen sponge under her feet, and cold droplets from the ceiling hit her head. Revulsion struck her when she saw the corner of the room where Aunt Edna's books had been stacked.

Choking and coughing on the gases hanging in the air, she took a few steps toward the box fragments and burned survivors. It had taken her hours to lug all the boxes up here and stack them in this corner. They'd towered four feet high. But now . . . Aunt Edna's gift to her was rubbish.

Christy turned toward the bookcase that had housed her mystery collection. Those books too were scorched beyond recognition, the middle shelf disintegrated, its remnants strewn across the floor.

Kneeling, her jeans were instantly soaked. Christy picked up one of the fallen books as carefully as if it were a wounded animal. The first letters of the author's name were still readable on the spine, and she knew this worthless piece of charred pulp had once been her most treasured possession, *Murder on the Orient Express* by Agatha Christie. She held its soggy remains to her chest.

Arson?

Pulling herself off the floor, she dropped the book. The bedroom held more of the same. Blackened walls and water everywhere. A metal frame and springs were all that was left of her bed, her clothes completely destroyed.

Turning from the horror, Christy looked out the window. Only one or two pieces of jagged glass remained, leaving no barrier from the icy wind. The secondhand computer Hunter had given her that sat underneath the window had been transformed into a gnarled heap of plastic and metal, the keyboard keys melted together as one.

She could hear Mrs. Mendoza and the other neighbors gabbing in the street. Bunch of pigs. Reporter boy was only looking for a story, the more tragic the better. Mrs. Mendoza basked in the attention. This was the excitement of the year for them all. And she despised them for it.

"Anyone been up?" someone asked.

"I just wanna get back to bed."

"Got all her stuff, I guess."

That was the last straw. Christy stuck her head out the window. "Shut up!"

Faces shot toward her.

At the top of her voice she cursed them all.

"What's she doing up there?"

"Hey, you better come down, lady."

She retreated and grabbed for the only object on the computer table that survived the heat, a ceramic mug, and hurled it across the room where it shattered against the wall. She threw the skeleton of the lamp, the melted keyboard, everything she could see, until the table itself crumbled to the floor.

Sick, Christy collapsed with it, too spent for tears. She took in gasps of the putrid air as the plink, plink of dripping water played on.

❧

Vince relaxed in his recliner by the gas fire, stroking Socrates' velvety fur. The lithe animal purred in his lap, kneading his leg.

"There," Vince whispered. "Happy now?"

He puffed on his cigar, every few minutes taking a sip of brandy from the rare tumbler he'd bought online from a dealer in Wales. While Christy drank for the buzz, he drank for the experience. The sensation on his tongue, the aroma in his nostrils, the texture of the glass against his fingertips. Vince held the tumbler up to the fire's light, and the amber liquid glowed. Fire. That's what alcohol was. Play with it and you'll get burned, which is why he never did. It brought too much pleasure for him to ever risk having to give it up. He never drank more than one glass a day and was proud of his strength to control himself.

He returned the tumbler to its coaster, glass clicking on marble. All the lights remained off, along with the heater. The same way his own father used to keep the house most evenings.

Vince stared at the mesmerizing flames and suddenly saw Father's angry face dancing in them, appearing like he had the night Vince discovered his mother's empty closet as an innocent eight-year-old boy. Those eyes. Those powerful hands that could strike without warning.

"She left because of you."

"Dad . . ." He backed away from his father.

"She hated you. That's why."

"No!" Tears stung Vince's eyes. "She loved me. She did!"

Father grabbed him by the front of his shirt, eyes bugging in fury. "You drove her away, boy."

Curling his fingers around the recliner's armrest, Vince brought himself back to the present, alone in his own dark study where the shadow of his hunched form projected onto the bookshelves. Driven her away. His own mother, Abby, and now Christy.

He gripped his head in shaking hands, breathing long, slow breaths. It had to stop. These women couldn't keep leaving him like this.

❧

Christy spent the rest of the day back at the White Horse. After drinking for a few hours, by midnight she found herself parked between two semis at a truck stop with the engine running for warmth and a fresh bottle of sherry stashed under the passenger seat.

All night trucks released their air brakes and rumbled past her window. Jolting awake sometime past four, she reached for the sherry and poured some into her plastic travel mug. She yearned for the buzz to help her sleep again, but it didn't come. Instead of bringing numbness, the alcohol pushed her deep into depression. The shock had passed, and she was now forced to face the truth.

Everything was gone.

The firemen had let her collect what she could, but that only amounted to a few dishes and silverware. Not a scrap of clothing. She was stuck with the shirt on her back and her fleece jacket, both reeking of smoke and useless against a frosty night.

She never had gotten around to buying renter's insurance. What little cash she had would probably run out by tomorrow. Her credit cards were already close to their limits. How could she live off that? Finding a new apartment would take time, but even if she did find something, she knew she couldn't scrounge up even enough for a deposit.

There was a chance Harvey would let her live at Aunt Edna's house until it sold, but pride kept her from calling to ask. If she did, he'd know she'd destroyed Aunt Edna's books. How could she face him now? The thought of returning to Vince actually came to mind, which disgusted her.

Christy swallowed more sherry and regarded the passenger seat. A small piece of paper sat next to the bottle. She picked it up and reread May's address and phone number.

As the sun began to rise, Christy slogged to the truck stop restrooms. Her mouth felt as dry as cotton, and she had the start of a bad hangover. A tourist with a camera around her neck held the bathroom door open, but Christy didn't have the energy to say thank you. At the first grimy sink she splashed cold water on her face. Maybe she should pick up a newspaper. The classifieds might have something. She might be able to—

She stopped herself. Did she really want to plan for the future? Maybe no future was the best future of all.

Christy hung on to the sink with both hands and looked at her sorry, dripping face in the mirror. Arson. The cops weren't ruling it out at this point. Could Vince hate her enough to set that fire? Had she pushed him too far at the White Horse? She couldn't even remember what she'd said in the haze of her martinis.

He was the only one she could imagine doing something like this, but she had trouble believing it even of him. He was crooked, sure. But was he capable of arson?

After visiting the nearest stall, she bought a cup of coffee that tasted like flavored water, but at least it was hot. Back in the car she melted into her seat, cradling the Styrofoam cup and turning the engine back on for the heat. What a total mess she'd made of her life. Here she was, thirty-three years old, a homeless piece of garbage with no hope of ever amounting to anything. What if she did find a place to stay? even a job? Right. She had no skills. No degree. The best she could hope for was another minimum wage deal that barely paid the rent.

And the next decade would hold more guilt and heartbreak. But then she'd be old and ugly. No man would want her. If only she'd been home when the fire broke out and died of smoke inhalation. That would've been a blessing, because life sure was a curse. Why should she keep going now?

Mindlessly, Christy glanced at her cell phone, still plugged into the charger cord in the lighter. There was one new voice mail. Must've come in while she was in the bathroom. Dialing in, she listened to Vince's voice: "Christy, whenever you get this, call me. Give me a chance to help you. There's still time to work things out."

She threw the phone onto the seat. "Just leave me alone! Leave me alone!"

⁂

The Happy Trails Motel was anything but happy. Tonight only the *V* and *c* in *Vacancy* were glowing, and foot-high weeds grew underneath the sign. Most of the lightbulbs outside the rooms were missing. Christy counted three cars in the lot.

She parked directly in front of room 112 and walked to the door with her car key brandished and ready to jab eyes. The door was made of thin fiberboard, flimsy enough for one good kick to bust it in. The chain was missing, the dead bolt broken.

Flicking on the light, she recoiled as a cockroach scurried across the shag carpet. Stains and smears were all over the walls. One of them even looked like dried blood. She clutched the cheap suitcase she'd bought at Walmart. How was she going to sleep in a place like this?

By making herself, that's how. She had no alternative. It was either this or another night in the car, and the pain in her back screamed in protest at that idea.

She chucked her suitcase at the only chair and turned on another light. Peeling back the wrinkled bedspread, she checked underneath each pillow for more roaches, then eased herself onto the mattress, which groaned against her weight.

This was the end of the road.

The way she saw it, she had four possible courses of action. One, move back in with Vince. It was better not to even think about him. Any conversation with Vince in this state could scatter what little resolve she had left. She was vulnerable enough right now to be seduced again.

Two, wait this out until Aunt Edna's money came. Next to impossible with the little she had. Harvey would lend her anything she asked, but she wasn't going to drag him into this.

Three, take what cash she did have and buy the biggest bottle of the deadliest pills she could find. This idea was more appealing with each passing minute. But there was a fourth idea.

Still lying on her back, Christy dug the paper with May's address out of her pocket. She had it memorized but read it once more anyway, then let her arm flop to the bed with the paper still in her hand. She never thought she'd be the one to initiate anything with May. Meeting at the funeral had been hard enough. But May was the only family she had left. For some reason that was starting to matter.

Christy drew her cell phone from her purse. What was the worst that could happen? May could reject her. She wasn't sure how that would feel. She didn't want to get hurt or to hurt May again, but seeing her after all these years gave Christy a glimpse of what it could have been like between them. They could've been close. Been friends. She never realized how much she'd lost by running away.

But May knew nothing of how she'd lived her life these past fifteen years. The last thing Christy wanted was to expose her closet skeletons. If she couldn't forgive herself, she couldn't expect anyone else to, either.

She punched in the number but waited to push Send. Just a quick phone call. Only a conversation. She wouldn't have to see May face-to-face. But what would she say? What if May asked questions? What if she was mad at Christy for ditching her at the funeral?

Christy took a deep breath. *Come on. Just go for it.*

She touched the Send key. Her pulse boomed.

On the third ring a woman's voice answered. "Hello?" It wasn't May.

"Is . . . can I speak to May?"

"Sorry. I don't know where she is right now. Can I take a message for her?"

Christy's heart fell. "No, that's okay. I'll try later." But as she set down the phone, she knew she wouldn't.

12

Hunter penciled a neat thirty dollars on the flyleaf of *Custer and the Great Controversy*, then glanced at the antique clock above the door. It was nearly closing time, and he was looking forward to it. With Christy gone, his workload had doubled. He knew he should've started searching for someone to take her place, but mentally he wasn't ready for that. He couldn't bring himself to put in the ad. Perhaps it was irrational. What she did was inexcusable.

The bell above the front door jingled, and a man in a three-piece suit entered. Hunter put him in his sixties—receding hairline, bespectacled. Some sort of businessman.

Hopefully he wasn't planning on browsing. Hunter hated when people showed up five minutes before closing and expected you to stay open while they searched the shelves, only buying a three-dollar paperback in the end.

"Can I help you, sir?"

The man came toward him. "I'm looking for Christy Williams. I understand she works here."

Hunter reached for another book. "Actually, she's out for a couple days. But I can give her a message when I speak with her again, if you'd like."

"That leaves me in a bind," the man said, extending his hand, which Hunter shook. It was a little sweaty but iron firm.

"I'm Harvey Kurtz. I've been a friend of her family's for many years. I haven't been able to contact her for days. I was hoping to catch her here, but it looks like I'm out of luck. Thanks anyway." He turned to leave just as a customer appeared at the counter with an armful of books to buy. Folks were trickling in from all corners of the Barn with their purchases.

Hunter would have to check them out. But something in him didn't want to let Mr. Kurtz go. A friend of Christy's family? He didn't even know she *had* family. Everything about her personal life was a mystery to him. And now Hunter was watching his chance to find out walking away.

"Sir?" he called after the man. "Can you wait a minute? I'd like to talk to you about Christy, but I have to help these people first."

Twenty minutes later Hunter locked the store's door and pulled two chairs toward the potbellied stove. Its warmth was welcome. When the sun went down, the room chilled exponentially.

He shook Mr. Kurtz's hand again. "Hunter Dawson. Thanks for waiting. We've been friends, but she hasn't told me much about her family. I hope you don't mind, but I was wondering if you could tell me a little more about her. How long have you known her?"

"Her father and I were in the Marines before she was born." He folded his hands in front of his chest. "And you?"

"I hired her four years ago," Hunter said, hoping Mr. Kurtz was picking up his genuine concern for Christy. Even after all that had happened, he wanted to help her if he could. There had to be more going on than he knew.

"Maybe I could ask you a few questions as well," Mr. Kurtz said. "I feel responsible for my late buddy's daughters. I get the feeling Christy's in trouble, but I'm not sure why. Is she okay?"

Hunter took a moment before answering, then looked the older man in the eyes. He hadn't discussed Christy with anyone but Pop before, but something about Mr. Kurtz made him want to. He could tell they had something in common. They were both worried about her. What if she really was in trouble?

"Did you know she has a drinking problem?" Hunter asked quietly.

Mr. Kurtz sighed. "I suspected it."

"She's been late to work many times—due to that, I'm guessing."

"Her parents were alcoholics," Mr. Kurtz said. "They were both killed in an alcohol-related accident fifteen years ago. They were coming home early from a business trip so they could be there on her eighteenth birthday."

"Wow," Hunter said.

"Yeah. How's that for a birthday present? She never told me, but I know she felt responsible. Can you imagine what that would do to a kid? A couple days later she dropped out of contact with me and her relatives. I found her, but she's been very guarded with me."

"Maybe she was hiding the drinking?"

Mr. Kurtz removed his glasses and placed them in his pocket. "I think so. I'm a little concerned. She hasn't returned my calls for days."

Hunter watched the stove and shoved a log inside. Sparks shot out. He closed the door, thinking about the Hemingway in Christy's car. How could she stand there and deny any involvement as emphatically as she did? Everything pointed clearly to her as the culprit. Maybe that's what bothered him. The facts fell into place too neatly. Or was he letting his growing feelings for her cloud his judgment?

"She's had some other trouble too," Hunter said.

Mr. Kurtz's eyebrows rose, but he let Hunter continue.

"We've had some valuable books stolen from the store. I've wondered if it was an inside job, but I haven't been able to prove anything. Just two days ago another rare book went missing from that case over there." He pointed toward the display beside the register. "I found it in Christy's car."

Another raise of the eyebrows from Mr. Kurtz.

"I'm having trouble believing she'd do something like that, but I also found out she's been dishonest with me before. That's why I wanted to talk with you. I need to know more about her so I can figure this out."

"What was her explanation?"

"She denied taking it and accused her ex-boyfriend, who also works here, of trying to frame her."

Mr. Kurtz tapped his thumbs together. "Could he be?"

"She lived with him for a while, and he wasn't good to her." Hunter didn't look at Mr. Kurtz. He could only stare at the glowing embers through the stove door. Abby never breathed a word either, but her bruises and quiet fear spoke for her. Abby finally escaped by moving out of state. She said it was because she wanted a change in scenery, a new life, but Hunter knew she left to escape Vince. He hated him for that. "I wouldn't put it past him."

Mr. Kurtz got a determined look in his eye. "Well, let's get to the bottom of this, shall we?"

❧

Christy shifted her car into fifth gear and focused on the red lights of the semi in the distance. A snow squall had overtaken her, and she could barely see the road. She wanted to think she was being gutsy taking this step, but she knew better. She couldn't do anything for the right reasons. Everything she did revolved around her stupid self.

All night she'd debated. Between that and worrying about some pervert breaking into her room, she'd gotten no sleep. By 5 a.m. she realized it was pointless to keep trying and checked out of the motel. After studying the map, she was on the road by six.

Heading toward Elk Valley. Toward May.

Christy kept pace with the 18-wheeler long after the snow cleared. It was desperation that drove her, really. Nothing noble at all. And what would May think of her unannounced visit? The sixty-four-thousand-dollar question.

Deep in thought, she hardly noticed as the miles flew by. Their childhood had been normal enough. School. Goofing around. They'd never been best friends or anything, but Christy had always loved May.

Later—in her teens, after Dad lost his job—the dynamics changed, and she didn't remember being home much. She always found excuses to be gone, especially at night when her parents drank. There were times May begged to come with her, but she always said no. It wasn't cool to have your little sister tagging along in the backseat.

Things changed even more when Christy was seventeen. She met Kyle, a guy already in his second year of college. They began dating, and she was introduced to a whole new set of friends who weren't afraid to have a good time, even if it meant breaking the rules.

When Mom and Dad died, she turned to those friends, especially Kyle. He dropped out of college and asked her to move away with him to Kansas. It had been such an easy out. Escape from it all. She'd felt twinges of guilt over leaving May, but her sister was tough, and she had Aunt Edna as guardian. Those rationalizations had enabled Christy to brush the guilt away.

Only within the last few days had she taken an honest look at her actions. What she did must have hurt May incredibly. She hadn't even said good-bye. If ever May had needed love and assurance, it would have been then, but Christy abandoned her.

Stopping at a gas station, Christy fueled up, hoping she had enough credit left on her Visa, then pulled to the edge of the lot and sat for a minute in the morning sun. *Shrug it off. That was fifteen years ago. Things have changed. May isn't a kid anymore.*

Yeah, she knew that. It was part of the problem. A kid might be more willing to forgive and move on. But why should May forgive her? Christy remembered the night they'd found out about Mom and Dad, how she'd cloistered herself in her room, listening to May sobbing in hers. Sometime later that morning May came knocking at her door asking to come in. Too absorbed in her own grief and guilt, Christy had yelled for her to go away.

Christy reached under the seat and pulled out her bottle of vodka. She had her usual sherry in the suitcase, but the vodka was perfect now. She tipped a small shot into her coffee. It wasn't much. Just enough to calm and give courage. She would drink it only once every five miles. Besides, vodka was hard to smell on the breath, especially mixed with coffee.

It was almost ten when she turned off Interstate 25 and onto Route 160 in Walsenburg, and it wasn't long before she arrived at Pronghorn Drive. May's road. Christy downed the last of the spiked coffee.

She made the turn and drove slowly down the narrow road, checking each widely spaced mailbox for a number.

The note called the ranch the Triple Cross. Maybe there would be a marker or something.

Scrub peeked through the snow in the field on her left. To the right was a huge stand of pines, their boughs dusted with snow. Up ahead were the craggy Spanish Peaks, dwarfing everything else. What had gotten into May to live out here in the middle of nowhere?

After three miles she saw the sign, and her determination withered. Logs formed a canopy at the beginning of a long dirt drive that bent around the pines and disappeared from sight. Three black metal crosses, the middle one slightly taller than the rest, poked up from the top log, and hanging beneath them by a rusted chain was a wooden sign. Triple Cross Ranch.

This was it.

13

When Christy approached the buildings at the end of the driveway, she almost did a 180. Her body felt like rubber, and her armpits were moist with sweat in spite of the cold. She really was crazy to have come here.

The Honda dipped into an icy rut, barely making it back out as she approached the cluster of buildings. First was a barn. She could tell by the hints of color under the eaves that it had once been red, but it was now a weathered brown. Dead ahead was a one-story house with a tin roof. She recognized the Dodge pickup from the funeral, parked near the house with a second truck beside it.

Don't park there. The last thing she needed was someone seeing her before she was ready. Instead, she pulled up behind the horse trailer beside the barn. She still faced the house, but at a glance her car wouldn't be easily noticed.

Christy turned off the engine and sat for a minute, unable to move. She might not even like May now that her sister was a religious nut. They had nothing in common anymore, and sooner or later May would find out what a loser Christy really was. The big sister who'd ruined Aunt Edna's prized possessions and couldn't even hold down a job.

She didn't have to do this.

Christy reached for some courage and took one more swig. Yeah, she did have to. She had nowhere else to go. Even this godforsaken place was better than living in her car.

But what if May didn't want her? That scared her more than anything. She didn't know if she could survive May's rejection.

Go. Just go.

Christy unclipped her seat belt. She should never have attended that funeral. None of this would be happening if she hadn't seen May and found out where she lived. What had she been thinking?

One step at a time. That's all I gotta take.

She got out of the car, closing the door as quietly as possible. She stared at the house, in plain view now. Why was she so afraid to do this? May had hardly been unkind at the funeral. She'd actually seemed pleased to see her.

Christy forced herself to walk. She made it to the front porch decorated with chalky plastic outdoor furniture, not letting herself hesitate a moment longer. Knocking softly, she waited.

Nothing.

She tried again with the same result. Surveying the yard, she saw no one, and all she could hear were cows bellowing from the nearby pastures. She walked around the house. There was a side door. She knocked on it and was again met with silence. Without thinking, she tried the knob and was surprised to find the door unlocked. She cracked it. "Hello? Anyone home?"

The house was silent, and she held on to the door, stuck, not knowing what to do. This was her out. Time to leave.

But she didn't. The truth was, she hadn't just come looking for a place to stay, though that's what got her started in this direction. She ached to know what May felt about her. Christy stepped inside, shutting the door behind her. She'd be careful not to disturb anything.

She found herself in the kitchen. The linoleum floor had probably once been white but was now a dingy yellow. It was worn smooth in spots, especially in front of the door and where the chairs slid away from the kitchen table. Several bowls, a pot, and three mugs lay soaking in an avocado green sink, but the counters were clean. A cast-iron woodstove sat in the corner. She felt little warmth from it.

Unable to resist the temptation to snoop, Christy wandered farther into the house searching for clues of May's life. In the living room she first noticed a gun case and counted five rifles and shotguns behind the glass. How often were they needed?

She glimpsed an unmade bed in the first room off the hall. Was it her sister's? She went to it. The room was nothing fancy; that was for sure. The plain bed was full-size, with the sheets and blankets in a rumpled heap at the foot.

Christy homed in on the small bookcase next to the bed, quickly scanning it. There were a few novels in the Grisham vein and some worn paperback classics. A book called *The Whole Truth* by James Scott Bell lay spread-eagled on top of the shelf, apparently May's current read. A few titles Christy considered more literary, like a copy of *No Life for a Lady* by Agnes Morley Cleaveland, a classic book that chronicled the author's girlhood on a New Mexico ranch in the 1800s. The bottom shelf had books similar to those May had given Aunt Edna, creased devotionals and a couple of versions of the Bible.

She found another bedroom, much neater than the first, and at the end of the hall was a small study with two desks.

She paused in its doorway and wished for a cigarette but decided against lighting up inside. It was a simple home, but at least May *had* a home. And it was clear she wasn't alone. More than one person lived here. Was May shacking up with that guy at the funeral?

Christy entered the study. One of the desks was messier than the other, like the bedrooms had been, and Christy focused on it. She guessed it was May's. Her sister never had been all that neat. Some old mail lay scattered across the surface, and she picked up an empty envelope addressed to Mrs. Ruth D. Santos and Ms. May A. Williams. The return address was a bank's. Who was Ruth Santos?

She looked over the desk for what could have been inside the envelope. That's when a small framed photograph caught her eye. Christy lifted it off the desk and saw herself. Her tenth-grade class photo. May kept it on her desk after all these years?

Sitting down, she stared at the old picture. She didn't remember giving it to May, but perhaps she'd found it in Mom and Dad's things after they died. Seeing herself set out in a place of prominence brought questions for sure and a glimmer of hope. May might not be holding a grudge after all.

She traced the brass frame with her finger. Then again, May could have it out to curse her face every time she saw it.

A door slammed.

Christy leaped to her feet, ready to run. She wasn't supposed to be in here! She couldn't let May find her snooping like this.

Clanging came from the kitchen. A refrigerator opened. A radio came to life, blaring a Toby Keith song. Then scuffling and clicking came down the hallway. Before she could react, a small black and white dog rounded the corner and sent out a startled howl at the sight of her. He kept barking, hackles upraised.

She took a step back from the dog and froze. The animal growled deep in his throat. If she could only get past him before she was discovered by whoever was in the house, she might be able to escape out the front door. Her gaze darted toward the hall. She took a step forward.

The terrier curled his upper lip, another low growl escaping his throat.

"Shh," she whispered. "You're gonna get me in trouble."

The growling stopped for an instant, and she thought she noticed the dog's tail wag slightly at her voice.

"Good boy," she said, and hanging on to that minuscule sign of friendliness, she took a risk and smoothly lowered herself into a crouching position on the floor. Patting her leg, she spoke as gently and quietly as she could. "Come here, fella. Come here."

His tail was definitely wagging now, and the growling stopped entirely.

"That's it. Good dog." She held out her hand, hoping to entice him to sniff. "I'm not gonna hurt you."

He cautiously approached, and she was careful not to make any sudden moves as she kept her hand outstretched. Her voice was calming him. "There. That's it. Good boy."

The dog gave the tips of her fingers a lick as if to taste-test if she was serious.

"That's right. It's okay. No need to bark." She reached for him and scratched the coarse fur of his neck. "Now listen. I've gotta get out of here, okay?"

"You do?" The man's voice came out of nowhere.

Christy looked up to see the same guy she'd met at the funeral standing in the doorway. He was wiping his fingers on a greasy rag.

She jumped to her feet. "I can explain. I—"

He held up his hand. "No need. It's freezing out there. I'd wait inside too." She could barely see his smile through that thick handlebar mustache. "Christy, right?"

She nodded, relieved he was letting it go. "I can't remember yours."

"Jim." He pointed at the dog, who was now leaning against her leg. "This here's Scribbles. He's all bark, as you can see."

Jim stuffed the rag into the back pocket of his tan coveralls, which were shredded at the cuffs and unzipped to his waist. She caught a whiff of manure and oil. He looked different without a cowboy hat, plenty of gray intertwined with his sandy hair.

"Sorry none of us were here," Jim said. "I was working on my truck, and May and Ruth are in town at Walker's pickin' up an order."

"I might not be able to stay anyway."

"That'd be a shame. May's been wanting to see you again." Jim stepped into the hall. "Wanna join me for some coffee?"

With a shrug, she followed. Scribbles bounced in front of her as if the whole incident in the study never happened. She sat down at the wooden kitchen table, uncomfortable with a man she didn't know. But maybe he'd be able to tell her more about May. "You live here?"

Jim was scrounging in a cabinet and didn't answer until he found a can of Maxwell House. "Got the trailer out back. May and Ruth have the house."

So May *wasn't* living with him. She watched Jim measure heaping scoops into the filter. When she counted ten, her expression must have changed, because he looked over at her and laughed. "This time of year we make it strong."

"This time of year?"

"Calving season. We're up at all hours checking the mamas. Coffee's our sleep substitute." Jim turned down the radio, the kind that was mounted underneath a cabinet, and as the coffee brewed, he leaned against the counter.

He pointed at the stove, where a bottle, filled with what looked like skim milk, sat in a saucepan slowly heating. "Colostrum. I got a calf in the shed right now that's not nursing yet. They gotta have this stuff within the first half hour, antibodies and all. We've got a bunch in the freezer for emergencies."

Jim tested the water with his finger and turned up the stove. "You meet Ruth?"

"Was she at the funeral?"

"That was her."

"We didn't actually meet."

"She's the backbone of this place. You'll like her."

Christy didn't appreciate the way he assumed she'd be staying.

Jim took two of the dirty mugs from the sink and slid them toward the maker. She managed to keep from grimacing when she realized he was planning on reusing them without washing them first.

"How long have you known May?" she asked. If she was going to sit here with this guy, she might as well pump him for all the information she could.

"About six years. She started working for Ruth, then bought into the ranch five years later. They hired me shortly after that."

Hired hand? Christy wondered how he felt working for two women. It didn't appear to be much of an issue the way he said it—not like it would be for Vince, who vowed no female would ever give him orders.

After a minute the maker gurgled and sputtered as the last drops of the syrupy brew dripped into the pot. Jim filled the mugs. "How do you like yours?"

"Black."

"Best way," he said, placing hers on the table and sitting in the chair opposite, holding his cup between both hands. Half of the fingernail of his right thumb was missing, and the part that was exposed looked painfully raw. Another finger was black and blue under the nail, with several small cuts adorning the others. She couldn't help comparing them to Vince's spotless, manicured hands.

She tasted the coffee and managed to keep from reflexively spitting it out. It was strong, all right. But she would have drunk it whether it tasted bad or not. The vodka was already wearing off, and with all the apprehension working through her body, she craved a good shot of something.

The silence between her and Jim became thick. What could she say to this tough cowboy who knew more about her own sister than she did? She looked at him and caught him staring at *her* hands. She realized they were trembling and gripped her coffee mug. Hard.

"May know you were coming?"

She decided not to lie. "No," she said, keeping her eyes downcast.

"I think she'll be thrilled." Jim took a long gulp of his coffee, then reached down to pet Scribbles. "This guy was your aunt Edna's, you know. May's had him only a week."

He'd changed the subject when she started squirming. Was her discomfort that obvious? "A ranch must be a great place for a dog."

"Great place to get in trouble, and he sure does." He told her how Scribbles had already managed to get himself into several scrapes, including getting kicked by an angry mother cow.

After a few minutes Jim finished his coffee with one more tilt of his head and stood. "I've gotta feed that calf. You're welcome to come along." He pointed at her fleece pullover. "That won't cut it, though."

She looked down at her clothing. She'd lost her parka in the fire. Without waiting for her to respond, Jim grabbed a worn brown coat from the rack by the door and flung it at her. "Try that on. You'll need it."

It smelled like horse, and even though she was almost

positive the flaky stain on the front was dried animal saliva, she put it on anyway.

"Take these, too." Jim handed her a pair of leather work gloves, then picked up a soiled gray Stetson from the counter and set it on his head. She decided he looked better in a hat. Jim took the bottle from the stove and held the kitchen door open for her, leaving her no choice but to join him. Scribbles bolted past both of them, jumping at snowflakes, which had started falling again.

Jim walked through the yard and around the barn to one of the smaller outbuildings. "I've got a couple others I'm watching too. They should calve soon, but if they don't, I'll need to give them a hand."

"How do you do that?"

"Pulling. You let 'em do it on their own if at all possible, but if it gets to be too long, it's better to get the calf out. Less risk. We try to do it mostly by hand here. Some folks use a mechanical puller all the time, but you can pull too hard that way sometimes. I've seen calves' hooves pulled right off with one."

Christy winced.

The door to the barnlike structure creaked as Jim opened it. "Welcome to the calving shed." He flipped a grimy switch beside the door. Bare white bulbs illuminated a wooden, straw-strewn walkway. A loud bellow came from one of the stalls. "Kinda makeshift, but it does the job." Jim leaned over the second stall's door and waved a hand toward her.

She looked over Jim's shoulder. A calf with brown matted fur sidled next to its mother, who stood almost as tall as Christy. Her huge tongue licked the calf's face, throwing its head back with each swipe.

"Mama's doin' her job," Jim said. "Baby just needs a little jump start, that's all."

Christy continued to watch the drama, but her thoughts wandered. She kept imagining what she'd say to May. It really would be better if she left. She could ask Jim to give her sister a message, like she'd only had an hour and was really disappointed it hadn't worked out. That would sound good.

"What time are you expecting May back?"

"Within the hour, I guess."

She turned away from him, pretending to be absorbed in watching the cow and calf. But with each passing second, the tension built in her chest. She realized something. May didn't need her. She had friends who cared and stood by her side in times of need. What would Christy be but an old ghost coming back to haunt her? She didn't have any right to butt in on her sister's life like this.

"I know May wants to see you."

That got her to turn around. Jim was flaking off hay into

the corner of one of the stalls for the cow inside. "She's been praying for you," he said.

"Yeah, probably that I'd go to hell."

Jim looked at her, his expression unchanged. "The opposite, actually. And also that you two would have the chance to spend some time together."

"You know, I don't understand something. What happened to her? Our parents weren't religious. I don't even remember going to church at Easter."

"I'm sure she'd be happy to talk about it."

Christy didn't know if she would let that happen or not. Religion had to give May double the reason to be disappointed in her. Yet she hadn't seen any kind of disapproval in May's face.

"What're you thinking?" Jim asked. "That she's gonna pound you over the head with her Bible?"

She couldn't tell if he was joking or serious. It was hard to see through that mustache. She'd play it like he was serious. "I guess I am."

"She isn't like that."

"What *is* she like?" Christy stood in the open doorway, her back to Jim, who'd stepped inside the stall with the bottle. She watched the falling snow and wandering cattle. "I only have memories of a fifteen-year-old girl."

He didn't say anything right away, and she was glad of it.

Maybe that meant he would give her a good answer. "Your sister's a strong woman," he finally said. "She's independent, and if she sets her mind to doing something, it'll get done."

It calmed her a bit to hear his response. That was the personality she remembered. The same stubbornness that often got May into trouble as a kid.

"She likes to have fun," Jim continued.

"Always did."

"I suppose she hasn't changed much, then. But her aunt taught her about God. You heard her at the funeral. That's her story."

Christy dropped the subject. She faced the stall door and watched him. He knelt in the straw, his gnarly hand gently cradling the head of the calf, his other holding the bottle in the animal's mouth. Liquid dribbled down the calf's chin as it noisily suckled. Jim spoke to it softly. "There you go, little girl. Drink up."

She was getting colder and thrust her hands in the pockets of the coat, wondering if it was May's. The dog pawed her knee. She squatted and rubbed his ear, clueless what to do next. She hadn't come all this way to hang out with a rugged cowboy.

Scribbles's sharp yap startled her, but it sounded different than with her in the study. He barked with happiness and excitement as he flew out the door.

That could mean only one thing.

She stood up, a wave of what felt almost like excitement hitting her. Quickly brushing off her jeans, she ran a hand through her hair and hoped she looked okay.

When Scribbles bounded back through the door, tail wagging with abandon, May was behind him.

14

MAY BROKE INTO a huge smile. "What are you doing here?"

Before Christy could do or say anything, she was encircled in a hug, even bigger than the one May had given her at the funeral.

"I'm so glad to see you again," May said into her shoulder, then let her go. Collars of several shirts stuck out at her neckline. She wore a hat similar to Jim's, with nicks in the edges and mud splatters all over the felt. Christy almost smiled. Here was the grubby little girl who could never seem to stay clean.

"Sorry I didn't call ahead."

May shook her head. "What, are you kidding? I just can't believe you're actually here. You know how often I've wished this would happen? that you'd show up and surprise me?"

Actually she hadn't pictured May wishing it at all.

"So I take it you two have met?" May said to Jim.

"Yes, ma'am," Jim said with a chuckle but didn't mention Christy's trespassing. Maybe he knew the embarrassment she felt about it.

May's face lit up, and she clasped Christy's arm. "Wait right here. I've gotta get Ruth." She ran out the door, leaving Christy alone once more with Jim.

"I told you," he said. "She's glad to see you."

Christy wanted to believe him. It felt better than she could have imagined to hug her sister again. But why wasn't May upset with her for leaving the funeral?

May reappeared with the lady who'd accompanied her at the church. Shorter than May and round in the middle like a tomato, the older woman's dark face was a sea of wrinkles, no doubt from countless hours of outdoor exposure.

"Here she is," May said. "Can you believe it?"

"Great to finally meet you," Ruth said, the skin around her eyes crinkling into deep crow's-feet. She gave Christy a firm handshake with both hands. "My name's Ruth."

May touched Christy's arm. "I've gotta check the fence to find where some of the cows are getting out. Come with me."

"In the snow?"

"It isn't too bad. We'll take the horses."

She hesitated. "I haven't ridden in years."

"I'll give you a gentle one." May's eyes were pleading, and Christy couldn't refuse.

As they walked away together toward the barn, she glanced back at Jim, who winked at her, then busied himself with the hungry calf.

❧

Pulling up to apartment building C, Harvey wished he'd driven his older Buick. It would have blended in better than the Mercedes. As it was, he checked the locks twice before leaving the car, knowing they would offer little protection in this neighborhood. Any car thief worth his salt wouldn't let a lock faze him.

Harvey studied the dilapidated building. Two windows on the third floor were boarded over with new plywood. The bricks around the wood were stained with soot.

Christy lived here?

Inside the dark stairwell, shouted profanities reverberated through the walls from somewhere in the building. The argument faded as he climbed the stairs and reached the third floor. He checked the apartment number he'd written on the back of a business card—306. It took only a second to realize which one it was. The numbers of each apartment were glued to the wall on the left side of the doors. Number 306 had plywood nailed crudely over its doorframe.

A sick feeling grabbed his stomach. Where was Christy? What happened here?

Harvey knocked on several doors, getting no answer at two and a shout to "Go away!" at another. Finally, he was rewarded when a red-haired guy with a pimply face and no shirt answered at one of them.

"I'm trying to find the person who lived at 306," Harvey said, pointing down the hall. "Christy Williams."

"Who?"

"Christy Williams. She does live here, right?"

The guy hung out his doorway to see the boarded-over door. "Hey, man, I don't know for sure. Maybe. They move in and out of here, you know?"

"Know anything about this fire?"

Red Hair squinted as if trying to think. "No one was in there when it happened, I'm pretty sure. Cops came, and some guys were poking around afterward. They think it was arson. Made the TV."

"They arrest anyone?"

Red Hair shrugged. "Dunno."

"Any idea where I could find the girl who lived there?"

Another shrug from Red Hair.

Harvey thanked him for his time and returned to the first floor. He knocked on more doors. Someone referred him to the landlady, and she confirmed that Christy had lived in apartment 306.

"Do you know where she is now?" Harvey asked as Mrs. Mendoza walked out, barefoot, closing her door.

She looked him up and down. "You a reporter?"

"No."

"Cop?"

"Just a friend of Christy's."

Mrs. Mendoza threw her hands up. "What do I know? She could be in Timbuktu. Didn't know she had any friends."

"How about a forwarding address?"

"Never gave one."

"What can you tell me about the fire?"

Mrs. Mendoza perked up at that question and told him the whole story, emphasizing every part she'd played.

He learned nothing new, except that Christy had been out all night and came home after the fire was extinguished. "Did you see Christy leave?"

"Sure, but there was nothing to it. Just drove off. I'll tell you, though—" Mrs. Mendoza stomped her foot—"she owes me a month's rent!"

He made a mental note to have his secretary send the woman a check.

A few minutes and plenty of gossip later, Harvey got back in his Mercedes. If it was arson, was Christy a target, or was it random criminal mischief? Who would want to do something like this to her? And where was she now?

He drove away with too many unanswered questions.

※

"Christy, meet Spirit." May led a huge dappled gray horse from the corral and walked him over to where she was standing outside the fence.

"Wow." Christy cautiously approached them. Even through his shaggy winter coat, powerful muscles bulged in his chest and shoulders. "Is he a stallion?"

May laughed. "He'd like you to think that. Actually, he's a gelding. Here." May handed her Spirit's lead. "You hold on to him while I get Nugget."

"Nugget?"

"She's the paint in the corner over there. The one you'll be riding."

Spirit nudged Christy's shoulder, throwing her off-balance. "Hey, hey. Careful now."

It had been over twenty years since she'd been around horses. When she was twelve and May was nine, Mom and Dad had given them both a year's worth of riding lessons. She hoped she still remembered what to do.

"Those riding lessons sure paid off, didn't they?" she called to May, already halfway across the corral.

"Best gift I ever got!"

Spirit snorted, and Christy patted his neck, which sent a cloud of dust into the air. How did she end up here, standing in the middle of May's cattle ranch holding a horse that looked like he could clobber her in one stomp? Watching May, she wondered what her sister was thinking. Could she really be happy to see her?

A few minutes later they had both horses in the barn, restrained with cross ropes hanging on each side of the aisle. When they were attached to their halters, the horses couldn't move much in either direction.

"I don't remember how to do any of this," Christy said. Even back during their lessons she'd asked May to saddle for her more than once. She'd never been interested in all the brushing, hoof picking, and tacking up. She'd just wanted to hop on, let her hair fly, and look like Elizabeth Taylor in *National Velvet*.

"Well, I'll let you off this time." May circled a currycomb through Nugget's coat, completely at ease around the animal. Like she was born to be doing this. Even at their first riding lesson, when all Christy could do was tell the front end of the horse, May got it. Something had clicked for her, and she'd soaked in every one of the instructor's words.

Her sister swung the saddle onto Nugget's back as effortlessly as if she were flinging on a blanket. That had to take strength.

"So what brought you all the way out here?" May asked.

Not sure how to answer, Christy grabbed the second brush May had brought from the tack room. She might as well give a half-truth. "Seeing you at the funeral . . . I guess I just thought it was time to, I don't know, catch up."

May reached under Nugget for the hanging girth strap.

"Um, should I start brushing Spirit?"

Slipping the leather straps into the buckles, May pulled them tight. She checked her work, then tightened them even more. "Gotta get these on when they're breathing out. Nothin' worse than a loose saddle. I got thrown once by rushing this part."

Christy wanted to ask May how long she'd been working here, how she'd met that woman Ruth, where Jim fit in the picture, and a host of other questions, but she didn't for fear it would open herself up to questions in return.

Fifteen minutes later they were finished, and Christy was staring at Nugget's saddle, wondering how in the world she was going to climb on. She knew enough to mount on the left side, but before she'd ridden only ponies, not full-grown, towering horses.

"Want a leg up?"

"If you don't mind." Christy bent her knee and May supported it, giving her a lift as she pulled herself into the saddle. Atop the animal, she smiled down at May. "Nice view."

May patted her leg, then just stood staring at her, hands on her hips.

"What?"

"I'm glad you're here."

"Let's just see if I can keep from falling off."

"You'll do fine. Nugget's a sweetheart." May led Spirit toward the gate, gesturing for her to follow on Nugget.

Christy watched her sister's back for a moment, surprised at the emotion rising in her throat. They'd lost so much time.

"See, I knew you could manage it," May said.

Christy held the reins loosely in her right hand and wrapped the other around the saddle horn. She was doing her best to look as cool and comfortable as May did riding Spirit in her chaps and boots. "Just don't ask me to do anything."

"All you do is hang on. Let ol' Nugget do the rest."

They were following a fence with the beautiful mountains on their left. May explained they were looking for a break where cows had been getting out. Twice this week the neighboring ranchers—a couple named Jan and Keith

Mercer, according to May—had to bring back cows that had wandered into their herd.

After a moment May said, "I wasn't sure I'd ever see you again."

Now that they were truly alone, was May finally going to let her have it for being such a rotten sister? It was easier not to respond. Christy jerked loose the pack of squashed cigarettes in her back pocket, bumped one out, and attempted to light up with one hand, concentrating on enjoying the familiarity of the process. It was the only thing familiar about this whole experience. But the wind kept blowing out her lighter.

May glanced over at her, and Christy expected a glare of disapproval. Wasn't smoking considered a sin? Instead, without a word, May rode closer to her and cupped her hand over the tip of the cigarette, effectively shielding it from the wind. Christy was able to light it without any further trouble.

"Uh, thanks," she said.

May's response was a smile, and they continued riding for a few minutes in silence, Christy's horse walking automatically behind May's.

"So what're you doing these days?" May called to her.

An innocent enough question. "I work at a bookstore in Longmont."

May turned around in her saddle, nodding in approval.

"Really? I can picture that. Remember when you used to read to me before bed?"

"And you always fell asleep before I finished."

"I still remember some of the stories."

"You do? Which ones?"

May thought for a second. "Those sisters during the Civil War."

Christy tapped ash off her Winston, letting herself smile. "*Little Women*?"

"I guess."

"I think I read that to you a couple times."

"And that series about those four kids who travel to a different world."

"Narnia."

"That's it. I liked that one."

Another minute passed with only the sound of their creaking saddles and the plodding of the horses' hooves. Christy was glad May's back was to her. She'd be even more uncomfortable facing her sister. This whole thing was crazy. In a million years she wouldn't have pictured horseback riding in the middle of nowhere with May. She had no idea what to say. It was stupid to hope they could pick up where they'd left off and put the past behind them. Sooner or later they'd have to talk about why she'd left, and Christy dreaded it.

"Chris, how old were we when we got our own rooms?"

She clutched the saddle horn with both hands, cigarette and all. It had been a long time since she'd thought about any of this, and she wasn't sure she liked it. "I was twelve."

"Those were good days. Remember PYA?"

"PYA?"

"You know, Pretend You're—"

"Asleep. Sure, I remember."

"Think Mom and Dad knew?"

"Probably."

May threw another glance in her direction. "Harvey told me about Aunt Edna's books."

Christy sucked at her cigarette. She'd been afraid of this. She'd wondered how May would feel about her, the alienated sister, being willed an equal inheritance plus the books, when May was the one who'd been the dutiful niece. How was she going to tell May the books were gone? Easy. She wasn't. "I was surprised she gave them to me."

"Why?"

"I hardly knew her."

"But she remembered how you loved books. And she never forgot how you'd drool over her library. She told me that the day before she went home."

The lack of spite in May's response puzzled her. If only she'd known this great woman like May had. But she'd had her chance and passed it by. As a teenager she'd thought of

214

Aunt Edna as an old-fashioned spinster, part of a generation that would keep her from having fun or would try to mold her into some Goody Two-shoes.

"I'm glad you got the books."

"A lot of them were gifts from you."

May smiled. "Never had to worry about birthdays or Christmas."

"But most of them were religious titles."

"Well, God was Auntie's first passion. Books were her second."

Here was an opportunity to broach that subject, though she'd tread carefully. "Her religion . . . it rubbed off on you, I guess."

May slowed her eager mount so he would walk in step with Christy's. "I suppose it did."

She chose not to take the conversation any further for the time being. They spent the next few minutes riding without talking, both of them focused on the fence. Then May gestured to the hill looming in front of them. "That's Squatter's Mountain. My favorite place to go when I want to be alone."

"You can get to the top of it?"

May reined in her horse and stared at the hill, mesmerized. "See that trail?" When she pointed, Christy thought she saw a break in the trees at the base. "Come warmer weather, it'll make a great hike."

The snow had let up, and they were close enough to see the top of the peak with its rocky outcroppings. Aspen skeletons and ponderosa pines graced its slopes. Christy didn't have to be an outdoorswoman to appreciate the beauty.

"I can't even imagine losing it."

Christy twisted around in her saddle to face May. "Losing it?"

May sighed, wiping her eyes with the back of her gloved hand. "We've been behind on the mortgage payments for a long time. We have to pay it off in sixty days or they'll foreclose."

So that was what the envelope from the bank was about. "You're kidding? Can't you sell some of the cattle or something?"

"It still wouldn't be enough, and if we did, where would we be then?" May stared at the peak, her voice getting quiet. "This time I think we're at the end."

Christy didn't know what to say. What could she, of all people, offer that would be any consolation? Yet her first instinct was to somehow comfort her obviously distraught little sister, a feeling she was glad she still had.

"Anyway," May said, urging her gelding forward with a click of her tongue, "we've got a fence to check, and I'm sitting here blubbering."

It took Christy longer to start up again. She couldn't take her eyes off Squatter's Mountain.

When they trudged into the kitchen two hours later, Ruth was stoking the woodstove, Scribbles by her side. "You both look freezing."

May wriggled out of her coat and started peeling off layers. "Those cows'll need wire cutters if they want to get out now."

Ruth brought chairs to the stove.

Christy sat in one of them, her open palms stretched toward the warm metal. May stripped down to a T-shirt and jeans. She was just as skinny as ever as she sat on the floor beside Christy, tugging off her boots. Her cheeks were chapped from the cold, and she wiped her runny nose with her shirt. Seeing her sister like this reminded Christy of how May would play for hours on end outside, even in the winter.

She tried to comb her damp hair with her fingertips. It was hard to stop thinking of May as her kid sister and get used to the fact that May was a thirty-year-old woman, living her life just fine without Christy.

A series of short knocks came at the kitchen door.

May rose to answer it. "Whatever you're selling, we don't want it."

"Guess you won't be having dinner, then," came a female voice.

"In that case . . ." May swung open the door, and a woman

around their age stepped inside. She plopped two pizza boxes on the counter and a plastic grocery bag on top of them.

"Hope you guys are hungry," the woman said, hanging her parka on the rack by the door and turning toward Christy and Ruth. Surprise flashed in her eyes when she saw Christy. "Whoa." She came over and gave Christy a firm handshake like Ruth had. Over her shoulder she asked, "Is this who I think it is?"

May beamed. "Sure is."

"Nice to meet you. I'm Beth." Then she pointed at May. "Let's get this straight right off the bat. Whatever you do, don't listen to anything this girl says about me."

May laughed, but Beth kept a straight face. "Two facts you need to know: I do not have a bottomless pit for a stomach, and I hate your sister."

Christy found herself smiling. Beth certainly was friendly.

"I'd like you to meet a good friend of mine," May said. "She's our vet, and between her and her dad, they doctor every sick cow, horse, dog, cat, goat, and sheep within a hundred miles."

"And iguana," Beth chimed in.

"Iguana?" May said. "When?"

"Two weeks ago. Had to break it to the owner that Bob was really Bobina."

Ruth explained to Christy, "Friday's our game night."

"How are you at cards?" Beth said, pulling up a chair next to her by the stove, which let Christy get a good look at her. The wool sweater, hiking boots, and lump of turquoise dangling from her neck with a silver chain pegged her as an outdoorswoman like May, but she had more meat on her bones than May did. And her clothes didn't have the holes and tears she'd seen in May's either.

"Not that good," Christy said.

Beth shielded her mouth to keep May and Ruth from hearing. "Neither am I. But it's fun anyway."

May let out a whoop as she discovered something in Beth's grocery bag. She held up a box of Triscuits for Christy to see. "Normal people go to bed, and if they can't sleep they count sheep jumping fences. But I swear, Beth here, when she gets insomnia, she counts Triscuits leaping gracefully over a lunch plate. She brings these *every* time."

"So I like them," Beth said. "Sue me."

"And she can eat the whole box!"

"What is this? Tattle-on-Beth night?"

May pulled her jacket from the rack and stuck her boots on again. "No, it's your-turn-to-decide-what-to-play night, and when I get back, you better have made up your mind."

"Where're you going?" Christy asked.

"Checking on those cows in the shed. Won't be long."

Beth quickly added, "I'll go with you," and before Christy could think of anything to say, they were both out the door.

❦

May shoved her hands deep into the pockets of her coat. She'd left her gloves inside.

Beth hurried to walk beside her. "Something wrong?"

"Just needed to get out and think for a minute."

"If you want to be alone, I can—"

"I'm glad you came," she interrupted. "Maybe I can bounce my thoughts off you." Beth was always a good sounding board.

May led the way to the calving shed, not really needing to check the animals. Jim had just been in here, but she'd give them a glance so she wouldn't be lying to Chris. Inside, May dropped onto a bale of straw.

"How long has she been here?" Beth sat down next to her.

"Since this afternoon. She just showed up."

Beth whistled.

"What do you think of her?"

"I just got here, remember?"

"Any thoughts would help."

"She looks like you."

That got May to smile. Ever since she was a kid, she'd

always wanted to be like her big sister. Chris was beautiful, and May was the scrawny girl with scars on her knees. May remembered often sneaking into Chris's room to play with her makeup and perfume. Even though she now realized it must have been obvious to Chris what she'd been up to by the mess she'd left behind, her sister never scolded her for it.

"I was thrown when I first came in," Beth said. "But I remembered that photo you showed me."

"Try walking into this shed expecting to find Jim and the cows and discovering the sister you thought wanted nothing to do with you."

"Surprise, surprise."

"No kidding." May pulled a piece of straw from the bale and twirled it in her fingers. "She ditches me at the funeral, then comes gallivanting out here expecting me to welcome her with open arms? No apologies, no nothing?"

"Maybe that's why she's here. To apologize."

"Well, she didn't exactly take the bait when I gave her the chance."

Beth rested her elbows on her thighs. "At least you know where she is now. She's not dead. She's right here in your house."

"What even gives her the right?" May bent the piece of straw in half, then quartered it. She'd done her best this afternoon to be nothing but kind to her sister. That was the

Christian thing to do. But it hadn't been easy. She kept waiting for Chris to answer all the unspoken questions she'd kept bottled inside over the years. When she hadn't, it only deepened the scar on May's heart.

May leaned back against the stall, closing her eyes. "I used to lie awake at night wondering how she could hate me so much she had to leave. What if she still hates me?"

"I doubt she'd be here if she did."

May rubbed her eyes. "I thought I forgave her. I really did. But seeing her again like this . . . And now I gotta go back in there and treat her like some prodigal."

"How long is she staying?"

"Another thing she didn't bother to tell me." May got up, brushing the straw off her jeans.

"Weren't you the one who *wanted* to spend more time with your sister?"

May shook her head. "I sound horrible, don't I?"

"You could just think of it as a chance to show her what true forgiveness is all about. Maybe she's never experienced that."

"If only I knew what happened to her," May said.

Beth smiled. "You'll never know out here."

15

"COFFEE?" RUTH ASKED, holding up the pot.

Christy shook her head. What she really wanted was a good hard drink. Normally by this time of day she'd be winding down with a glass or two of sherry.

Ruth poured herself a cup at the counter. Christy hadn't minded her company. She'd kept up the conversation, talking about the early days of the ranch when her husband, Luis, was still alive, telling how they'd married young and spent the first years working on other ranches. Buying the Triple Cross had been their dream realized. They'd endured many trials and shared many joys, but when Luis's horse threw him on a remote corner of the ranch, nothing prepared Ruth for the stiff, bloated, and very dead husband she found three days later.

"Luis loved this place," Ruth said, her voice cracking slightly as she returned to her chair with her own mug and an ashtray for Christy. Christy guessed Ruth's emotion wasn't only because she missed her husband. She hadn't forgotten what May had shared about the ranch's financial situation.

Christy lit a Winston, marveling at the thought of one woman running a ranch completely by herself like Ruth had in the years after her husband's death, before May or Jim arrived. How had she endured the isolation? And what about the fear of something terrible happening to *her* with no one to know for days?

If anyone could handle it, Ruth looked like she could. Her weathered features spelled endurance, and with her sleeves rolled up to the elbows, Christy saw her forearm flex with each lifting of her cup. Yet her eyes revealed a gentle spirit. She bet those same arms that could surely throw forty-pound hay bales into the back of a pickup would just as deftly coax a stray dog to food or rescue an injured bird.

"How'd May come to work here?" Christy asked. She still hadn't figured out what had brought her sister and this aging woman together.

"I met her four years after Luis passed," Ruth said, smiling.

"It was actually the dust cloud I saw first. Then this old truck rattled up the drive with a skinny girl behind the wheel. I was sitting on the porch, and she marched right over and asked to work here. I liked her boldness, and she could ride. But she admitted she knew little about cattle. I decided to try her out anyway. I wasn't gettin' any younger, and the stock was becoming more than I could handle by myself."

Ruth slurped her coffee. "One thing's for sure. I never regretted my gamble. Your sister worked her tail off that first year and wouldn't let me pay her until she could hold her own. Don't remember her complaining either, though there were nights she'd be so exhausted I'd find her asleep on the porch. I liked her spunk. She had the guts to come here and go for it. I saw fire in her eyes. Fire to learn. She wanted to work here so bad, even though she knew it wouldn't be easy."

From what Jim said earlier, Christy figured May had been eighteen or nineteen at that point, and five years later she bought into the place. When Christy was that age, she'd accomplished nothing but squandering all her parents' life insurance money.

"She was just a kid," Christy said.

"Yeah, but you start 'em early in this business. 'Course, most grow up with it. That's another thing about May. Wasn't raised knowing cows and had to learn from scratch. Took her fair share of tumbles, bites, and kicks."

Christy fell silent, and Ruth did the same, but somehow it wasn't uncomfortable. Ruth didn't fill the space with meaningless chatter. She let Christy sit warming by the stove with her own thoughts.

Several minutes later May and Beth returned. Beth blasted the radio to play the Top 20 country countdown. A deck of cards was produced, and they broke into the sausage and cheese pizza.

Hearts was chosen as the first game by Beth, who joked about not being able to make any decisions without tremendous inner turmoil.

During the game Christy observed the interaction of the three women. The person joking with May should've been her. Instead, someone else was filling her role. Why would May even want a relationship with her again? Forget what Aunt Edna wrote; Christy wasn't needed. May had these people in her life now, and Christy was insane for thinking there might still be something between them. Being family wasn't enough.

She tried to focus on the game, but it was getting harder to do. She really needed a drink.

Two hands later Jim blew in from outside, stomping the snow off his boots. She noticed it was now dark outside. "Ladies," he said.

"Hey, grab a chair," May said. "We're just gettin' started."

Jim shook his head and pulled a slice of pizza from the box on the counter, eating it without a plate. "Got that carburetor replaced in your truck, Ruth," he garbled, his mouth full of pizza. "Couple more inches came down. You guys feel like sledding?"

May brightened and looked around the table. "How about it?"

Beth readily agreed, and Ruth was game. Then May looked at Christy.

She wasn't sure what to say. Were they kidding? "You all go ahead. I can wait in here." Maybe if they left, she could finally get the drink she craved.

"If I can do it, you can," Ruth said.

"I'm not—"

"Come on. It'll be fun," Beth said.

They weren't going to let her off easy, and it was starting to irritate her the way they were pushing, but then she realized it was the perfect excuse. "All right, all right," she said, lifting both hands in surrender and trying to sound jovial like them. "Just let me grab something out of my car."

She slipped out before they could respond. They'd think she needed an extra sweater or a scarf.

It took her three tries to unlock her car with her hands shaking so badly, but when she finally closed herself inside, she eagerly pulled out the bottle of vodka. Unscrewing the cap, she sniffed the aroma, similar to that of rubbing alcohol, then took a swallow. It burned as it slid down her throat and poured into her stomach. Just a few swallows would be enough to get her through. They wouldn't smell it on her, and here in the shadow of the barn behind the horse trailer no one would see her.

Popping open the glove compartment, Christy pulled out Aunt Edna's soiled letter. "Listen," she said as if her aunt could hear, "I've tried to do what you wanted, 'kay? But she doesn't need me, and I don't need her, either. Too much has happened. It's been too long."

She rubbed her eyes. She was getting tired, and she really should've left by now. But one glance at the newly fallen snow confirmed that was impossible. The roads out here would be bad, and she didn't have tire chains or four-wheel drive. She'd have to stay the night and hightail it first thing in the morning. Christy turned on the engine and cleared the windshield with the wipers. It felt great to have a break from all the "fun" that was going on inside.

Guzzling more vodka, she leaned back into her seat and imagined what May and her friends would really think if the truth about her life were known. What they'd do if they saw her now. Gone would be the hospitality and friendliness. These were religious people who lived right. They would never understand.

She better get back. May was probably wondering what was taking her so long. She switched on the interior light to stash her bottle. Only then did she see Jim walking around the horse trailer toward the car. She felt a rush of panic. Had he seen the alcohol? She doused the light and hid the bottle under the seat, clambering out of the car and locking the door.

"Get what you needed?"

Christy nodded, then realized she was empty-handed. Hopefully he'd assume she'd taken lipstick or something else that could easily be pocketed.

"You know, we don't have to go sledding if you don't want to," he said. "I'm sure the girls will understand."

As crazy and childish as sledding might be, she didn't mind as much now that she'd given herself some strength. And she had a voyeuristic curiosity to see how May lived. "Like Ruth said, if she can do it, I can."

Making her way around the car, she hurried to the house. The kitchen was a flurry of activity with everyone bundling up against the cold. May loaned her a pair of boots, and Beth had an extra ski cap. Now she would have hat hair like all of them.

She followed them out to one of the pickups, and Jim jumped in the driver's seat. Ruth and Beth sat with him in the cab.

May climbed into the truck bed and held out her hand. "We'll sit back here. Cab only fits three."

Christy wasn't pleased with the idea of riding in the back of the truck, but she grabbed May's hand anyway, hoping this would all be over soon. They crouched across from each other, Scribbles leaping over the two toboggans already in the bed and lying low beside May.

"It'll be bumpy," May said. "Hang on. Jim doesn't slow much for the dips."

The truck rattled across a wooden bridge over a small, half-frozen stream. The sky was almost clear now. As the moonlight reflected off the snow, it created a world of blues and grays that reminded her of the magical land of Narnia written about in the classic series by C. S. Lewis. She half expected to spot a fawn or dwarf peeking around a distant tree trunk. Instead, through the creaks and groans of the truck, she heard cow bellows and saw their forms moving in clusters toward the truck as it passed.

"They're hoping it's feeding time," May shouted over the din.

For the first time, Christy laughed, but not because she thought anything was funny. What a simple life May led. No booze, no cigarettes, no drugs. She bet May was even still a virgin.

Christy looked into the cab at the back of Jim's head.

And he was another case study. He obviously wasn't getting any from May or the other women. Most of the men she'd known, except maybe Hunter, had only one thing on their mind. But Jim had had several opportunities to hit on her earlier today and hadn't. He and everyone else had been nothing but kind. Why?

The truck dipped drastically, and her back thrashed against the metal side. Because they didn't know her, that's why. She was just May's older sister coming for a visit. Everyone be on your best behavior for the visiting stranger.

They stopped at the crest of a hill Christy couldn't believe they actually planned to use for sledding. Jim positioned the lights to shine on the run, which looked more like a cliff. These people were either on something or crazy.

"You'll love this," May said, jumping over the side of the truck. Scribbles did the same.

Christy took the longer route, opening the tailgate and carefully climbing down.

"Who's first?" Beth said, stealing a sled from the pickup and pitching it in the snow at the top of the gigantic hill.

May took the second and threw it alongside the first. "We oughta let Chris go. She's the guest, after all."

"No way," Christy said. "One of you. Make it back alive."

Ruth moved forward. With her leather cap and white

scarf she looked like a flying ace. All that was missing were goggles.

May pushed Beth. "You go too." Then, cupping her hands to make the words echo, she announced, "Ladies, take your mark."

Beth and Ruth stepped back several feet behind the sleds. Christy realized with surprise what they were planning. Two grown women, one practically old enough to be her grandmother, were doing the belly flop.

"Get set . . ."

Beth and Ruth tensed.

"Go!"

They ran for the sleds, lunged, and sent themselves zooming over the edge. Their screams lasted all the way to the bottom.

May yelled, "Who won?"

"I did!" Ruth shouted.

By the time the racers tramped back up the hill, both were winded but thrilled. Man, they got pleasure from the simplest things around here.

"You're next," Beth said, handing Christy the sled's rope.

She took it but not without protest. "I really don't think so."

"Come on," May urged, leading her to the top. "You don't have to do the belly thing. Just sit down and we'll push."

"Why don't we double up?" Jim said.

She shot him a look. Did he mean she and him?

"Beth and I'll take one, May and Christy the other," he added.

She was tired of the nagging. Maybe if she took a run, they'd stop bothering her. She slowly placed herself at the front of the toboggan, and May got in behind her, holding on to her waist.

"Trust me," May whispered into her ear. "It'll be fun."

The hill looked even more frightening when she was about to throw herself down it like a kamikaze.

"Ready?" May asked.

Christy wasn't. Not at all. She glanced at the others. Beth and Jim looked ridiculous, filling up the entire sled probably meant for one ten-year-old. They spilled over the sides like a swollen loaf of bread in its pan. Beth gave her the thumbs-up as Ruth got ready to push both sleds.

The violent shove came, and Christy's heart dropped with the sled. She screamed as stinging snow kicked up into her face, and they whipped forward, faster than she imagined possible. She couldn't see a thing as they plummeted through the darkness.

"Stay straight! Straight!" May yelled as the sled tilted. She jerked Christy to the left, trying to compensate. Too late. They both tumbled from the sled only halfway down the hill. Christy landed on her face, her mouth and nose crushing into the snow.

By the time she rolled onto her side, Scribbles had reached May, attacking her with his tongue. May giggled, playfully trying to push him away.

Way up at the top was Ruth's form, shrouded in the headlights. Beth and Jim's run was just ending. She could see them as specks in the distance, standing and giving each other high fives.

"Didn't I tell you to keep it straight?" May said.

Christy shook her head, fell backward into the snow, and laughed. Really laughed. Laughed so hard she started coughing and her sides ached. What a gas. She'd actually done it.

❧

Hunter propped his feet on the checkout counter, *For Whom the Bell Tolls* resting in his lap. He'd just gotten off the phone with Mr. Kurtz. What could they do now? Christy's apartment was destroyed, and no one knew where she was.

He picked up the Hemingway. In the beginning he'd tried to be objective. Christy wasn't exactly without her share of blame. But as time went by, he kept remembering the way Vince had treated Abby. Any man who would abuse a woman like that didn't deserve to be trusted. Somehow he'd known

Christy was telling the truth about Vince framing her. He just had to find some way to prove it.

Turning the book around, he stared at the author's photograph.

And saw it.

Hunter's feet were off the desk in a second, and he straightened in his chair, seizing the book with both hands. He gawked in disbelief at the words beneath the author's picture. How had he missed them?

Photograph by Arnold—Sun Valley.

Five words, but the most important point in distinguishing a first state dust jacket from a second state. A first state had no photographer credited. The second state did. A multi–hundred-dollar difference. Hunter distinctly remembered looking for the point when he bought the book from that elderly man. There was no way he would have forgotten to check.

The truth startled him. This wasn't the same book he'd displayed in the case.

Flipping to the flyleaf, he would have sworn it was his own handwriting that advertised the price and edition. And Hemingway's signature was unmistakable on the title page. But anyone who was smart enough to switch the dust jackets surely could manage to switch the books and forge a signature too.

It would be easy enough. A first edition book with a second state dust jacket could be bought for a couple hundred. The actual book would look exactly the same; it was only the photographer's credit on the dust jacket that would be different. Forge a signature, and at first glance, the book would look identical to the one you stole. But why go to all that trouble?

Hunter stared at the wooden beams on the ceiling. What if the purpose of the fake was to incriminate someone else? Then the thief could keep the real first for himself. Hunter placed the book on the desk. It made absolutely no sense for Christy to have created this duplicate to leave it in her car in plain view.

Hunter scooped up his phone and punched in a number. "Eric? Hunter. I need you over here right now. . . . Yeah, now. It's very important. I'll owe you one."

Replacing the receiver, he regarded the book. He'd have to check the signature first. Eric was an expert with celebrity signatures, specializing in authors. He'd verified the authenticity of Hemingway's before Hunter paid the guy.

If this was forged, he'd know for sure within the hour. And if so, it would mean the *real* signed first edition was still out there. Find it, find the thief. That would be enough proof to convince even Pop.

Hunter's wheels started turning. He knew where to look.

16

MAY FLIPPED THE page of her Bible, pulled her covers to her chin, and rested back on her pillow. She tried to read the words slowly, but she was having trouble concentrating. She kept thinking about Chris sleeping on the sofa. She'd brought a suitcase. Without even checking with her. Was she just assuming May would put her up, no questions asked?

With effort, May reined in her thoughts. *"Dear children,"* she read, *"let us not love with words or tongue but with actions and in truth."*

She was trying to do that. But what if Chris never apologized? What if even now she was just using her?

"'*If anyone says, "I love God," yet hates his brother, he is a liar. For anyone who does not love his brother, whom he has seen, cannot love God, whom he has not seen.*'"

May closed her Bible and turned off the light, staring at the ceiling. If only she could pick up the phone and call Aunt Edna. Auntie would understand more than anyone. What would *she* say about Chris?

Emotion pushed up May's throat when she thought back to the day of her baptism. Auntie had found her crying in the church bathroom right before the ceremony. She remembered being just as angry with Chris then. With all the families packing the church that Sunday, Auntie would be her only relative.

May could still hear the old woman's soft voice. "You have a choice, honey. You can hold on to this unforgiveness and let it consume you. But I guarantee *you're* the one who's going to suffer. Not Christy."

"She should be here," May had sobbed.

Auntie gently held her by both shoulders, looking right into her eyes. "Yes, she should be. But I'm here. Your church family is here. And more importantly, the Lord is here with you. He will never leave you or forsake you. He's a friend that sticks closer than a brother or sister. If you never see Christy again, you will always have Him."

May rolled onto her side in the dark bedroom. She'd kept the unforgiveness in her heart all these years. Instead of being angry, she should be praying for Chris. That's what Auntie would've done.

※

Christy snapped awake on the sofa, clutching her blanket, gasping for air. Her heart hammered against her ribs. Vivid was the tiny hand with two fingers ripped off and the bloody stump on the leg where the foot should have been. Blood was everywhere, mixed with shards of bone and pieces of skin and cartilage.

She dug her head into the pillow. She wasn't supposed to have seen. The nurses, catching her horrified gaze into the trash can, had rushed her from the room, chatting about coworkers, new cars, and clothes as if nothing had happened. As if their frivolous chatter would erase the sight from her mind.

Never.

Christy tried to stifle her cries and come back to the here and now. She was in May's house. May's living room. In the darkness here on May's sofa. But the repulsive dream remained, each frame a permanent snapshot in her mind.

It might have been possible to forget if it had been only a nightmare. Everyone knew dreams were figments of the imagination. But this one wasn't just a dream. It was a hellish memory. Those scenes actually happened to her fourteen years ago. And to him.

Throwing back the blankets, Christy knelt, shaking, in front of her suitcase. She flipped it open and groped under a sweater. Her fingers found the cool bottle of sherry, and she carefully removed it from the suitcase and held it up so the one dim light from the kitchen caught the green glass. This was the only thing that had ever been able to make the dreams fade.

A fresh pack of Winstons in one hand and the sherry in the other, she dropped onto the sofa and unscrewed the bottle. Lifting it to her lips, she tried to fill her mouth with as much as she could on the first stinging swallow. She ripped the cellophane off the pack of cigarettes, poked one in her mouth, lit it, and greedily sucked.

She leaned back into the cushions. Somehow she knew it was a boy. Sometimes an infant, sometimes a toddler, he haunted her at night. Only this time she'd seen him as he was: a mangled corpse tossed in the trash bin. Christy covered her mouth to muffle another sob as tears fell down her cheeks. He'd been innocent. He hadn't deserved what she did to him. She was the one who deserved to die, not him. She was the guilty one.

The minutes passed as she took leisurely swallows of sherry, and her eyes were drawn toward the gun case. The spotlight from the barn reflected off the glass of the case like an eerie white eye. Just a few feet away. Within easy reach. How many times had she planned suicide? Twice she'd had pills in her hand. But she'd never gone through with it, mainly out of fear she wouldn't be able to finish the job properly. But with a gun . . .

Everyone was asleep. If she could just find the shells, it would be simple to remove one of those guns and end the madness. . . .

Before the sound of footsteps registered in Christy's brain, May was already halfway down the short hall, coming straight for her. "Hey, Chris, I—" Her sister's eyes locked on the sherry in Christy's hand. "I . . . thought . . ."

Christy scrambled to get it out of sight.

May glanced at the floor where she'd set it, then back at her face. "My turn to check the cows. I was hoping you were awake so maybe you could join me."

How could she have forgotten? May told her they checked the cattle around the clock this time of year. She should've known she'd be caught.

"You go right ahead," Christy said. "I'm going to the bathroom and back to bed." She stuffed the cigarettes into the waistband of her sweatpants and stood up with the bottle of sherry held against the side of her that was farthest from May. She attempted to scuttle around her sister.

But May caught her arm. "I'd love the company."

She pulled away.

"Just thought it might be nice," May whispered. "We could talk."

She stood with her back to May, wanting to snap something nasty. But she had to get a grip. May hadn't done anything. Wasn't this what she came for? Finding out what May was really like? Did she want to wreck any chance she had of knowing May again? If only May hadn't seen her this way.

Christy slowly turned around. What a loser she must look like. "Okay. I'll go with you."

"Meet me outside in five minutes," May said and quickly slipped into the kitchen.

As soon as she was gone, Christy hid the sherry back in the suitcase. Then she sat on the sofa, checking herself. She didn't think she'd drunk enough to affect her abilities. Her dream was still clear. That was a good sign. If she was drunk, the dream would've faded.

Please don't let me make a fool of myself.

When Christy finally stepped out into the night, bundled in the layers and coveralls May had left out for her, the cold still took her breath away. Inside May's pickup wasn't much warmer, but at least they were sheltered from the wind. Christy shivered against the vinyl upholstery, watching the snowflakes swirl before the headlights. She should never have agreed to this.

May started the truck, and with a groan and a lurch they headed toward the pasture in the same direction they'd taken to go sledding. "Keep your eyes peeled for new calves," May said, jumping back inside after closing the gate behind them. She grabbed a handheld spotlight powered by a cord in the cigarette lighter and swung it along the fence where some cows had gathered.

Christy clung to the door handle as they rocked over the bumps. Should she address what happened in the house? Surely May was wondering. Christy watched her hang out the window with the spotlight aimed underneath a stand of cottonwoods. What did May think of her now?

"Look." May pointed toward the trees. One of the cows stood hunched over a steaming calf. May leaped out, leaving the headlights pointed toward the animals.

Christy reluctantly followed, clomping through the snow behind her.

"Past couple years we've had to watch the herd even closer than we used to during calving season. Coyotes love veal for breakfast." May stopped a few feet from the animals and squatted to watch them. "I love wildlife, but coyotes . . . they do brutal things to calves. If they just killed and ate, I could deal with that. But they'll usually only eat the hindquarters and leave the poor calf suffering."

Christy shuddered at the thought. That's why they had those guns.

In a few moments the new calf was trying out its wobbly

feet. With determination he planted one shaky hoof and then another on the ground. Falling once, he tried again, tottered, but finally managed to steady himself enough to nuzzle up to his mother's udder.

"I never get tired of watching that," May said. "Amazing, isn't it?"

"Sure."

"It's an awesome privilege to witness a life begin."

Christy was silent. Not the sanctity-of-life thing. Not now. She went back to the truck, leaving May to continue her philosophical musing by herself. Christy watched her from the cab and thought she saw May bow her head. Great. She was praying. What could that mean?

When May returned, she switched the heater fan to high.

"Don't you ever get lonely out here?"

"Sometimes. But town's not too far away."

"You've got a lot of guts to be doing this." She meant it as a compliment.

May seemed to take it that way. "Or stubbornness."

"This was your dream, wasn't it?" Christy's voice got quiet. "And now it's come true."

May nodded, but she didn't verbally respond. Christy guessed why and cursed the bank that would sell her sister's life out from under her. One look into May's eyes and she knew how much this place meant to her sister.

"What about you?" May gave the truck gas, and they were moving again. "Did your dreams come true?"

Christy kept her eyes focused out the window. May had already found her half-drunk. Didn't that tell her enough? "I never had any dreams. You had enough for both of us."

"You know, Ruth wasn't even looking to hire anybody." May shook her head, smiling. "But I knew about her from some friends and how she was alone, doing all this by herself. One day I just came barreling out here and asked for a job."

"She told me."

May chuckled. "Can only imagine her version of the story."

They spent a few minutes searching the fields for cows needing assistance, and May explained how they kept the cattle corralled in the fields closer to the house during calving season. Christy didn't know how they could keep this schedule up for two months. May must be exhausted.

"It's funny," Christy said. "Neither of us got married."

May directed her spotlight toward a bunch of cattle huddled under some more cottonwoods. "Not many guys could put up with me."

Christy thought of Vince. In the beginning of their relationship she'd imagined he might be the one. She used to lie awake at night daydreaming about what it would be like to spend the rest of her life with him. The feeling was all too short-lived.

"So you were never engaged or anything?" Christy asked.

"Nah. I haven't dated much since I've been here."

"But don't you ever wish you had a guy in your life?"

Her sister shrugged. "Don't think about it too much, really. I'm so fulfilled here, and frankly I don't have time for that kind of stuff."

"What about Jim?"

May laughed. "What about him?"

"Seems like a nice guy."

Her sister laughed again. "He's like a brother. And I'm his boss."

"Hey, you never know."

"No, I *do* know." May glanced over at her, a little more color in her cheeks. "I don't want this to sound weird, but knowing I'm loved by God . . . that's all I need."

Christy gave her an incredulous look.

"No, really," May said. "Think about it. How many guys do you know who'd love you no matter what you looked like or what you did? Even on bad hair days."

They both laughed. Christy thought of Vince again and how she was always trying to please him. No matter how hard she tried, he'd still criticize her. One day she wore too much makeup, the next day when she adjusted the application, too little. Even dyeing her hair for him wasn't enough.

"I kept thinking, years ago," May continued, "if He loved me enough to die for me, then I could trust Him with my life. Does that make sense?"

It was Christy's turn to shrug. Yeah, it made sense for people like May and Aunt Edna. They hadn't screwed up their lives like she had.

"What do you think about God?"

She decided to be honest. "I don't. Not if I can help it."

"He loves you. You do know that, right?"

"That's awfully easy for you to say. But fifteen years hasn't gone by without . . . In case you haven't noticed, I've changed."

May backed off, waiting a few seconds before answering. "I've changed too. Remember when we were talking about Aunt Edna rubbing off on me? Well, she's the one who showed me all this. I always thought you had to be a saint for God to love you, which I'm definitely not, but I found out that isn't true."

Good old Aunt Edna. Christy stared out the window, wanting to believe May. But her sister didn't have all the facts. "I've done some awful things, and what I did to you . . ."

May brought the truck to a stop and faced her. She started

to say something, then looked away. "When you left, my heart nearly broke."

Christy tensed, but when May glanced over again, her eyes held no malice. "I thought I forgave you years ago, but I'll be honest. When you showed up today, I started to wonder if I really had."

Christy couldn't meet her sister's eyes.

"I don't say that to hurt you. No matter how bitter I was, I never stopped loving you. You'll always be my sister. We've got the same blood running through our veins."

"You loved who I was."

"No, I love *you*. And so does God."

Christy managed to keep from rolling her eyes. "Hard to believe. What if . . . I killed someone?" She didn't wait for an answer, realizing that was saying too much. "I mean, what about thieves, rapists, drug dealers? What's God think of them? He can't love trash like that."

"Somehow He does."

"Can we please keep driving?"

❧

Vince shut off the TV. The hotel room went black except for the red glow of the clock beside the bed. Rolling onto his side, he stared at the empty pillow next to his head. If Christy were lying beside him, he would reach out and rest his hand on her warm back, relishing that she was his. His prize. His possession. His alone. Then sleep would come.

Vince grabbed the pillow and threw it to the floor. But Christy wasn't lying beside him, and the darkness and silence he usually cherished mocked him tonight.

She thinks she can dump me.

I'm alone.

I drove her away.

He tossed to his other side. But he would get her back. One way or another. Walker's Feed Store had all that he needed. He thought about the supplies he'd purchased earlier today and stashed in his rented Blazer: snow boots, a pair of snowshoes, goose-down jacket, insulated hat, flashlight, batteries, rope, tarp, shovel. He was going into this prepared, for once thankful for Christy's sloppiness. By leaving that name and address in her car, she'd made things easy for him.

❧

They found the heifer straining in the snow, almost hidden against the fence. It took Christy and May half an hour to lead the animal to the calving shed and get her secured in one of the stalls.

"She's in hard labor and making no progress," May said. "Gotta take a look."

May unzipped the top half of her coveralls, tying the arms around her waist. She peeled off layers down to a long-underwear shirt that had the right sleeve cut off. Pulling a plastic bottle from one of the shelves nailed to the shed's walls, she squirted it all over her hands and right arm. Christy guessed it was disinfectant.

With a clean rag soaked in more of the liquid, May washed the genital area of the cow who lay huffing in the straw. Kneeling behind the animal, she gently pushed her hand and arm inside the vagina.

"It's okay, girl," May said, leaning into the cow, palpating with her fingers, a worried look on her face.

Christy stood behind May, admiring her sister's skill. She seemed to understand what the cow was thinking and be completely in tune with the animal's pain.

"Your arm starts to ache after a while," May said. "Contractions are pushing against me. But I can feel the calf's front leg is caught. No wonder it wasn't coming. I think I can straighten it, but it's not gonna do much good." She struggled, slipping in the straw. Despite the cold, a sheen of sweat appeared on May's forehead.

Christy stepped closer. It *was* amazing. She couldn't deny it. Her kid sister was bringing a new life into the world. How many people could do that?

May pulled out her arm and stood back, seemingly

unaware of the crimson strands of mucus hanging from her arm. "Push, girl, push," she said.

The cow obeyed, but after several contractions only the tips of the calf's hooves were visible.

Christy watched the animal, whose eyes were wide and distressed, her breaths coming in chugs now. There was no way she could understand what was happening. She didn't know the pain would soon end and she'd have a new child to nourish and protect. It was her instinct to give life, no matter the cost. There were no options.

"We're gonna need to pull it." May produced two chains and looped one around each of the calf's hooves above the joint. She attached a handle that looked like the top of a shovel to each end and nodded toward Christy. "Take one."

"But I . . . I don't know what to do!"

"Just grab it!"

She didn't take offense at May's sharpness but lowered herself to the straw beside May, gripping the handle. This calf's life was now partly in her hands.

"We're gonna pull with her contractions," May said. "On my word, okay? Pull . . . *now.*"

Christy tried to copy May, who used her foot and pushed against the cow's rump for leverage.

"A little harder."

Christy leaned back, using her weight, and she felt some

give from the calf. Slowly the legs slid farther out of the vagina. A white nose appeared. She smiled when she saw it. "It's coming!"

"One more, mama," May urged the cow. "Give us another one. Good girl. Chris, get ready."

When the contraction came, she gave it her all, gritting her teeth. The head appeared. Then, in one smooth motion, the calf was lying at their feet in a steaming heap of fur and afterbirth. She stared at the helpless pile, waiting for it to move. Christy looked at May, who only sighed and nodded grimly. The calf's chest was still.

"Shouldn't you do something?"

"It's dead, poor fella. I could tell when I touched him inside."

Mama bawled and looked back curiously at the calf.

"Sorry, girl." May stroked the cow's rump.

Christy dropped her handle in the straw. "What happened?"

"Not sure. Umbilical cord could've tangled up, I guess."

She looked at the calf again, a messy heap that never had a chance, his swollen tongue lolling from his mouth, his dead eyes half-open. A sickening heat rushed up her neck. She'd seen something like this only one other time in her life.

After removing the chains and retrieving the handles, May dragged the limp calf out of the stall.

Christy followed mechanically and slumped onto a bale of hay, holding her head in her gloved hands. But the instant she touched her face, she felt bloody wetness against her cheeks and jerked her hands away.

May sat beside her, and together they stared at the calf. The irony. Less than an hour before they'd been watching a healthy newborn nurse for the first time. Now they were gawking at a carcass. It wasn't fair.

"They say when losing a calf quits bothering you," May said, "get out of the business."

Christy couldn't speak. She was suddenly overwhelmed with exhaustion and grief. Please . . . she couldn't lose it here. But she kept seeing that body in the trash can. How could she even think about fairness? At least both calves tonight had an equal chance. They both had mothers that tried.

"I'm glad it still gets to me in a way," May said. "But I always think about the things I should've done."

Christy swallowed. "You're just going to leave it there?"

"I'll move him outside. Tomorrow I'll take it to the grave-yard." May got up and took hold of the calf's back legs, dragging him out of the shed. His body scraped the floor and left a dark trail.

Christy knew he probably hadn't suffered. Just never took that first breath. Fate had been kind. He hadn't felt the agony of being ripped apart piece by piece. She squeezed her head with both hands.

When May returned, she sat down beside her again, and it was all Christy could do to keep from running away.

"You okay?" May rested her hand gently on Christy's shoulder.

She nodded, but the tears poured out of her. She turned her head away.

"We did all we could." May obviously thought she was bothered about the calf.

"You don't understand. I'm not talking about the calf." Christy faced May again, and before she could stop herself, she blurted, "May, I did kill someone."

17

AT SUNRISE MAY knocked on the sliding glass door of the Eckerts' kitchen. In a moment Beth appeared, hair tousled. When she saw May, the lock clicked, and the door slid open.

"What's the matter?" Beth still wore her bathrobe and held a bowl of half-eaten Cheerios.

"I've gotta talk to you," May said. "Sorry it's so early."

Beth stepped back to let her in, and May closed the door.

"It's Chris," May said, taking off her jacket and hanging it on the back of a chair.

Beth took a big bite of cereal and spoke with her mouth full. "What about her?"

"Listen, I hate to bother you like this. Ruth left for town early. Otherwise I'd be talking to her."

"As you can see, I'm extremely busy." Beth held up her bowl and smiled. "Dad left early on a call, and Mom's still asleep. What's going on?"

May sat down in the chair, running her hands through her hair. She didn't know how to start. She'd thought it was the dead calf upsetting Chris. Her city-dwelling sister had probably never seen such a gory sight. She never expected to hear what Chris revealed. "She told me she killed someone."

Beth's smile disappeared.

"Last night I had to pull a dead calf. It upset her a lot. I was trying to comfort her; then out of the blue she shocked me with that. I tried to get her to explain, but she clammed up."

"You're kidding." Beth pulled out a chair across from her. "Is she serious?"

May had wondered that all night. Could it really be true? It would explain her sister's aloofness, but she just couldn't picture Chris taking anyone's life. Was she drunk last night when she said it? Mom's and Dad's personalities had changed completely when they drank. Dad got angry. Mom got mushy.

"And that's not all," May said. "Earlier, before she told me, I found her drinking. Right in the living room. She had a whole bottle of something."

"So maybe she wasn't all there when she said it."

"But you should've seen her. The agony on her face." May ran her hand across one of the cloth place mats. "What if she's running from the law? Maybe that's why she's here. To hide out."

Beth pushed her cereal aside. "She actually said she killed someone?"

"I know. It's hard to believe."

"She seemed distant last night, but . . ."

May threw her hands in the air. "What am I supposed to do?"

"It's not like you can force her to talk about it."

"But you think I should I bring it up?"

"I . . ." Beth rubbed her chin, staring at the table. "I wish I knew what to tell you."

May hung her head. "And I can't believe she's drinking after what alcohol did to Mom and Dad. She hated their drinking just as much as I did. If anyone should know better . . ."

May stood and walked to the door. The sun was just rising and, like Midas's finger, turning everything golden. Jim would be feeding hay by now. Chris was probably still asleep. "I wish I could've done something before she ran away. Maybe if I could've kept her from leaving, none of this would've ever happened."

"You were a kid."

May stared out the glass door, her breath condensing on it. "What does she want from me?"

"To know you again?"

"I'd be surprised."

"People can change," Beth said.

May sighed and returned to the table. "I want to believe the best of her. I really do. And I do love her. I just wish I knew what she's done."

❧

Christy awoke in an empty house. She sat up, her hands and arms trembling even more than they had yesterday. She hadn't drunk nearly as much as she'd needed last night, and she could really feel it now.

As soon as she dressed, she went for her car. Again she locked herself in the Honda and pulled out the vodka. This time she let herself drink more, but she still tried to monitor how much. She had to appear normal if anyone showed up. The vodka soothed like ice on a burn. Numbed her pain. It was hard to keep from guzzling the whole bottle.

She'd been an idiot to get caught drinking. And then to run at the mouth like that to May. Now her sister knew how screwed up her life really was and how she'd spiraled into a weak, desperate nobody.

Christy drank for the next ten minutes and thought about what she was going to say to May, but she emerged from the car with no answers.

"Was wondering where you got to."

She jerked toward the voice. Jim. He stepped around the horse trailer.

She stammered, "I was . . . getting something out of my car." Oh, good, that sounded intelligent. Same excuse she'd given last night. "This makes the second time you've startled me out here. I don't appreciate that."

"And this makes the second time you've run to your car for booze."

His bluntness caught her off guard. "Excuse me?"

"That's not cream soda in there now, is it?"

Be calm. Don't react. "I don't know what you're talking about." Denial was the only defense she knew.

He laughed, and it grated on her nerves like nails on a blackboard. "Relax. You're not anywhere I haven't been. I used to run for my drinks at all hours. Sometimes hid my stash in the hayloft like a good ol' drunk."

"Did you hear me? I said I don't know what you're talking about."

"Whatever. Only you're not hiding anything." Jim started to walk away.

Without thinking, Christy caught up and jerked on his

arm. He swung around and she flinched. They stood facing each other, Jim looking intently into her eyes. Didn't she know better than to come at him like that? Yet he just stood there, not even angry. Not even close to hurting her.

"You're out of line here," she said, pointing at his face. "You don't even know me!"

"No, I don't, but normal people don't keep liquor in their cars."

Christy squared her shoulders. "What's it to you?"

"Just trying to help."

"Save it. I don't need your help. So what if I have a drink now and then? I don't have a problem."

"That's what I used to say."

She wanted to slap him for that remark but instead pivoted on her heels and marched toward the house. He followed her.

"Just leave me alone, okay?" Christy yelled over her shoulder. He was punching every one of her buttons, and she couldn't take much more. He came into the kitchen behind her anyway. What was he trying to prove?

On the counter were two plates full of bacon, eggs, and toast, each covered with saran wrap.

"For you and May," Jim said with a wave toward them. "Ruth made it."

Christy wasn't hungry. She chose to ease her inner seething

by finding a cup and pouring herself some coffee from the ever-present, steaming pot, hoping Jim would get the point. He remained hovering in the background. So he was obstinate as well as nosy.

She held up her coffee cup. "This better? Or is caffeine a no-no with you too?"

Jim just watched her, leaning, almost sitting, on the kitchen table. He crossed his arms.

"Don't you have to clean some stalls or something?"

"You know anyone named Vince?"

Christy almost dropped her mug and ended up spilling some on the floor.

Jim found a towel in a drawer and handed it to her. "I take it that's a yes."

"Why do you ask?" she managed. She had to keep her wits. Had to.

"Is he bad news?"

"Why do you ask?" Christy repeated.

"A man by that name was looking for you."

"Here?" She set her mug down. She would surely drop it if she didn't. "When?"

"Guess you were still asleep. Early this morning."

Her voice was taking on a desperate tone, which she tried to suppress but couldn't. "What did he say? Did you tell him I was here?"

"I said you were out, and I didn't know when you'd be back."

Christy was surprised he'd lied for her.

"Something about him I didn't like," Jim said.

"What else?"

"He wanted you to call him. And he said to tell you he'd taken care of your apartment, so you don't have to worry."

She stared at Jim as fear enveloped her. Taken care of her apartment? Right now her apartment and all her possessions lay in a heap of ashes. Was Vince playing games? Up until this point she'd managed to choke her suspicion that he'd set the fire—he wouldn't do that to her!—but his indirect message removed all doubt. He was saying something else too: *Beware. I found you here, and I can do a lot worse.*

Christy took a breath and tried to settle down, taking everything in. Vince had definitely planted the Hemingway in her car. He'd succeeded in killing her career and her reputation at the Barn all because she knew too much. She'd gone too far. She had dirt on him. Worse, she'd rejected him. He'd probably rationalized in that sick mind of his that if he tormented her enough, she'd eventually give in, come back, and do his bidding. That could explain the fire. And he could've easily copied her keys. Maybe he'd truly thought it would drive her back to him. But it didn't, and she wasn't coming back. Maybe he was finally realizing that, and it had provoked him to stalk her all the way to the ranch.

Whatever the reason, the truth was terrifying. She was the only one who had evidence, her own eyewitness testimony, to connect him with the thefts and embezzlement at the Barn. If she disappeared, Vince's world would continue spinning according to his plan.

"Christy?" Jim's voice sucked her out of her thoughts. "What's wrong? Who is this guy?"

She shakily pulled out her cigarettes and lit one before responding. He deserved an answer, but how much should she reveal? "I used to live with him," she said, then waited for Jim's puritanical reaction.

He only nodded. She appreciated that more than she could ever tell him.

"We worked at the same place and soon started a relationship. But I didn't know the kind of man he was. Later, I learned." She tapped ash into the sink. "I moved out a few weeks ago. He hasn't gotten over it."

"What does that mean?"

She clenched her jaw. "I didn't tell anyone I was coming here." She'd thought May's ranch would be safe. But now it wasn't at all. Not safe for her or even for May.

Christy was suddenly telling Jim more. "And I haven't been very truthful with May. Don't get me wrong, I came here to see her, but I also don't have anywhere else to go. There was a fire in my apartment three days ago, and I lost everything. What Vince said about my apartment? The cops suspected arson, but I wasn't sure."

Jim stood a little taller and uncrossed his arms.

"He's crazy enough to have done it. And now that he's found me, I can't stay here. He's likely to hurt May to get at me. Or burn something else. I'm not willing to put May through anything more on my account, especially with what you guys are facing already."

"He wouldn't try anything with all of us around."

She let out a sarcastic laugh. "Don't underestimate him like I have."

"Don't underestimate me."

Christy almost laughed again at the way he said it. There was certainty in his eyes. And if it was a matter of pure physical strength, she bet Jim could whoop Vince bad. He wouldn't have a chance against a man who worked his muscles every day. But Vince wouldn't go that route. He'd likely formulate some devious plan and find a cowardly way to strike, like torching a barn or poisoning the cattle. She couldn't sit around and wait to see what method he chose. Vince wasn't going to ruin May's life too.

"I have to leave," she said, throwing her cigarette butt into the sink and heading toward the living room and her suitcase. Besides protecting her sister, it would also solve the problem of what to do about her little show last night. If she was gone, there would be no more conversations. She had already wrecked any chance of having a friendship with May. This might be for the best.

Jim was right behind her. "Wait a minute. You're safest here. Out there you'd be alone. Here, we won't let anyone hurt you. One man can't fight four."

"You people can't stop him. I'm telling you."

"And what's to keep this guy from following you once you leave?" His voice contained a hint of frustration.

She stopped. He was right. That was probably what would happen. Somehow Vince would hunt her down and make her pay. But at least if she left she wouldn't be dragging May into her problems. Hadn't she done too much of that already?

"What about May?" Jim said. "You'd leave without talking to her?"

"You can tell her for me."

"No."

"Why not?"

"Your relationship's none of my business. But I'm not going to hurt her, and you know it would." His next words were soft and sincere. "You're safest with us."

Christy wished he could be right, but he didn't know Vince.

"Think this out. Talk to May. We can help you."

It went against all that was screaming in her head, but she finally gave in. She could see Jim wouldn't let her do anything else. And it was true that rashness wouldn't get her anywhere. Maybe she could even smooth things over with her sister if she stayed a little longer.

She'd stay one more day, but that was it. Tomorrow would be another story. It was Sunday, and May had already talked about going to church. Christy could make her getaway then, without anyone to stop her.

❧

Early on Sunday morning, a familiar voice woke Christy from her sleep on the sofa. She opened her eyes to see May kneeling beside her. Christy eased up on an elbow and smiled at her. She'd spent the whole day yesterday following May around, helping her and Ruth tag and vaccinate the calves in the second-day pens, and then riding along as Ruth, May, and Jim moved the yearling bulls closer to home. Amazingly, May never brought up the drinking or anything else, and Christy had almost enjoyed herself. Almost. Vince was still lurking out there somewhere.

"Good morning, sleepyhead," May said cheerfully.

Christy groaned and fell back onto her pillow. With the checking for calves going on through the night, her sleep had hardly been restful. "Don't you people ever sleep in?"

"I wish," May said, smiling. "Hey, after breakfast we're going to church. Come with us?"

Christy sat up, struggling with how to respond. She didn't want to hurt May, but church really wasn't an option. This was her only chance to leave. "Not this time. Some other, okay?"

May swallowed the answer like a champ, but her disappointment was obvious. It made Christy reconsider for a second. She hated to let May down, but she couldn't afford to get sentimental now. She had to get out of here.

"Okay, then," May said. "We won't be long. There's a storm on the way, so we'll get back as fast as we can."

All through breakfast Christy acted bright and pleasant, but she kept catching Jim watching her from across the table. Each time their eyes met, she'd look away. After helping with the dishes, Ruth announced it was time to go, and Christy almost sighed in relief. They'd never have left her if they'd known about Vince. She was grateful for Jim's silence, but it surprised her that he was going to let her stay alone.

She saw them out the back door, then raced into the living room. Checking to make sure what little she'd brought was stuffed in her suitcase, she stripped the sofa of its sheets and blankets, neatly folded them, and left the pile on a cushion.

In the kitchen she jotted on a scrap of paper, *Something came up at work. Had to leave. Sorry. I'll keep in touch. Thanks for everything. Love, Chris.* Closing Scribbles in the house, she hastily strode to her car.

She threw her suitcase so hard it bounced on the backseat. She'd convinced herself Vince was the real reason she was leaving. If he burned her apartment, what else would he do? She didn't want to find out. She had to escape and hole up someplace he would never find. Where didn't matter. She'd check into another dumpy motel or something.

Christy opened the passenger door and reached across the seat to start the car and get the defrost going. This was supposed to be easy. She'd done her duty just like Aunt Edna wanted. They'd spent time together. She didn't need to feel bad about anything. But why couldn't she have just explained her situation to May like Jim suggested? Instead, she'd hidden it all, as usual, and hadn't breathed a word. If she left now, in May's eyes she'd be abandoning her. Once again.

She fished the ice scraper from the glove compartment and slammed the door. That's when she saw Jim come out of his trailer. She swore when he walked toward her. "I thought you left for church," she said.

"Didn't change your mind, did you?"

Christy brushed a thin layer of snow off her windshield.

"So now you're leaving."

"What gave you that idea? Was it the suitcase or the keys?"

"Why won't you talk to May about it before you go?"

She rolled her eyes. "Because I don't want her to know I'm a loser, all right?"

"She's not gonna think that. She cares about you."

Christy stomped around him to the back window.

"That what you really believe?" Jim said.

"You think you know something about me? Well, you don't know half my story. And May doesn't either."

"Your sister loves you. Period."

With the windows clear she went for the driver's door, but Jim stood directly in her way. "Would you step aside?"

"And I know she'd only want to help. We all do."

Christy wasn't putting up with this anymore. She said in a low voice, "I'm asking you to let me by."

"Look, she's about to lose everything here. The ranch and now you too. Don't just walk out on her like this."

Her silence was the only answer he was getting.

He stepped out of her path and pointed to the car with a shrug. "Go ahead. Run away."

She hesitated, then swore at him again. "You've got a lot of nerve."

"But I'm right."

That's what bothered her. How could he see through her so easily?

"It's always easier to run," Jim said. "I oughta know. Ran from God for almost twenty years. About as long as you, no doubt."

"God doesn't have anything to do with this."

"Then why not go to church with May?"

"I told you already. Because of Vince." But even as Christy said it, she had a feeling Jim was seeing through this excuse too. Vince was a real threat, but he was also her scapegoat. If she had any backbone whatsoever, she would have opened up to her sister, then left. She started to walk to the driver's door, then turned around. "Why are you doing this?"

"Because you remind me of myself." Jim tried to look into her eyes, but she wouldn't let him. "I used to be like you." For a second he almost appeared self-conscious, trying to find the right words. "I can see you need what I've found."

Her gaze dropped to his muddy boots. "Right. I'm sure you say that to a lot of women."

For the first time Jim seemed taken aback. "As hard as it might be for you to believe, people can care for each other without having ulterior motives. I don't have one. You can believe that or not, but it's true." He walked toward one of the pickups, and he didn't look back.

Christy stood still, the cold wind flipping her hair into

her face, her shoulders hunched. She heard his engine roar to life. Saw him drive toward her. Jim unrolled the passenger window and stopped beside her. They studied each other in silence.

"Where you going?" she said.

"Church." He smiled a crooked smile, one she could barely detect. "Wanna come?"

18

CHRISTY NEVER WOULD'VE guessed it was a church. From the outside it looked like any other shop on Main Street, but it took up three storefronts.

"We're hoping to have our own building soon," Jim said, circling twice before finding a space at the edge of the packed lot. "Almost outgrown this place." The sign said worship started at 11:15. She wasn't sure which was worse: milling with people she didn't know beforehand or coming into a service already started.

A cute elderly couple greeted them with smiles in the lobby decorated with fake plants. Music emanated from closed doors behind them. The couple was dressed nicely, and Christy immediately felt self-conscious about her jeans and sweatshirt. Even Jim had on clean denim and a bolo tie.

"Good to see you, Jim," the old man said, extending a hand, which Jim heartily shook.

"Same to you, Carl," he responded, then introduced her to the couple he called the church's faithful greeters. "Any seats left?"

"Pretty full today, but we'll find you something." Carl opened one of the doors, and the music boomed. Guitar, piano, drums. Somewhere a tambourine rattled. Christy saw rows and rows of people, maybe two hundred, standing, most clapping and singing to the music.

Carl scanned the room. "I'll get some more seats." He returned moments later and set two folding metal chairs against the back wall.

Jim thanked him. Christy did the same, thankful he'd put them in the back.

Above the heads of the crowd she could see the song leader, a twentysomething guy who strummed a scratched guitar and belted out the song into a standing mike. Jim started tapping his foot and soon was clapping with the rest, singing "I'm So Glad Jesus Set Me Free."

Christy determined to remain a spectator and kept her hands at her sides. When the song was over, some of the people raised their hands and spoke fervently to the ceiling in a bizarre way. Were they trying to talk to God?

As things calmed down, a man in his fifties with a shaved head took the platform. "Praise God. Folks, He's right here with us, ready to meet you where you are."

She looked around. God? In this place? There were no pews. The carpet was ratty. A ceiling tile was missing right above the guy's head. If God was anywhere, she guessed He would at least want a church with stained glass and hymnals.

"Who's he?" Christy whispered to Jim.

"Pastor Walt."

A pastor in black jeans and a belt buckle the size of her purse? He wasn't even wearing a tie.

"Thank y'all for coming out this morning," the pastor said with a slight Southern drawl, setting a huge book on the podium. That would be his Bible, no doubt.

Just then she thought she saw May. About halfway up and over on the side with Ruth. Christy glanced at Jim as he reached into his coat and brought out a thin leather volume with the words *New Testament* in gold on the cover. Had she come here only to prove to him she wasn't a coward? She remembered the things May had said the other night and had to confess they'd made her wonder. May had something in her life that was keeping her happy and optimistic even in the face of losing her beloved ranch. What if what Jim said was true? What if this cowboy sitting beside her really did have something she needed?

Yeah, she was curious. She could admit that. Christy eyed the pastor as he walked back and forth across the stage.

"I grew up with an abusive father," he said. "And a mom who tried to ignore it. My little brother and I lived every day fearing when our next whippin' would be. When I was fourteen, I could take it no more, and I ran away from home. Had no intention of ever returning, and I didn't. Left my brother to fend for himself. Living on the streets, I quickly learned I could trust no one. I became hard and tough, stealing what I could to stay alive."

Christy shifted in her chair, thinking of her own childhood. They had something in common. He abandoned his brother, she her sister.

"By the time I was seventeen, I'd sent three men to the hospital with serious stab wounds, dealt drugs, and stolen cars. It was then I discovered motorcycles. Got me a Harley and knew I'd found something goooood."

The crowd chuckled.

Walt returned to the podium and held it with both hands, almost as if it were the handlebars of his bike. "Met a guy in a motorcycle gang, and he introduced me to the biker world. It was all I never had. A family. Men to look up to. I did whatever it took to be accepted by them. If that meant breaking into a store, I did it. If it meant beatin' somebody up, I did that. Then one day I realized I was gaining respect. I had people looking up to *me*, something I'd never experienced before.

"I had power. But the thing was, when I got home and was by myself, I'd look in the mirror, and I wouldn't see a big tough guy. I'd see a scared man who was searching for love."

Walt stepped off the platform and paced slowly across the front of the room. "Then one night a bunch of us decided to have some fun. We'd been partying, and we got the idea that robbing a gas station would be a thrill. But something went wrong. When I showed my gun and demanded cash, the guy behind the counter pulled out a piece of his own and fired three rounds. All of them got me. And the thing was, my buddies, the guys who were supposed to stick by me when times got rough, ran. They left me there in a pool of my own blood waiting for the cops. I'm told I almost died, but no one visited me in the hospital. Guess they were too scared the cops would get 'em. That hurt more than the bullet holes. I felt betrayed. And I had plenty of time to think about it, 'cause it was right from that hospital bed to a prison cell for me." He shook his head. "A lot of time to think. Was convicted of armed robbery and got six to ten.

"But I'll tell you something," Walt said with a smile. "I'm glad I got convicted."

Christy wasn't sure she'd heard him correctly. How could he be happy for that? When she'd been in that awful cell two weeks ago, she'd even been willing to go back to Vince to be free again.

"You know why?" Walt continued. "Because in that prison I met God. There was an old guy with a cane who visited us inmates, and he started talking to me. He told me God loved me and wasn't looking for me to clean myself up before He'd accept me. The Lord just wanted my heart."

Christy glanced toward where she'd seen May, remembering their conversation last night. They made it all sound so easy.

Walt started walking down the aisle. "Somewhere along the way that old guy cracked through my facade. Maybe it was because of the genuine care he had for men he knew had committed heinous acts. And once there was a crack, my walls started falling away piece by piece. I'm glad I got sent to prison, because I never would have listened anywhere else. Guess it was my rock bottom."

She crossed her legs uneasily. Hadn't she hit rock bottom too? She was homeless, jobless, and hated herself.

"It seemed impossible for God to love me," Walt said. "But I knew I needed His love. Deep inside, I knew."

Walt was silent for a moment, then came farther down the aisle, closer to where Christy was sitting. She could see the lights reflecting off his shiny head. "If God had waited to love me until I stopped cussing and drinking and otherwise got my act together, I wouldn't be here today. When I gave my life to Him, a peace like I'd never known flooded over me."

Christy found herself looking away from the guy. Peace. She wondered what that felt like.

❧

"Don't look now," Ruth whispered in May's ear, "but guess who's here."

May leaned closer to her friend. "Who?"

"Christy."

She twirled around. "Where?"

"Shh." Ruth put her hand on May's arm. "Against the back wall with Jim."

May could barely believe it, but there she was.

❧

"I was still locked up," Walt went on. "God hadn't magically thrown open the prison doors, but inside I was free; my burdens were gone." He placed his hand on the shoulder of the man closest to him, a large guy with tattoos on his arms who nodded like he knew what the preacher was talking about. "I want y'all to do something for me. Close your eyes, everyone. Now imagine you're on death row."

Christy didn't do it at first. What was this about? But as he continued, she found herself obeying and closed her eyes.

"You're about to be executed," Walt said. "They've got you tied to the bed. You're terrified, shaking. It's over. You're done. You don't look, but there's a poke in your arm, and you know it's truly the end."

Walt stopped and let the silence hang over the room. "Suddenly, the door bursts open, and a stranger rushes inside. He stops the guard ready to release the lethal fluid meant for you. You watch as the guard reluctantly steps away from his post, and the stranger unties your arms and legs.

"You're shocked when the guard leads you away from the death room and outside the prison gates, where he releases you. 'You're free,' he says, and you can only stare at him in astonishment. 'But what about my crimes? I was sentenced to die,' you say. The guard smirks like he can't believe it either, then says with a point in the direction of the execution chamber, 'That man in there. He just died in your place.'"

When Walt stopped speaking, the packed room remained as quiet as the death chamber he described. Walt looked in Christy's direction, and their eyes met. "That's what Jesus actually did for all of us," he said. She could swear his gaze was on her. "He loves you that much."

She looked away, warmth coming to her cheeks. Why was he staring at her?

Walt returned to his podium. "Our sins will send us to eternal punishment. That's just the way it goes. Like a death sentence. We can't change it unless we receive what Jesus did for us. Once I realized what He did for me and accepted it, my life was never the same."

Christy stared at her hands as he went on. She wanted to believe what he said, just like she wanted to believe May, but nothing in life ever came without strings attached, right? What was the catch here?

And what was she? A weak, pathetic woman who settled for sleazy men and the low life. Why would God want her?

The preacher asked everyone to close their eyes and bow their heads, and Christy complied with only half of the request. She would keep her eyes open this time.

"Would you be so bold as to lift your hand if you're ready to give your life to the Lord?" Walt said.

A hand or two shot up.

Christy wanted to respond, and this surprised her. But if she raised her hand, committed to change her life, it would only last till tomorrow. She didn't know how to walk the straight and narrow. She'd still be the same alcoholic who'd hooked up more than once with guys she'd just met in bars and the same wretch who'd ended the life of her own child with an abortion. She was weak. There was no changing that.

And though the urge was powerful, Christy knew she couldn't respond. She didn't have the guts.

❧

"I see your hand, sir," Pastor Walt said, acknowledging the man with a smile. It was all May could do to keep from checking on Chris. Had the message gotten through to her sister?

"Thank you, ma'am. I see your hand."

She pictured Pastor Walt seeing Chris's hand come up, maybe slowly, and he'd thank her too with a smile.

"Yes, sir, you're making the best decision of your life."

May continued her desperate prayer for the Lord to soften her sister's heart.

"I see you, ma'am, way in the back."

❧

Christy turned to Jim. "Can we go?"

Jim glanced at the preacher. "Now?"

She nodded. It wouldn't be easy to explain why, and she hoped he wouldn't ask. She wanted to get out before this thing ended. She needed to think about it alone. If she could leave now, she'd have a little time at the ranch to prepare herself before May returned, and then she would say good-bye. "Please, Jim."

He looked at her with a kind expression she didn't understand, then reached into his coat and placed a small bunch of keys in her hand. "You can take my truck."

Her gaze went from the keys to his face, unsure if he was serious.

"I can get a ride with May and Ruth," Jim said.

His trust caught her off guard. The preacher was still talking, asking the people who raised their hands to come to the front. *Go for it.* If she left now, no one would notice.

"Thanks," she said and slipped out before she could change her mind.

❦

May's eyes flew open. Seven people stood at the altar. Four men, three women.

No Chris.

Her hopes deflated. She'd thought for sure the woman raising her hand in the back had been Chris.

"Let's give our new brothers and sisters a hand clap," Pastor Walt said.

May did, though her heart wasn't in it. After she'd realized Chris was here, she'd pinned everything on this service. And she couldn't have planned it better herself. The music. Pastor's testimony. The invitation. Even so, she should've known better than to assume Chris would respond so quickly. She had no idea what baggage her sister carried.

May allowed herself a peek toward the back. There was Jim. And beside him, where Chris had been, was an empty chair.

19

CHRISTY PARKED JIM'S truck outside his trailer, got out, and stood for a moment beside it. He was right. She had been running.

When was she going to stop hurting May? Sisters were supposed to care for each other, treat each other like May and Beth had the other night. There was an unspoken sisterly affection between those two. Christy wished her relationship with May was like that.

Glancing up the drive, she suddenly felt vulnerable. She was alone. In her haste to leave the service, she'd forgotten how isolated this ranch was. When would the others return? A splash of dread hit her. What if Vince came back now?

Christy decided not to be around to find out. After borrowing a coat and some gloves from the house, she found a halter in the barn. She would take a ride. By the time she returned, May would be home, and Christy would've figured out what to say.

Spotting May's gray gelding among the horses in the corral, she went for him. Wasn't his name Spirit? It took her fifteen minutes to catch him. He seemed to enjoy playing with her, darting out of reach every time she got close. He finally fell for the carrot she swiped from the fridge, and Christy led him to the barn, pleased with her success.

She secured him with the cross ropes she'd seen May use. She wasn't exactly an equestrian; that was May's department. But the little she'd learned from taking those few riding lessons as a kid had come back to her when she and May rode together.

"Think we can do this, boy?" Christy said, stroking the nose of the beautiful gray. He didn't flinch. She hoped May wouldn't mind her taking him. As she awkwardly began the process of tacking up, her mind drifted to what that preacher said.

"If God had waited to love me until I stopped cussing and drinking and otherwise got my act together, I wouldn't be here today."

She ran a brush over Spirit's shaggy winter coat, a cloud of dust puffing upward with each stroke. Was he for real, or was this guy just another preacher working the crowd to get an offering?

"A peace like I'd never known flooded over me."

Christy tugged off the halter and, imitating May, pushed the bit of the bridle against the horse's mouth. His lips wrinkled back as the metal clinked on his teeth, but he finally took it. She pulled the bridle over his head, reattaching the cross ties.

The peace thing. That was the difference in May. Despite all her financial troubles, even the impending loss of her ranch, there was still peace in her eyes. To have that herself . . . Christy couldn't quite imagine it.

She lifted the saddle at her feet, ready to hoist it onto Spirit's back, and she could almost see that preacher staring at her again. It was creepy the way he seemed to know her thoughts. It made his words cut right through her. There was something real about the guy, and she found herself believing him.

With a heave Christy threw the saddle onto Spirit's back, hanging on to the stirrup to keep it from flying over the other side. Spirit stayed calm, and she petted his neck in thanks. Struggling to snag one of the two hanging girth straps— cinches, May had called them—she finally managed to catch it by practically crawling under Spirit's belly.

That preacher had been out there and experienced some hard stuff, like she had. May had talked the same way he did about God's love. Jim, too. Could they all be wrong? Christy pulled on the strap, knowing she had to get it as tight as possible. But even when she jerked upward using her whole body, she was still unable to tighten it to the worn hole she guessed was where it should be.

A noise came from outside. Could that be a gate closing? Was May back already? Popping her head out the door, she skimmed the yard. It was still. Jim's truck sat where she'd left it. Not a soul in sight.

The snow had started again and was coming down in huge flakes, the wind ratcheting up. She took a moment to enjoy the bucolic view of cows scattered throughout the pastures and the snowy mountains. May sure did have it good out here. Christy leaned against the doorway with one hand. "God?" she whispered. "Are You really like they say?"

Returning to the barn, she tightened the second buckle on the girth strap with the same mediocre results as the first. She couldn't pull it past the first two holes. Tugging on the saddle, she checked for looseness. Not too bad, she guessed. She shortened the stirrups, then stood back to admire her handiwork.

Christy stroked Spirit's neck and congratulated herself for remembering how to do everything. Then, after zipping up her jacket, she donned the ski cap Beth had lent her for sledding.

"Ready, boy?" she said and undid the restraining ropes.

"Well, well. Isn't this a sight."

Her heart stopped at the voice, and Christy caught her breath in horror. She swung around, her worst fears confirmed.

❧

As soon as the service was over, May and Ruth headed straight for Jim.

"Where'd she go?" May asked.

His look was sympathetic. "Left before it was over. I gave her my truck."

"You *what?*"

Jim pulled on his coat. "I couldn't make her stay, and I thought she might need time to think."

May couldn't help grimacing in frustration. Perfect. This was just like Chris's other disappearing act at Aunt Edna's funeral.

Ruth patted May's back. "Hang in there."

She tried to smile but ended up shaking her head. For a moment she'd thought she was making headway with her sister. "She wouldn't come when I invited her this morning."

"It's only because she's going through things I can relate

to," Jim said. "And I pushed her the way I needed to be pushed years ago."

All the events of the past forty-eight hours flashed through May's mind. What should she have done differently? She hadn't brought up Chris's drinking or what she said about killing someone. She'd decided to let Chris explain in her own time. That hadn't been easy, but it was what she felt God would want her to do. Had staying silent been a mistake?

"What am I doing wrong?" She longed to reach Chris so badly, but it wasn't working. Who did she think she was, anyway? Why would Chris even want to listen to her, the kid sister? "I'm trying to be real. I even told her exactly what I was feeling."

"It's not you," Ruth said.

"Sure feels like it."

The three of them walked toward the door. Jim held it open for the two women, and a wall of glacial air blew inside. Snow was already floating down.

"If it helps, she was listening closely today," Jim said.

May blew on her hands to keep them warm. "I was hoping she'd go up front."

Ruth added, "It was only one sermon."

Jim smiled. "Ten years ago I would've been written off as a lost cause too. It took a lot more than a sermon to get through to me."

They crossed the parking lot toward May's truck. She hadn't known Jim before he was saved, but he'd told her the story of how the foreman at the ranch where he was working had reached out to him and eventually led him to God. Apparently he'd been a hard nut to crack. That foreman could have given up. But he didn't. She wanted to be like that for Chris.

"It's not up to you to convert your sister," Ruth said. "You just need to love her. God'll take care of the rest."

May unlocked her truck. Why was trusting God always so hard?

❧

Christy could only stare numbly at Vince. No one would hear her scream.

"What's this? A new side of you I don't know about?" Vince laughed, leaning against the doorway, his arms crossed. "I'm sorry to say it, but you don't make a very good Dale Evans."

"What do you want?" Her voice was cold. She would have to play this carefully.

Vince stepped inside. He was uncharacteristically dressed in outdoorsman clothes—canvas pants, snow boots, a down parka. "And your manners always have been horrible."

"You're not welcome here," Christy said, still holding Spirit's reins firmly in her left hand.

He slowly unzipped his parka. "Can't a man visit the girl he loves?"

She squeezed Spirit's reins until the leather dug into her palm. Could she stall him long enough for Jim and the others to get back from church? "Let's both just get on with our lives. You go your way. I'll go mine."

"You know, your apartment is a wreck these days."

Even though Christy already knew he started the fire, hearing him say it made her feel sick. Anger boiled in her gut. She looked past him, yearning for the door.

He moved toward her. "There doesn't seem to be anyone around, does there? Looks like we're all by ourselves."

Heat flashed up her back at the mistake she'd made. She'd known Vince followed her here. She was an idiot to come back alone. "I just want to get on with my life," she said slowly, carefully, enunciating each word and trying not to show fear. "I have no interest in getting you in trouble."

"You really want to know what I want?" Vince smiled, then said softly, "You."

Her skin crawled. "I want you to leave. Now."

Vince turned in a circle, surveying the barn. "What kind of place is this?"

"A place where people work hard and care about each other. Something you know nothing about."

"And I suppose little sis taught you that?"

Christy forced herself to breathe. What did he know about May?

"News flash. I'm about to teach you something far more important. Something you should've learned a long time ago."

Their eyes locked. His were full of hate. She'd seen this look before. Only now, instead of appearing in flashes right before striking her, the hate was a constant stream of electricity charging his eyes.

Moving back, she gripped the gelding's reins tighter. What could she do? Running wasn't an option. He would easily catch her. If she could only mount the horse.

Vince methodically stepped nearer.

There was only one thing she could do. Christy lifted her chin, feigned confidence, and boldly walked past him, leading Spirit behind her. She would bluff her way out of here, whether she felt confident or not.

"I'm not finished."

Christy kept walking.

In an instant, he spun her around, shoving her body into Spirit. The horse panicked and jumped away, ripping the reins out of her hand.

Vince's fist landed on her cheekbone, and she stumbled

to her knees, vaguely aware of the horse bolting out the door. Throbbing pain pulsed across her face.

Vince was upon her. He grabbed a fistful of her jacket and yanked her to her feet. "Learn *this*, darling." He stuck his face in hers. "I don't take no for an answer."

She closed her eyes, gasping for air. If she resisted, he'd make it worse. "Please, don't."

"You pitiful excuse of a woman." He hit her again, a swift bash to the left temple, and let her crumple to the floor. "Worthless piece of trash."

Christy's ears rang as the room turned black around the edges of her vision. If only she'd lose consciousness. He could do what he wanted and she wouldn't feel it. Christy lifted her head, trying to see. "I . . . I promise I'll never tell a soul. But please . . . don't do this to me."

Vince picked her up by the jacket again, shoving her against a stall door like she was a rag doll. She groaned as pain shot through her back. He'd pushed her against the metal latch, and it dug into her ribs.

His nostrils flared. "Look at me."

She tried to lift her arms, but he had them pinned to her sides. She was crying now like a blubbering fool, begging him to let her go.

Vince slammed her into the door again, and her head snapped back against the wood. "Look at me!"

Christy raised her eyes to his face, now a grotesque carica-
ture of the handsome man she'd met four years ago. How
could she ever have loved him? Why hadn't she seen?

"I've given you more than enough chances."

"Please . . ."

He backhanded her across the face, and she fell to her
knees again, clutching her nose. Warm blood dripped onto
her fingers and ran down the back of her throat.

"What did I see in you? You're certainly nothing to look
at." Vince pulled a wad of rope from his jacket pocket. "Not
even worth the air you breathe."

A rope? That's when she realized the awful truth. He
wasn't just doing this to frighten her into submission. He
intended to kill her . . . slowly. No doubt purposely choosing
a method that would force her to suffer and sputter her last
breath in a plea for mercy.

Every ounce of survival instinct she had kicked in.
She searched the barn for a weapon. Bale of straw. Horse
comb. Bottle of saddle soap. Shovel. She locked onto that.
It leaned against the wall by the door. Could she crawl fast
enough?

Vince kicked her in the thigh, and her quad muscle
knotted. "Get up."

Christy rose in a slow, defeated way. If she could just take
him off guard . . . Halfway to her feet she lunged for the

shovel. Grasping it with both hands, she willed herself to focus on Vince and swung at his skull.

The shovel met its mark with a revolting thud. Vince's hands flew to his head, and he sagged to the floor, moaning, cursing.

She ran. Into the yard, past the pickups.

The house! Get to the house! Lock the door. Maybe she could figure out how to use one of those guns before Vince could break in.

And then Christy saw the most beautiful creature in the entire world—Spirit, a snowy apparition standing in the middle of the yard, as if waiting for her. For a split second she hesitated. Should she race for the house or try to mount the gelding when she could barely see straight?

Vince decided for her. He appeared in the barn doorway still holding his head, his eyes ablaze. She wouldn't make the house.

Adrenaline propelled her to Spirit. She stumbled to his side, frantically gathering the reins. She raised a foot of lead, nearly losing her balance.

A glance behind. Vince ran toward her. Clutching Spirit's mane, she summoned all her strength, pulled herself up, and made it!

So did Vince. He was at her again, seizing her leg and jerking her down.

"Let go!" She tried to kick him in the chest.

His grip tightened around her thigh and calf, twisting her leg. One more second and she knew he'd have her on the ground, and she'd be as good as dead.

Christy slapped the reins like a whip at Vince's eyes. He screamed and let her go.

She whirled Spirit away toward . . . what? There was nowhere to go except over the gate and fence. And she could barely ride, much less jump. Was there enough room for Spirit to gather speed? She urged him with a kick to his flank, and he shot forward, straight for the fence.

Vince yelled obscenities after her.

The fence sped closer.

She dug her heels into Spirit's side, hanging on to the saddle horn and his mane. "Faster, boy!"

Spirit didn't balk at the fence. He leaped through the air, cleared the boards, and they landed on the other side with such force that the air whooshed out of Christy's lungs, and her face smashed into his neck, sending another bolt of pain through her already-tender nose. But she was still in the saddle.

Christy didn't realize a gun could be so loud. The shot cracked through the air like thunder. She whirled around in the saddle to see Vince standing at the fence with a pistol trained directly on her. All she could do was keep Spirit running. She had no idea the range of that gun.

"Go, Spirit! Go!"

Probably as scared as she was, the horse obeyed, speeding into a canter.

Two more shots came back-to-back.

Crouching as low as she could without falling off, Christy thought of pleading to God for help but didn't. She'd gotten into this mess all by herself. It was up to her alone to get out of it.

❧

May walked into the kitchen. "Chris?"

A note on the counter caught her eye. It had been a while since she'd seen that familiar handwriting. May pulled it closer. *Something came up at work. Had to leave. Sorry. I'll keep in touch. Thanks for everything. Love, Chris.*

May stuffed the note in her pocket and went outside. Chris's Honda was still parked behind the horse trailer. She walked to the car and stared inside. A suitcase sat on the backseat. Okay . . . so where was Chris now?

In the calving shed, May found Ruth preparing a syringe.

"Scours," Ruth said. "Number 209's calf."

"You seen Chris anywhere? She's not in the house."

Ruth shook her head. "Maybe she went for a ride. Spirit's not in the corral, and I know I put him in there this morning."

May pulled out Chris's note and handed it to Ruth. "She was planning to leave. Without saying good-bye."

Ruth read it, then put an arm around her. May leaned into the older woman.

"She might not realize what she's doing to you, *chica*," Ruth said, gently brushing a strand of hair out of May's face. "And it's obvious she's hurting."

"I know. I see it in her eyes, and it makes my heart break."

"She needs your acceptance now more than ever. It doesn't mean you condone her sins. You love her in spite of them."

"Like that Scripture. Judge not, lest you be judged."

"That's right." Ruth squeezed her shoulder. "I meant what I said in the parking lot. You're not doing anything wrong. The other night when we were playing cards, I saw her watching you with longing in her eyes. And when you and Beth went outside, I was talking to her. Every question she asked was about you."

"Really?"

"I think she just needs time."

❧

Christy finally slowed down for Spirit's sake. She had enough sense to know he couldn't keep up a gallop for long. She let him slow to a fast walk as she craned to look back, her whole body trembling. She couldn't believe it. Vince tried to kill her. He wanted her dead.

She wiped some of the blood from her nose. She kept sniffing, trying to keep more from flowing, but it still drizzled onto Spirit's mane. Her face ached, and the spot on her back where the stall's latch had caught her sent a sharp pain up her spine. The ranch house was now hidden behind the hills, but she still didn't feel safe. Pulling on the gloves she'd stashed in her coat pocket, she held her fingers to her nose and tried to calm herself. What should she do? Was Vince following her? She cast another glance over her shoulder. There was no sign of him. But that didn't mean anything anymore.

Christy pulled the ski cap down over her ears as the whiteness eddied all around her. Zero cows out here. Only freshly accumulated snow spread over the hills and that mountain May had called Squatter's Mountain straight ahead. Spirit was taking the same route she'd ridden with May the other day.

She couldn't go back. Not without any idea when May and especially Jim would return from church. Vince could be following her this very moment.

She tapped Spirit's flank.

❧

"What is it, boy?" May found Scribbles behind the barn, hackles upraised like a patch of needles and barking at a Chevy Blazer. What in the world? Where did *that* come from?

She scratched the dog's back. "Settle down." Wiping the snow from the car's blacked-out passenger window, she tried to see in. All that was visible was a map on the seat.

Ruth and Jim were in the house fixing dinner. She'd been busying herself outside, waiting for Chris to come back from her ride. May took Scribbles with her and stuck her head in the kitchen. "Guys? You know anything about that Blazer behind the barn?"

"Blazer?" Ruth asked.

Jim stood up from the table, and May was surprised to see alarm on his face. "A green Blazer?"

"Uh-huh."

"Show me."

She brought them to it and stood with her hands on her hips. It was a new model, unusually clean for this area. "Know whose it is?"

Jim didn't seem to hear the question as he tried all the truck's doors.

May and Ruth looked at each other.

"Jim, what's the matter?" Ruth said.

He turned to face both of them. "I *have* seen this truck before. Early yesterday a guy named Vince drove up in it and said he was looking for Christy. When I told her, she freaked out. It's a long story, but I think he's been stalking her."

"What?" May said.

"He was mad 'cause she broke up with him."

"And when were you going to tell me this?"

"I was hoping she'd talk to you herself." He scowled at the Chevy. "I should never have let her come back alone."

May felt the muscles in her entire body tense. "What are you thinking? Is this guy dangerous? She should've been back by now."

"She was real scared of him finding her. That's why she wanted to leave." Jim used his sleeve to remove the snow from the rest of the windows, peering in each one.

Ruth turned toward the barn. "I'll saddle the horses."

⚘

Christy stopped Spirit to smoke a cigarette amid the first few trees at the base of Squatter's Mountain. Her pulse had steadied almost to normal, and she felt safe enough to take a minute to rest. But her hand still shook as she lit up, and it wasn't from needing a drink this time. Were the others home yet? Would it be safe to return?

Easy. Calm down. I'm okay. For now.

She sat quietly smoking for a moment, the only sounds the creaking of the saddle leather at her slightest move and Spirit's heavy breaths in the cold. The snow was quickly piling up all around her.

A twig snapped.

She jumped and spun around in the saddle, studying every degree of her surroundings. Even though she saw nothing, she urged Spirit forward. She couldn't let herself be an easy target. Forget the weather. She had to get going! Vince left her no choice.

Christy turned Spirit onto that trail May had pointed out on their ride. A gust of wind sent a huge clump of wet snow down her neck. She grabbed at her collar too late. Ice shocked her skin, and she had no choice but to bear it until it melted and warmed to her body's temperature.

For several minutes she maneuvered the horse through the trees, unable to avoid branches whisking into her face and thighs. A couple times on the incline the saddle slipped dangerously sideways when she least expected it. She'd known the girth wasn't tight enough, and she was really paying for it on these hills.

"Come warmer weather, it'll make a great hike." What had May meant? She hoped this trail was safe for horses.

Leaning forward as Spirit climbed higher, Christy wove her gloved fingers through his mane. "You can do it," she grunted. The farther she went, the safer she'd be. Vince would never find her on Squatter's Mountain.

Spirit labored up the slope, his hooves sinking through snow and hitting the rock beneath. He was struggling to keep his footing now, but they finally made it to where the hill leveled off, and she rode him through a small clearing. Looking back, she checked to see how far they'd come, but she couldn't see anything past the pines.

A mental picture of Vince hiding behind one of them forced her to plow on, and she didn't look back again.

❧

May met Ruth walking out of the barn.

"Nugget's gone," Ruth said. "And she was in her stall before we left."

"Maybe Chris took her?"

Ruth glanced toward the corral. "Then where's Spirit? Last time I checked, one gal can't ride two horses."

"You think that guy . . . ?"

"That's exactly what I'm thinking."

May sprinted for the tack room. They had to find Chris.

❧

Was she still on the trail?

Christy gripped Spirit with her legs until they were full of fire. Winding through the switchbacks had kept the climbing to a minimum at first, but now she was hugging the horse's neck to keep from falling off as they struggled up another arduous grade. It was getting scary. She knew the smart thing would be to turn back, but what if Vince was waiting for her at the bottom? Maybe she would have a better view at the summit.

Spirit balked at the next incline, and she had to force him forward. He finally obeyed, his hooves grabbing at the slope, and she felt her hold on his mane slipping. She looked down. The left side of the trail dropped fifteen feet into a ravine. She held the saddle in a death grip. A branch slapped her face on the cheekbone where Vince hit her in the barn. She managed to keep from instinctively letting go and reaching toward the sting.

"Go, boy!"

Spirit valiantly pushed on, but no matter how hard he tried, he slid backward. This was crazy! She had to get off and lead Spirit the rest of the way. Flipping her foot out of the right stirrup, she clasped the saddle horn with both hands, shifted her weight, ready to dismount. There was just enough space to get off without sliding into the ravine.

Mistake. The saddle flipped to the left before she had a chance to get her right leg over. Spirit clambered to keep his footing, but it was too late.

They were going down.

Spirit's whinny mixed with her scream. All Christy could do was watch helplessly as the ground raced to meet them.

And before she could react, the horse's mammoth body slammed on top of her and they both tumbled down, down into the ravine.

20

"See anything?" May reined in her mount as Ruth rode toward her. One look at the older woman's face and May knew the answer.

"Nothing. Passed Jim, and he hasn't either."

The three of them had been out for over an hour, and now the snow and wind, which had already covered any tracks, were picking up. There wasn't going to be much more daylight. May struggled to keep from completely panicking.

"It's time to call . . ." Ruth sat straighter in her saddle, her eyes focused on the horizon.

May followed her gaze. A distant gray speck was coming

quickly toward them and growing into the form of a horse. "It's Spirit!"

They sat on their mounts silently watching him approach at a gallop, the stirrups from the twisted saddle he wore swinging and beating against his flank.

"Dear Lord," May whispered.

The saddle was empty.

❧

Christy came to, retching. She tried to roll onto her side, but excruciating stabs of pain shot up her left leg. Then she was spewing bile onto herself and the snow. Coughing, sputtering, she struggled to breathe. What happened? Where was she?

The deep purple sky was barely visible through the tree-tops, and only as icy flakes lit on her face did she remember where she was. Spirit had slipped on the trail. She had no idea how far they'd rolled or even if the horse was still alive.

Pain raced across her forehead, and she jerked off a glove with her teeth to feel for its source. Her fingers dipped into a wet wound, still bleeding. She could move her arms without any trouble. Good. They seemed all right, anyway. But her ankle . . . any attempt to move it brought jabs painful enough to make her scream. At least she wasn't paralyzed. Weakly raising herself on an elbow, all she could make out were the dark shadows of her lifeless legs.

Despite agony and dizziness, she forced herself to sit and explore her leg with trembling fingers. Running them across her thigh and downward, she felt a tear in her jeans and sticky blood again. Her knee was bruised and swollen, but it was still in one piece. Wincing, she stretched her hand toward the spot that hurt the most. She hated the idea of touching it. Christy gritted her teeth as her fingers crept down her leg.

A larger tear in the fabric. More warm stickiness as her fingers reached a break in the flesh. Gently she slid her hand farther down and felt a sharp object sticking out of her ankle.

A splintered bone?

Easing back into the snow, she shut her eyes in torture. "Help! Please, somebody help me!" But the second the words escaped her, she realized with dread what she'd just done. If Vince heard her, she could've just signed her death warrant.

She must have blacked out again, because the next thing she knew her body was shaking uncontrollably in the cold. There was no light of any kind. A shower of dry, biting snow blew onto her face. Hugging her ribs, she pulled her fingers together within the palm section of her gloves in a futile attempt to warm them. She wanted to yell for help again, but Vince could be ten feet away. That was when reality hit.

He was the only one who knew where she was.

❧

"Chris!" May called.

Aiming her Maglite into the night, it did little to penetrate the thick darkness and whirling snow. If only they'd found her before nightfall. The blizzard was in full force now. Would it ever let up?

The first thing May did when the riderless Spirit returned was call Beth's cell phone. Since the stirrups on Spirit's saddle were way too short for a man, they knew for sure Chris had been the one riding him. And if a search was to be conducted, she couldn't count on anyone more than Beth and her parents, Sam and Peggy. They'd arrived in record time, followed by their neighbors Jan and Keith Mercer.

Now they had to search in the dark. Beth rode beside May, the beams from their flashlights intertwining over the hills. Following Spirit's returning tracks had been easy enough at first, but the tracks had deteriorated until eventually the wind wiped them out entirely. Which meant all they had to go on was the general direction from which he'd come. They'd split into four teams of two with May and Beth on horseback and the others in their vehicles.

Everyone was keeping in touch by radio, and May reported into her handheld, "This is May. Nothing yet, guys."

"Same here," came Jim. "But we'll keep going."

A burst of static, then Peggy echoed the same.

"We'll keep looking," Keith replied.

May clipped the radio back onto her jacket. "Let's head up there," she said, pointing in the direction of Squatter's Mountain, trying to keep her worries under control.

This land wasn't too kind to folks who didn't know it, and she kept thinking of the horrific accidents many of her neighbors had endured. There was that experienced foreman whose horse spooked at a jackrabbit and dragged him to his death. The cowboy who barely made it back alive after being jumped by a starving cougar. The rancher whose horse threw him and left him paralyzed from the waist down. And then there was Ruth's husband. All of them were men who knew the ways of horses and knew their ranches even better than they knew their wives.

May desperately wanted to believe and trust the Lord that her sister was all right and that this nightmare would end better than those other disasters. At first she'd been okay, managing to convince herself that at any moment Chris would appear, maybe a little bruised, but none the worse for wear. But Chris hadn't shown up, and fear now seized her. Not only were the elements against her sister, but none of them knew where Vince was either.

Was he hurting Chris right now?

❧

Christy had to get warm. Her teeth chattered as she dragged her body inch by inch toward the trunk of the nearest tree. It was excruciating, but she had to have the little shelter it would provide. *So this is what it feels like to freeze to death.*

Another blast of wind. She willed her body toward the tree, aware only of its vague outline. Two last drags and she was underneath it. Clenching her jaw, she swore at the pain.

A series of eerie howls that sounded like a bunch of teenage boys pretending to be wolves set her nerves on edge. Coyotes. A whole pack of them, it sounded like, way too close. May's voice echoed in her mind: *"Coyotes . . . they do brutal things to calves."*

Could they smell blood? Did they attack people?

And what if Vince was stalking her right now? If he found her like this, she would be completely at his mercy, and she didn't doubt what he'd do.

Christy had to get up. She couldn't just lie here like a sitting duck.

But she didn't risk calling out again like she'd so foolishly done earlier. If Vince was near, that would only alert him to her location. Desperately, she listened for sounds of help. There were the coyotes again, then nothing. Nothing but the rustling of falling snow, like dry grass blowing on a windy day. Sounds of nature. No human voices. No sound of Spirit nearby. No one calling her name. How would May know where to look?

Christy took off her glove again and felt the wound on her forehead. It stung when she touched it. A drop of blood trickled down her face, and she wiped it, closing her eyes. She didn't know how long she could last out here.

❧

Vince stopped the horse to light a cigar, glad he'd had the presence of mind to bring one along. He had planned to smoke it in victory, but enjoying it in anticipation was satisfying enough.

He touched his fingers to his throbbing temple where Christy had dared to strike him. Instead of defeating him, the pain drove him on. And confidence pulsed through him like the nicotine pulsing through his cells.

The scream had been faint, but he was sure he'd heard it. If it weren't for the time he'd lost saddling this beast and the blasted weather, he would've caught her by now.

Coyotes howled in the distance, and somehow he felt akin to them. They were all hunting tonight.

❧

"Could she have made it this far?" Beth asked.

May turned up the collar of her coat. "How should I know?"

Beth quieted at her sharp answer.

"I'm sorry," May said. The cold and frantic searching were starting to wear on her, but that gave her no right to take it out on Beth. She handed her friend the radio. "Could you take this for a while?"

Beth did and reported, "No signs of her yet. Over."

May whispered, "Hang on, Chris. Wherever you are. Hang on."

❧

Christy clawed at the snow around the tree, hoping to find dead branches she could use for protection. All she found were frozen pine needles, and she had no idea what to do with those. She craved warmth, but she could only lie on her back shivering, fearing each breath would be her last.

How much time had passed? There was no way to know. She had to be missed by now. Had Spirit made it back, or was he lying dead nearby? Were her tracks still visible in this weather? If her tracks were visible, May wasn't the only one who'd be able to follow her. Or maybe no one even knew to look for her this far out.

Was she going to die out here? If Vince found her, she'd be dead eventually. But even if he didn't, she knew she was losing blood, and a night in this frigid air would be enough to kill even a healthy person.

Christy held her hands over her face and whispered into them, "I don't know if May's right about You or not. I want her to be. But she's so much better than me. She's a good kid. I never have been."

She took away her hands, and as she lay still in the snow, scenes of her past replayed. She saw herself leaving May. She was eighteen again, driving away knowing, but not admitting she knew, how it would hurt her sister.

Jump ahead a year. Christy was inside that abortion clinic allowing them to cut up her tiny baby like a hunk of meat. She'd known deep at her core what she was doing, but she hadn't allowed herself to think about it. She couldn't be a mother yet. Her whole life was in front of her waiting to be lived.

Yeah, a life of nights in bars just to forget that one day.

She thought of her affair with Vince and the other men she'd slept with in an attempt to feel loved and fulfilled. But instead, she'd always woken up in the morning with an even-deeper emptiness inside. It wasn't love. She'd used the men; they'd used her.

"I'm ashamed of my life," Christy said under her breath. "All I've ever wanted was for someone to love me. I've never felt it. That's why it's hard for me to imagine You could love me. I don't understand why You would. I don't have anything to offer You."

She looked up through the pines. Her eyes were getting better at seeing through the darkness. The tall silhouettes surrounded her like a massive army of giant soldiers ready to gun her down.

Please be listening, God.

❧

The urge was strong, and May couldn't ignore it. *Pray. Now. For Chris.*

She did. "Lord, I ask You in the name of Jesus to protect Chris right now. Satan, you are not getting her. I claim her for God. She *will* be all right. And we *will* find her."

Beth chimed in, "Amen."

They kept riding, but May felt no release. Something was very wrong.

❧

Vince dismounted and flipped on his flashlight, shining it through the trees. Once he got his bearings, he snuffed the light. No need to announce his presence.

The faint tracks he'd seen led him in this direction, but the snow had quickly erased them. The call had come from this way too, and here was a meager trail winding up the side of the mountain. It looked way too dangerous to ride any farther. He'd have to continue on foot. He secured his horse to a tree near the trailhead, as much out of sight as possible, and started climbing.

❧

Christy squeezed her arms tightly around her body and tried to ignore the excruciating pain. She was still shuddering uncontrollably. Why would God even listen to her? She was guilty.

But what about that pastor's message? He'd said God wasn't looking for him to clean himself up before He accepted him. God just wanted his heart.

He couldn't be talking about me. I'm worthless.

Tears welled up in Christy's eyes. How many times had Vince told her that?

"I'm a sinner," she whispered.

A picture flashed through her mind. It was May sitting beside her in the truck the other night. Christy saw again the earnestness in her sister's eyes when she'd said, "I love *you*. And so does God."

None of it made sense. God should've turned His back on her years ago. But if what May and that pastor said was true, He hadn't. He was up there now looking down on her. Waiting.

She lifted her eyes to the treetops, her tears warm against her cheeks.

"I've been . . . running from You my . . . whole life," she said, the words coming out in jerky sobs. Without thinking, she clasped her hands together. "I'm sorry." She didn't know what else to say. Just two words spoke her heart. "So sorry."

❧

"Which way now?" Beth asked.

May stopped her horse and panned her flashlight, trying to decide. Visibility was better now that the snow was easing up, but the wind was relentless. She wasn't sure why she was feeling a draw toward Squatter's Mountain. Chris would've been a fool to try to climb it in this weather, but Spirit could've taken her there. May had ridden him to the mountain so many times that he knew it by rote. "Let's at least go past Squatter's."

"May."

She clicked her tongue to get her mare going again.

"Hold up a sec."

"We've gotta keep moving."

"I just want you to listen to me for one minute, okay?"

"While we're riding."

"No, please listen now."

May lifted her light to Beth's face. Her friend's expression was grim.

"I'm gonna stay with you for as long as it takes," Beth

said. "And so are Mom and Dad. But I just want to prepare you. I mean—"

"I know."

"It's been a long time. It's twenty degrees out here, and even if—"

Holding up her hand, she stopped her friend. She knew full well what Beth was going to say. Even if Christy was alive, she wouldn't be for long in this weather. But she couldn't stand to hear anyone say it, including herself. "I can't think about that. I just can't."

Beth raised her own light to May's face. "Okay."

"She has to be all right. I don't know what I'd do . . ."

Beth nodded. "Then let's keep going."

❧

Christy wasn't afraid anymore, even though her limbs were stiffening and she was still in the middle of nowhere. It was like something had filled her so completely that there wasn't room for fear. Could that be peace?

Clouds were now visible moving across the sky. Then the huge smiling moon emerged and shone down on her. She closed her eyes. *Nice touch.*

What if Vince hadn't followed her after all? For all she knew, he was sitting warm and cozy in front of his fire back home.

Christy felt her consciousness drift. *No, stay awake!* She

tried to move her leg and a bolt of fire shot up to her waist. Staying quiet would kill her too. What if she called just once more? Once would be all she could muster anyway.

It would hurt. She struggled to form the words through her thick, numb lips. "Someone help me!"

She listened, but there was nothing, and unconsciousness quickly blacked out her pain.

❧

May abruptly turned in her saddle.

"What?" Beth said.

"You hear that?"

"No, what?"

"I thought . . ." Was her mind playing tricks on her?

Her mount let out a startled whinny, and she caught movement in the brush beside them. They both swung their flashlights around at the same time, only to catch a flash of gray fur.

"Coyote," Beth said.

"Yeah." But May thought for sure she'd heard something else.

21

CHRISTY OPENED HER eyes, but it made no difference. The moon was gone. What was that noise? Where was she? Maybe this was just a dream. . . . *Wake up.* . . .

Her eyes sealed shut. She wasn't shivering as much now. She would sleep for just a little while longer.

❧

May's heart battered her ribs as she kept her horse walking. Had she imagined Chris calling?

"It was a coyote," Beth said.

"Didn't sound like one." She called her sister's name again and listened for a response.

The radio crackled. It was Jim reporting his and Ruth's location.

"We're nearing Squatter's," May said. "Guys, I'm sure I heard something."

⁂

Vince chuckled. That was definitely a voice. He threw his cigar into a drift and trudged forward up the trail. Thrusting a hand inside his jacket, he felt for the pistol, his fingers tingling with anticipation. He could feel Christy's presence. Just a little more moonlight was all he needed.

⁂

"Beth, let's pray."

They'd reached the trailhead and heard only an occasional wind gust, but the uneasiness wouldn't leave May. Both of them stopped their horses.

Beth veered her flashlight up through the trees. "Wisdom, Lord. We need Your guidance."

Call her again.

The thought was clear, and May wasn't about to ignore it. "Chris! Are you up there?"

Silence.

"I know it's dangerous." May spoke into the radio. She was trying to convince Jim they had to start climbing Squatter's Mountain immediately. "But we won't take the horses."

"At least wait for us to meet you."

"We can't wait."

Jim protested further, but May had already made up her mind. "I'll keep in contact," she said and reclipped the radio to her coat, turning down the volume so she could barely hear his objections. Normally she wouldn't rebel against Jim's seasoned judgment, but this time she had to. She'd never been so sure of anything.

"Let's go," she said to Beth, dismounting.

Beth yanked the blanket roll from the back of her saddle as May aimed her light into the woods. The forest was in constant motion from the wind, and every shadow looked like a body. She started up.

"Hold on. Hold on," Beth said, lifting a hand. "Shh. Listen."

Swishing. A snort.

"Whose—?"

A shrill whinny shattered the silence. Both of their flashlights lit the spot it had come from, a few paces away. Nugget stared back at them, her reins wrapped around the trunk of a small sapling. It took only a second for May to realize what that meant.

"Chris!" she yelled and raced up the trail. She kept calling Chris's name and swinging her dimming flashlight beam back and forth as each step brought her to a higher altitude and closer to exhaustion. Her thighs and lungs begged her to stop or at least slow down, but she couldn't. Beth was calling just as loudly and managing to keep up.

May stopped for a moment, gasping and swinging her light among the trees off the trail. First she searched close, then slowly moved the beam outward to cover every inch. At each turn she expected to face that guy named Vince. What if he really was out here? That was a risk she had to take.

They came to the part of the trail they called Judgment Coulee. It was the steepest section, a hard climb even in good weather, and the left side of the trail dropped off into a small coulee, or ravine.

When her beam passed over the dark heap at the bottom, she almost missed it.

"There!" Beth grabbed her arm and fixed her light at the base of one more towering pine down below.

They both took one look and bolted.

May reached the body first, falling to her knees. It was Chris. She wasn't moving. Her eyes were closed, her mouth gaping. "No . . . please."

Christy groaned.

"Oh, thank You, God. Thank You." May stroked her sister's face. Chris reeked of vomit and blood, but May hardly smelled it. "Chris, we're here."

"Don't move her." Beth arrived and knelt beside May, running her flashlight beam over Chris's body, then focused the light on her ankle. There was the ragged edge of bone, and the snow beneath the leg was crimson.

Beth sprang into action and snatched the radio from May's coat. She called to the others, giving instructions to her parents about what medical supplies to bring. "We're going to need the backboard, more blankets, bandages. She's hurt pretty bad and in shock. Over." Beth handed May her blanket. "Try to get her warm without lifting or moving her. If you can, get it up to her neck. She's hypothermic by now."

As May did as she was told, Beth reported into the radio, "We're at the bottom of Judgment Coulee on Squatter's Mountain. Contact us when you're near. I'll meet you at the trailhead."

May looked down at her sister's bruised and bloodied face. She wanted to hold her, draw her close, and let her know everything would be okay, but they had internal injuries to think about.

Chris's eyes fluttered open.

"Hey, Sis," May said.

At first there was no recognition. Chris stared at May blankly, her blue lips moving like she was trying to say something. Her eyes closed, then after a moment opened again. "I'm . . . sorry," she said, barely loud enough for May to hear.

May held up her hand. "Don't worry. Nothing matters except getting you out of here."

Beth leaned toward Chris. "Where do you hurt?"

"Ankle."

"Anywhere else?"

Chris's face contorted. "Head."

May pulled the blanket up to her sister's chin. The cruel wind tore through the ravine, and she wished she could shield her sister from it.

"I thought I'd lost you," May said, starting to choke up. Back there when she'd wavered, when fear threatened to wash her faith away, she *had* doubted God. But He'd still come through for her. He'd still spoken to her and made sure she and Chris would have another chance to reconcile.

An eternity passed as they waited for the others and tried to keep Chris warm. When the radio came to life, it was Sam, who said they were nearing the trail.

"I'll go down and show them the way," Beth said, handing the radio to May.

"More help's coming," she said.

Chris's forehead wrinkled in agony. "It's my . . . fault."

"Shh." May took off her glove and touched her sister's blood-streaked cheek. It felt like ice. "Don't worry."

It seemed like hours before May saw flashlights bobbing up the mountainside toward them. "Down here!" she called, waving her own light.

Beth led the group. Peggy and Ruth followed, carrying blankets and first aid supplies. Jim and Sam brought up the rear with a sheet of plywood.

"Keith and Jan are up in the top pasture," Jim said. "They'll meet us at the house."

"She okay?" Beth asked, returning to May's side.

"She's drifting in and out." May squeezed Chris's hand. "We're gonna have to move you."

Sam knelt beside his daughter and hunched over Chris's leg and ankle, examining it like Beth had, with the care and precision of a man well accustomed to examining wounds. "Sweetheart, I'm going to put a splint on you so we can get you to the hospital."

Jim handed him a couple of two-by-fours, and Sam laid them on either side of Chris's leg. At his touch Chris cried out, and May could barely stand to hear it.

They used the plywood as a backboard and as carefully as possible slid Christy onto it, securing her with rope. What came next would be the challenge: carrying her up the ravine and down Squatter's Mountain.

May gave her sister another stroke on the cheek. "Ready?"

Chris managed to nod.

They took it three to a side, May and Jim right across from each other at Chris's head.

When Chris saw Jim, she tried to say something to him. "Is . . . did Vince . . . ?"

May perked up at the question, and she and Jim made eye contact. Had Chris seen that guy today after all?

"What about him?" May asked, but Chris couldn't rally a response.

It took two hours of slippery, treacherous creeping before they made it to the bottom of the mountain, where Sam and Peggy's Suburban and May and Beth's horses waited.

They hoisted the makeshift stretcher into the back of the Suburban, and May jumped in beside it. She covered Chris with more blankets as Beth, Sam, Peggy, and Ruth hurriedly piled in. Jim offered to bring back the horses.

May reached for her sister's hand and held it firmly in her own as they rumbled forward. "Hang on. You can do it."

But Chris gave no indication she heard. She'd stopped responding to their voices a while ago and lay still and lifeless.

It was another thirty minutes before they made it back to the ranch, and her condition hadn't improved.

Sam revved the engine, and they started down the drive toward the Spanish Peaks Regional Medical Center, in this weather another forty minutes away. As they passed the barn, May glanced at where they'd found the Blazer earlier that afternoon.

It was gone, and waiting at the gate was Nugget.

22

HUNTER SAT ALONE in the darkness, his eyes dry and begging for sleep. He'd nodded off once or twice already, and he could barely keep awake now. He'd been sitting here all night, waiting. His back was stiff, his body aching. Dawn was near.

When he heard the car, he was instantly alert. The garage door rumbled. Someone was coming. He froze.

A car door clapped shut. The door to the house squeaked open.

Hunter felt himself stiffen and tried to resist it. *Stay calm. Stay cool.*

Footsteps edged toward him.

This was the moment he'd been waiting for. Into the black study stepped a man. His silhouette was all Hunter could see. In one second the man would be getting a surprise.

Vince turned on the light.

"Nice place you have," Hunter said.

The look on Vince's face was worth it all. He whirled toward Hunter, eyes wide, mouth open.

Hunter immediately noticed the bruise on the side of Vince's head that hadn't been there two days ago. He leaned back nonchalantly in the white leather chair he occupied near the fireplace as if it were perfectly normal for him to be here.

"What are you doing in my house?" Vince was still in his coat, a parka Hunter had never seen before, looking tired, drained, and mad.

"You have some beautiful books, too." Cat and mouse. He had to put Vince on the defensive.

Vince's gaze shot to the shelves, then quickly came back to rest on Hunter. His eyes fell on the book in Hunter's lap.

Hunter waited a moment, then calculatingly picked up the book and paged through it. It was *For Whom the Bell Tolls*, and he wanted Vince to see that clearly.

"Answer me! How did you get in my house?"

He didn't tell him it was luck that Abby's old key still worked or that he'd brought along a crowbar as backup. "Was time I came for a visit. I wanted to chat with you."

"About *what*?"

"Maybe we could start with this." Hunter held up the Hemingway as he stood. "Where'd you get it?"

"You broke into my house to talk about a stupid book?"

"It's a very important book, and I think you know that."

"You're crazy," Vince said with a chuckle, doing a bad job of appearing at ease. His right hand was a balled-up fist. "And I know what you're thinking."

"What am I thinking?"

"That you've got me."

"Do I?"

When Vince spoke, his voice was deep. "You can't prove anything."

"Then what's this?" Hunter held up the book again. "Good enough for me. I know for a fact this book was stolen from the store, and here it is in your house."

Vince came toward him, and Hunter sized him up. They were almost the same height and build, but he was pretty sure he could defend himself if it came to that. He was quick, and chopping two cords of wood a week made him strong enough to easily take care of himself against a guy like Vince.

When they stood eye to eye, Vince laughed. "You think this little book is proof?" He grabbed it from Hunter's hand, and before Hunter could react, he ripped it in half down the spine. The sound of the tearing cloth was painful to Hunter, but he kept from flinching as Vince plucked out the title page with Hemingway's signature, waved it at him, then shredded it too.

"Proof?" Vince threw the pieces into the fireplace, where they sent up a puff of soot. "I don't see any proof."

"I had a feeling you'd do that."

Vince shoved him in the chest. "Get out of my house."

He stood his ground.

"Did you hear me, or are you as much of a moron as I've always thought?"

"Why'd you plant that book in Christy's car?"

"She got what was coming to her, and you're just jealous anyway." Vince grabbed the front of Hunter's shirt. "Get this straight right now. You don't have a thing on me."

Hunter deliberately waited to speak and placidly wrapped his fingers around Vince's hand, squeezing harder than Vince could have imagined him capable of. Harder. Vince managed to hide the pain Hunter knew he was inflicting. Had to give him credit for that. Harder. They stared each other down, Hunter boring his eyes into Vince's, never breaking the stare, as if they were two wolves challenging each other in the wild.

"I should've believed Christy," Hunter said.

Vince let him go and backed toward his desk. "You're too stupid to understand." He slowly eased into the chair behind his computer. "And so is your father. End of story."

Hunter seethed, and he couldn't quell his feelings any longer. Squeezing Vince's hand had somehow opened the door to his pent-up disgust for the man. His neck burned as he leaned into the desk with both hands, returning Vince's glare. "Actually, it's just the beginning."

Vince held a taunting grin. In one smooth motion he pulled a revolver out of his jacket, aiming it at Hunter's forehead.

Hunter didn't move. He'd known coming here alone had been foolish, but he'd chosen to override caution to prove Vince was the thief. While he'd expected some trouble, he hadn't expected this. "Shoot me and you'll regret it the rest of your life," he said, hoping there was still some sanity left in Vince.

"Get. Out."

Hunter leaned in closer. It took all his resolve to keep from punching Vince, gun or not. "If you ever touch Christy again—"

"Now!"

He knew he'd gotten all he was going to get. But it was enough. What Vince didn't know was that carefully stashed in his trunk was the real stolen first edition he'd found on the study shelves long before Vince arrived. The copy Vince tore up had been the decoy.

And only when he was safely back in his car did Hunter turn off the handheld recorder in his pocket.

❧

Christy gradually realized she was lying in a hospital room. She had no memory of arriving or how long she'd been here.

Daylight slipped through the slats of the drawn window blinds. She wasn't in her clothes anymore but a hospital gown. She touched her head with her fingers and felt gauze, not bloody flesh. An IV was taped to her hand. Very carefully, she tried to move her leg, but the lower half was immobile, in a cast. There was less pain than she'd felt on the mountain. Just a nice headache and a dull throbbing in her ankle remained. She could feel her warm blood coursing through her body. Lying still, she thought about that for a long time. A few days ago she would have been disappointed. Today she wanted to live.

Then she noticed the cot against the wall under the window. May lay sprawled on it, asleep. She was covered with a thin blanket, her coat piled on top, and her arm hung over the edge. Christy watched her sister sleep. How could she have put her through so much?

Eventually May stirred. Seeing Christy awake and staring back, she threw aside her covers and slid into a chair at the bedside, barely awake.

"Hi," Christy said, her voice hoarse.

May smiled, and it made Christy want to cry. After all she'd done, there was still love in May's face. Nothing else. No anger or disapproval. No hidden agenda in her smile. Genuine love. And she'd done nothing to deserve it.

Christy tried to smile back.

May rested her hand on Christy's. "How're you feeling?"

"Better, thanks to you."

"Your temperature was 89 degrees. It was a good thing we found you when we did. They took you into surgery last night after warming you up, and five screws went into that ankle."

"Can I walk?"

"With crutches for a while. There's some frostbite on your toes, and you had a concussion, but they say you should make a full recovery."

Christy feared the answer to her next question. "Is your horse okay?" Before May could respond, she added, "I had no right to take him without asking."

"He did better than you," May said. "Only a few scratches. Don't worry about feeling sorry, okay? It's really all right. I'm just glad you're alive. We almost lost you."

Christy knew the time had come to throw everything out in the open, but knowing was always easier than doing. She wasn't sure where to start. "Something happened to me up there," she said, stringing the words together as they came. If she took any time pondering how to spill her heart, she was sure she'd chicken out like she usually did when faced with doing something right.

"I was thinking about what you said to me about God, what all of you have said, and I want you to know I made it right with Him. Now I want to make it right with you." Christy shifted in the bed and touched May's arm. "Little sister, it's time I was honest with you."

May looked down at the sheets.

"When Mom and Dad died, I blamed myself. The only reason they were coming home early was for me. I can still see those officers at the door telling me they were gone." The memory choked her up even now, but she had to get the rest out. "I'm not saying that to excuse what I did. I realize now how much I hurt you by leaving. And I can't tell you how sorry I am for that."

May lifted her head, her eyes teary.

Christy grabbed hold of her hand, wanting her to know she meant every word. "I never hated you. It was never your fault. I was a selfish, rebellious teenager." She felt her own eyes tear up. "I couldn't take it. I ran off with Kyle. Remember him? I thought we were in love, but only I was. When I got pregnant, he ditched me."

She let go of her sister's hand for a second. She remembered begging Kyle to marry her, but he wouldn't hear of it. He'd stopped answering her phone calls, and she'd caved under the pressure, thinking getting rid of the "problem" would win him back. It hadn't.

"The other night when we pulled that dead calf, I told you I killed someone." Christy sniffed. "Well, I . . . I did."

She saw the surprise on May's face and could barely keep talking. "I had an abortion, and I've never been able to forgive myself. They told me it was just a blob of tissue, but . . . I saw." Christy stopped and let the tears run down her cheeks. "I *saw*."

It took Christy a moment to be able to speak again, but May let her take her time.

"The only way I could ease the pain," Christy finally continued, "was when I drank."

May spoke quietly. "Even after seeing what it did to Mom and Dad?"

"All I cared about was easing the guilt. And, temporarily, it always did. But it never lasted." Christy closed her eyes and longed for a drink even as she spoke. It would help her find the right words and speak her thoughts clearly. Yet somewhere deep inside a small impression whispered that she could do better without alcohol in her life.

May squeezed Christy's hand. That gesture gave her the strength to keep talking. "I've regretted what I did to you and my baby every single day. I was ashamed to come back. I didn't want you, Aunt Edna, or anyone else to see the mess I'd made of my life. I didn't think you'd want anything to do with me."

"Oh, Chris. That never was true."

"I should've explained, but I wasn't ready to let anyone in my world." A part of her still wasn't ready. The part that urged her to stop right here and let May believe better of her. She overrode it. Because as each truth poured out of her, she felt a new inner strength encouraging her to keep going.

"What about that guy, Vince?"

Defensiveness came immediately, and she felt herself recoil. How did May know about him?

"We found his car behind the barn when we came back from church," May explained. "But it was gone when we got back with you from the mountain."

"What about him?" Christy said, then caught herself. She couldn't close up now. She had to quit that with May. More than once her sister had proved she'd accept her just as she was. And there was still more to reveal. She reminded herself that telling May all this had been her idea.

"We lived together. He was good to me at first, but after a few months he started getting violent. I paid the price, and then I left him. He's been trying to get me to come back ever since." She licked her cracked lips. "He followed me to the ranch." She wasn't sure she could tell May the rest. But she had to. "He tried to kill me."

Shock filled May's face. "Kill you?"

"He showed up right before I went riding. But I escaped on Spirit." Christy talked quickly now, afraid if she stopped she'd never start again. "Here's another thing I wasn't truthful about. I told you I work at a used bookstore. I did. But because they found out about some shady stuff I did a long time ago, I was let go."

She told May how she almost went along with Vince's plan to steal more valuable books from the Barn and about Vince framing her with the Hemingway. But when she got to her apartment fire, she balked. She didn't want May to think she'd only come to see her because she was homeless. She made herself continue. "Vince set fire to my apartment because I wouldn't do what he wanted. It was completely destroyed. All my stuff is gone. Even Aunt Edna's books."

Christy didn't allow May to respond until she got the rest out. "That's partly why I came here. But I'd been wanting to come anyway. I was just so afraid to face you."

She waited for May's response, half expecting now to be the time of rejection.

"I'm glad you came," May said.

"Would you believe me if I said I am too?"

May stood up and hugged her, and this time Christy hugged back without hesitation.

"I love you," May said and then started crying, burying her face in Christy's shoulder.

Christy held her. "I love you too."

They remained like that for several moments. When they let each other go, something was different. Every last vestige of the wall Christy had built up between herself and May was razed with that one hug. For even though May knew everything, she still loved her. And in that moment Christy knew for sure God did too.

❧

Hunter pressed the Stop button on his handheld recorder.

Pop rubbed the side of his face and shifted in his chair. "Christy had nothing to do with any of it?"

"No." Hunter picked up the recorder. "It was all Vince."

"What about the deal with Fletcher? How could we ever trust her again?"

"Pop, that was a long time ago."

"True." His father let out a long breath. "But she could've told us what Vince was doing."

Hunter fingered the player. "You heard how he threatened me. And you saw how he treated Abby."

Pop sighed and nodded. There was real regret on his face. "I wish I could redo some things."

"We can do something now." Hunter slid the player across the desk surface.

Pop caught it. He leaned forward and grinned at him. "So tell me, what are our plans?"

❧

The next day Harvey surprised Christy with a hospital visit. May had just left to get something to eat in the cafeteria when Christy heard a knock and his familiar voice announce, "Room service!"

He stepped into the room dressed in jeans and a polo shirt, carrying an armful of flowers and his briefcase. The ever-dutiful lawyer. "How's our patient doing?" he said, stooping to kiss her forehead.

She hugged him as best she could from the bed.

"May called and told me what happened," Harvey said.

"Should be out in a few more days."

Harvey rumpled her hair like she was a kid again. "How's the pain?"

"They've got me doped up."

"Next time you start hankering for a scenic horseback ride, you might consider taking a few more lessons."

She laughed. "Agreed."

He sat down and rested his hands on the bed rail. "What did the doctors say?"

"Six weeks of crutches. No weight on it, lots of therapy. Tons of fun." Christy decided to hint at some of what she'd shared with May. "A lot's happened."

Harvey's face went grim. "I know about the fire. Found out when I went to see you a few days ago. I hope you don't mind, but when I couldn't get in touch, I went looking for you at work. I met Hunter Dawson at the bookstore, and we got to talking, sort of comparing notes. He was as concerned about you as I was, and he shared with me some of the things that have been going on in your life."

Christy felt her walls going up. She wrestled to stay open. "I guess he told you I was fired?"

"Not in so many words. But he also shared the circumstances of why it happened. That book going missing and all."

"He thinks I stole it."

Harvey tilted his head slightly. "Not exactly."

"He found it in my car."

"Yes."

"I didn't put it there. I hope you can believe me."

"I do, and Hunter wanted to." Harvey picked up her hand. "He told me about Vince."

She took a deep breath. It had been hard to admit her failures to May, and it was no easier with Harvey. "I wish I'd never met him."

"If only I could've helped you sooner."

"I was an idiot."

"He's a loser. What he did wasn't your fault."

She wasn't so sure but let him go on.

"Your friend Hunter and I decided to look into things together. When I found out your apartment burned, I got worried. That's when Hunter discovered that book in your car was a fake."

Christy tried to sit up. "What?"

"I didn't know exactly what he meant, but he explained how the dust jacket had the photographer's name on the back."

She thought out loud. "Making it a second state rather than a first."

"That's what he said."

Her mind whirred as she thought back to when she and Hunter stood outside her car. She'd seen it with her own eyes, but neither of them had checked the dust jacket. "What about the signature? I saw that myself."

"Forged."

Vince *would* be clever enough.

"We suspected Vince, but Hunter found out for sure. Went to his house looking." Harvey smiled. "He tells me he beat Vince at his own game by pretending to find the real book there. Apparently Vince all but admitted to being the crook, and Hunter got it on tape."

"He went to his house?" Christy could still remember the

rage in Vince's eyes when he'd attacked her in the barn. She wouldn't have been able to forgive herself if Vince had hurt Hunter.

"He really went to bat for you," Harvey said.

"Where's Vince now?"

"We don't know."

Her heart sank. "He's been following me." She told Harvey everything from how she thought Vince set the fire to him beating her up in the barn.

When she finished, Harvey looked like he'd been beaten himself. "Have you spoken with the police?"

"I haven't decided what to do."

Harvey held her hand in both of his. "We're going to put an end to this. I promise I'll help in any way I can."

"This time I'll let you." Christy squeezed his fingers. More people cared about her than she ever imagined.

"I was going to talk to you about Aunt Edna's estate," Harvey said. "But maybe we should wait for a better time."

"Actually, I'd like the distraction."

He hesitated, then opened his briefcase and pulled out some papers. "Are you sure? I need you to sign a few things."

"Just show me where."

He did, and while she read some of it, she felt it was finally okay to ask when the money would come. It would be just what she needed to get back on her feet.

"It really depends," Harvey said. "I'm trying to hurry through probate as much as I can for you two."

She went out on a limb. "You do know about the financial difficulties May's having, don't you?"

"Yes."

"Will she have enough now to save the ranch?"

"I'm afraid not."

Christy blew out a long breath. "You're the lawyer. Can't *anything* be done?"

"They're meeting one more time to beg for an extension, but it doesn't look like they'll get it. If not, it's really only a matter of time."

"She loves that place," Christy said. She'd witnessed first-hand what it meant to May. It was her future, her passion, her dream. Almost her existence. She would have nothing without it.

"I wish I could do something. I've called everyone I know, but that bank is sticking to their guns." Harvey handed her a pen. "Ready to sign those?"

She ruffled through the pages some more. Everything looked in order. She took the lid off his gold-nibbed pen and stared at it in her fingers.

"Problem?"

"No, no. The papers look fine. It's . . . I need to think about this."

❧

Two days later the hospital released Christy. She and May chatted the whole way back to the ranch. Nothing profound, but that didn't matter. Every conversation was a chance for Christy to get to know May again—her likes, dislikes, opinions. She loved every minute of it.

After settling Christy on the sofa, May left the ranch house for a few minutes to check the cattle. Christy tried to relax into the pillows propped behind her but instead kept fidgeting, unable to get comfortable.

Her body screamed for a drink, and she didn't know what to do about it. The painkillers she was taking didn't seem to help her cravings at all. For years, whenever she'd felt lonely or worried, alcohol had been her constant friend, always there, ready to offer comfort. Her first instinct was to find a glass and fill it. She'd had no choice about staying dry in the hospital, but now the only thing keeping her from that bottle of vodka in her car was her stupid cast.

Her inner war was still raging when she heard Jim enter the house. Did she have the courage to talk to him about it? "Jim?"

He poked his head into the living room, once again wearing worn and dirty coveralls like he had the day he found her snooping around. "Need anything?"

Christy hadn't spoken with him alone since the day of her accident, when he'd convinced her to go to church. "I need to talk to you," she said, clueless what she was going to say. But the urge to drink was becoming so strong she knew if she didn't get help soon, she would be finishing that vodka today, if she had to crawl out there to get it.

"Sure. What about?"

"I don't know how to say this. But I remember you telling me you used to drink." None of this would be easy to put into words, but she had to try. She wanted to do what was right. She wanted to honor God with her life, but she didn't know how. "Don't you ever want to drink anymore?"

Jim sat down on the sofa beside her. "Yeah, sometimes. But not as much as I used to."

"What do you do?"

He took a moment to answer, his eyes focused on the coffee table. Maybe she was being too nosy. "Honestly, I had a tough time in the beginning. Messed up more than once. Then a good friend gave me some advice. First, I needed to get myself to some sort of recovery group. Pronto. Then second, when I felt the need to drink, I should pray until the urge passed."

"And it worked?"

"For me."

"What if you don't know how to pray?"

"You just talk to God. It's nothing fancy."

Christy studied her cast. She'd hoped things would automatically be different. What she'd felt up on the mountain, that peace, was real. She knew that. The massive weight of all the guilt and shame she'd lugged around for fifteen years had beautifully lifted. So she was surprised to still have the same desires, the same addictions.

"I can't tell you how much I want a drink right now," she said, almost under her breath, not sure what Jim would think.

He sat quietly, just listening.

"I want to do the right thing, but I don't know if I can. I've been this way for so long."

"Christy," Jim said, and she tuned in to him. What he had to say meant so much right now. "The Bible says the Lord won't let you be tempted beyond what you can bear. You can be sure that any craving, any desire, can be overcome with His help. You just have to walk it out, day by day, trusting He'll help you. I know. I've been there."

She rubbed her forehead with both hands. "Guess you have."

"It'll be hard at first. I can't promise you a walk in the park. But I've been sober for almost ten years, and I'll tell you, it's worth it. Yeah, sometimes life'll throw you a punch. You wanna drink because that's what you've always done before. What do you do right then? Pray. Ask God to help you. Call someone like May or me. Join a group, maybe something at a church."

Christy took a deep breath. Pray. She'd have to be doing a lot of that. "The keys to my car are on the kitchen counter. There's a bottle of vodka under the passenger seat and a bottle of sherry in my suitcase. I'd appreciate it if you would get rid of them for me."

23

CHRISTY COULDN'T SLEEP. After hours of trying, she finally gave up and crept into the kitchen as quietly as she could with her crutches and cast. After filling a mug with coffee— she'd tripled her consumption since going cold turkey—she hobbled to the table with her steaming cup and sat in the dimness, the appliance bulb over the stove the only light.

Five days had passed since she'd come home from the hospital, and gone was the strain between her and May. Sure, they'd still managed to get on each other's nerves a few times, like when Christy tried to make herself useful by straightening up May's room and her sister had practically bitten her head off for it. But they'd agreed to talk things out now instead of holding in their feelings. It was new territory, but they both welcomed it.

Christy was only now starting to understand what changed in their relationship. Just being May's sister hadn't kept her from leaving fifteen years ago. It hadn't even given her the nerve to tell the truth. But now they had a bond even thicker than blood. Everything had changed up on that mountain. Somehow God's love for both of them had accomplished something their blood ties never had. May was no longer a religious enigma. She was a beautiful Christian woman Christy wanted to emulate.

Almost every evening they'd spent together sitting around the stove, talking and sharing. Sometimes Ruth joined them. She had a calm wisdom that made Christy want to sit at the older woman's feet just to hear her talk. A couple of times May got out her Bible and read a few passages, which they discussed. The whole book was full of new concepts to Christy, but May and Ruth were always patient. So was Jim. She'd had a few more lengthy conversations with him since her first day back. He'd even prayed with her. Christy felt like she could call them all friends. They'd seen her at her worst, and amazingly they still cared.

Last night Beth had come over. At first, Christy was unsure how that was going to work. She knew May and

Beth were close friends, and now that she was feeling closer to May herself, she didn't want to be jealous of their friendship anymore. Her concern hadn't been necessary. Beth joked with May just the same as before but readily included Christy in it too.

Christy slurped at her brew. She would've stayed on crutches for the rest of her life if it meant she could remain at the ranch. But she knew she couldn't. There were still things that needed to be resolved back home. Her arraignment for the drunk-driving charge was coming up at the end of the month. She'd decided to plead guilty and pay whatever price came—community service, probation, fines. They would be a reminder of who she'd been a short time ago and how she'd changed.

Even though she didn't feel much different now, she was sure what happened to her on Squatter's Mountain had been real. May helped her understand that. What changed that night was her heart. The inside. The hunger for her old ways would dissipate over time, with God's help, as she grew stronger in her faith.

She hadn't been able to quit smoking yet. One thing at a time. But she hadn't had one drink, which was a huge boost to her self-esteem. She'd actually succeeded at tightening her belt and taking the honorable path, something she knew she could never have done without her newfound faith. And she planned to take Jim's advice and seek out professional treatment too. She knew there was no way she could keep this up on her own. She needed the accountability.

A long talk with Hunter was due. She couldn't expect to get her job back, but she wanted to be as honest with him as she'd been with May. He'd believed in her when she hadn't believed in herself. He'd even risked his life for her. It was the least she could do.

And she had another appointment to keep as well.

Christy finished her coffee in silent reflection. Whether she liked it or not, tomorrow she'd be leaving this sanctuary.

❧

After a hearty farewell breakfast made especially for Christy, the two sisters stood at the corral fence together and took in the view, indulging in its beauty. The blizzard had cleared days ago, leaving in its wake a sparkling, snow-covered world. The mountains stood sharp, their tops cutting at the blue sky. Both women were working hard to keep it together.

"Now I understand why you moved out here," Christy said.

"Never knew it would become such a part of me." May kept her eyes focused on the mountains.

Christy knew what she was thinking. The bank hadn't agreed to an extension, and she admired her sister's strength at controlling her emotions. "It's gonna be okay. God hasn't forgotten you. I know it."

May put her arm around Christy. "Thanks, Sis."

Spirit sauntered toward them, hanging his huge gray head over the fence right beside Christy. "Hey, boy." She stroked his nose. "Forgive me for that wild ride I took you on?"

The horse nuzzled her jacket and May laughed. "Forgiven and forgotten," she voiced for him. "Now give me a carrot."

They spent several aimless minutes petting the horse, putting off the inevitable.

"This is a lot harder than I thought," May said. "I was just getting used to having you around."

"I'll be back. I promise."

May gave her a big hug.

"Don't cry," Christy said, "or you'll make me."

"There's something I want to give you." May let her go and pulled a worn leather book out of her jacket. She handed it to her. "I want you to have this."

Christy took it and instantly knew it was May's Bible. She eyed May incredulously. "I can't take this. Aunt Edna . . . she gave it to you."

"I want you to have it."

Christy held the book to her chest. It was highlighted, underlined, and dog-eared. A priceless treasure to May. "You've been so good to me," she said softly.

"I wrote a verse inside."

Christy opened the cover and read Aunt Edna's inscription to May, a sweet paragraph about her love and May's baptism. Beneath that in fresh ink was Ephesians 2:12-13. "Remember that at that time you were separate from Christ . . . without hope and without God in the world. But now in Christ Jesus you who once were far away have been brought near through the blood of Christ."

She looked at May, hoping her face was showing how touched she was.

"Auntie would be proud of you. Like I am." May wiped at her eyes. "Let's go get your suitcase."

They took their time walking back to the house, and May kept her hand on Christy's arm in case her crutches slipped. Jim had plowed the yard before leaving for town to pick up some fence posts, but there were still icy patches. She'd already said good-bye to him and to Ruth, who was off feeding the cattle with Scribbles.

May swung open the back door and they both stepped inside, the country station playing quietly from the kitchen radio. "Are you sure you're going to be able to drive with that thing on your foot?"

"Oh, definitely," she said. "I've already sat in the driver's seat and tried it out. I can completely bend my knee, so it's no problem. The hardest part is getting in and out."

May picked Christy's car keys off the counter and held them up. "I'll go warm up your car, then."

"Don't worry about it."

"Just take a minute."

She shrugged, and May disappeared out the door.

More than anything Christy wished she could stay. After so many years of emptiness, she felt like a parched sponge soaking up the love and acceptance May and her friends lavished on her. She wanted to bask in it, but she couldn't. Not yet anyway. Too much remained undone back home.

Christy hobbled across the floor. That's when Vince stepped into the kitchen through the living room doorway. She jumped back and stifled a scream.

He trained his pistol on her face and slid closer. His hair was a greasy, matted-down mess, and several days' growth of beard stuck out of his face. She recognized the wrinkled and untucked shirt he wore as one of his dress oxfords.

Christy prodded herself to breathe, keenly aware of the door at her back. Escape would be impossible with her bum ankle.

They stared at each other for what felt like hours. Why was she just standing there? She had to do something! But she was frozen. She couldn't make herself speak or run.

Sweat beaded on Vince's forehead, and she watched a drop glide into his eyebrows. Could she use a crutch to knock the gun out of his hand? Should she scream?

The perky DJ on the radio declared, "It's shaping up to be a beautiful morning. Clear, cool, and sunny. Now here's a classic from Mr. Randy Travis on KSPK, southern Colorado's best country."

"They wrecked my house," Vince said in a slow, deliberate tone barely over the first notes of "Deeper than the Holler." "And it's all your fault."

Christy found her voice but couldn't keep it steady. "What . . . did I do?"

"If you'd only listened," Vince said louder. "Why doesn't anyone listen to me?"

What if she kicked him with her good leg? Would the gun go off?

"They took my books."

He was standing so close she could smell his rank hair. If only she could get the upper hand. "Who?"

"I deserved them." His vein-streaked eyes widened. "They had no right to take them from me! And I can't go back there now. Everything's a wreck 'cause of your big mouth."

"Vince, I—"

"I told you not to tell Hunter." He gripped the gun so hard that she saw his knuckle bones move under the skin. "But you had to open your trap."

"I didn't say anything."

"You two had this all planned, didn't you?"

"No, we—"

"Shut up!"

She backed off. It was a dangerous game speaking at all without knowing what would drive him over the edge. But if she didn't keep him talking, there would be no reason for him to keep her alive.

"Thought you could pull one over on me?" Vince cocked his head ever so slightly, egging her to answer.

She gripped her crutch handles to keep her sweaty palms from slipping. Silence. Something told her to let him vent.

He reached out and touched her face. "We fit together perfectly."

Christy bit her tongue to keep from snapping a response. His disoriented mind was leaping all over the place.

"We could've had a family. I loved you. You were mine."

One foot separated her from that gun. She could see the bullet poised in the cylinder. What would it feel like to be shot?

"You'll always be mine," Vince whispered, his fingers snaking down her neck.

She closed her eyes. It would be better to die fighting. She tensed, ready to swing her crutch.

Vince abruptly pulled his hand away. She opened her eyes to see him stiffen, his gaze locked on something behind her.

She dared a look herself.

May was walking across the yard, coming back to the kitchen.

Christy ground her teeth together, her protective instincts coming to life. "Don't you dare hurt her."

Any movement toward the door could set him off. Alone, she might have risked bolting, crutches and all, but with May out there . . . she couldn't.

Vince grabbed her chin and pulled her face toward his, forcing her to look him in the eyes. "Get rid of her." He hid his gun hand under his shirt. "Or she goes first."

She knew he was serious. May was almost at the door.

Christy turned around and rested her right crutch against the counter. She twisted the door handle. What could she do? She had to keep May away.

"Hey," she called out, trying to give her voice a normal lilt.

May reached the stoop. "Ready to go?"

"Um, not quite."

"Decided to stay?"

"No, I . . ." *Think. Think! Find an excuse.* "Remember that guy I told you about at the bookstore? Hunter?"

"Sure," May said, then looked past her shoulder.

Christy smiled but didn't move from blocking the door. "Well, he came to visit me."

May half returned her smile, and Christy couldn't tell if she was buying the story. Waving at Vince, May said hi to him.

He waved back and grinned cheerily.

"Would you mind giving us a few minutes alone?" Christy said. "We've got a lot to talk about." *Please go away.*

"Oh, I'd like to meet him," May said.

Christy tried to fill the doorway with her body. "Later, all right?"

May slowly nodded. "How long will you be?"

"I'll come get you."

"I guess I can check on the cows," May said. "Sure you're okay?"

"Positive. Thanks, May."

Her sister turned, and Christy watched her only chance of rescue walk away. But it didn't matter. She had to keep Vince from hurting May. Christy faced him again.

"Come here," he said, pulling out the gun again.

Christy knew if she wasn't close to him she'd have no chance to strike. She picked her crutch back up and obeyed.

Vince smirked. "Hunter?"

"You're not gonna get away with this."

He laughed in mock surprise. "I'm not?" But when his eyes locked on Christy, the sarcasm drained from his face.

She had to stall him. But for what? So he could murder May too? Jim wouldn't be back for hours, and she had no idea when Ruth would return either.

Suddenly, the kitchen door burst open. Christy jumped,

and Vince leveled the gun on May, who stood planted in the doorway, wielding an ax she held with both hands.

"So you're the little sister," Vince said.

"That's right," May said.

Tears stung Christy's eyes. "Why didn't you listen to me? I told you to leave!"

"Drop that thing outside and close the door," Vince said. "Try anything, and big sis's blood will be on your hands."

May glared at Vince, and Christy could see her lips tighten, but she did what he said, then leadenly walked toward Christy until she was standing beside her in the middle of the kitchen. Her hand constricted around Christy's arm.

"You'll go first," Vince said, like he was bestowing May a gift. "Then I'll have Christy all to myself."

"You aren't getting anyone today, buddy," May said.

Without warning, Vince whipped the pistol at May's head. It sank into her face, and May groaned, almost falling against Christy as she collapsed to her knees.

"No!" Christy threw down her crutches and reached for May. Her hands grazed May's shoulders before Vince kicked her casted leg so hard that the pain rocketed to her hip. She plunged backward, landing on her elbow. Scrambling, she forced herself to her feet, fire bursting through her ankle. Fear turned to rage, and she would've flown at Vince right then if he hadn't aimed for the center of May's chest.

"Stay back!" Vince said. "Or she's dead right now."

She stared into his eyes. They oozed hate. Why was he doing this? How could she save her sister? "You came for me, not her. She didn't do anything to you!"

Grabbing May's hair, Vince wrenched her to her feet. May was obviously dazed and couldn't fight back, and blood dripped on the linoleum from the gash in her cheek. Vince jammed the gun against May's temple and smiled at Christy.

"Vince, don't! Please! Shoot me instead. I'm what you want."

He threw May's head back with a yank of her hair and crushed the gun even tighter against her head, glaring at Christy. "What'ya gonna do now?"

Tears fell down Christy's face. He was hurting May to torture her, and it was working. She was powerless to stop him. May was pulling in breaths through her mouth, each a ragged wheeze. Christy would do anything to take her sister's place.

"Hear me?" Vince spat in May's face. "You can't have her. No one can!"

"I'll do whatever you want. Just let her go." Christy could face dying herself but not May. She couldn't watch him kill May.

Vince released May's hair, shoving her away. Her sister tumbled to the floor, and he turned on Christy. She faced down the silver barrel. It was shaking. *Keep it on me, Vince. On me. I'm not afraid to die.*

He didn't seem to notice May staggering to her feet.

"We were meant for each other," he said. "Nothing can change that."

Christy swallowed. "You're right. Only leave her out of this . . . darling." She choked on the last word and thought she saw Vince's countenance soften.

"Let's talk about this," she said gently. He had to think she was coming around to his way of thinking. *Get him to relax. Set the gun down.*

His lips curled up slowly, a faint smile.

She didn't allow herself a glance at May, who she sensed was waiting for an opportunity to strike. Christy focused solely on Vince.

"You can't live without me," Vince said, and something ruptured in his face. "I won't let you."

She knew then it was over. His finger twitched on the trigger.

That's when May rushed him.

The revolver exploded, and May was instantly wrestling with both hands to keep Vince's gun pointed at the floor. Just as fast, Vince clamped his free arm across May's throat, and her face contorted, turning beet red.

Christy sprang toward them, dragging her hurt leg. She

joined her hands with May's around Vince's gun arm, digging at his clenched fingers. If she could just pull one out of joint! Pain would compel him to let go.

May jammed her knee into Vince's crotch, and he buckled with a curse but held on to the pistol, a pit bull in a death grip.

"Get . . . gun," May gasped.

Frantically, Christy struggled to hold his arm down and grab a finger, but they were clamped around the gun barrel like a vise.

Another shot blasted through the room.

Stalemate. They were getting nowhere. She could struggle with May and hope his strength waned before theirs, or she could let go and find something to use as a club. Could she get that ax? What if he overcame her sister before she could find something? May's face was turning purple. She couldn't hold him back for long.

Go! Christy dived for the first thing she saw. Coffeepot. On. Hot. Full of coffee. Her hand flew to the handle, yanking the pot from its base. She lunged toward Vince, lifted the weapon, and brought it down on the back of his head.

The glass shattered, and boiling coffee spilled down Vince's neck. He dropped May with a howl, flailing at his back. His pistol clumped to the floor.

Another shot blasted through the room. There was a bizarre moment of stillness as the acrid smell of gun smoke spread through the air. Christy looked up to see Ruth standing in the living room doorway, a rifle in her hands.

"Get on the floor, and don't move a muscle." Ruth kept her rifle zeroed on Vince.

He turned toward Christy, a splotch of red quickly spreading across his shoulder. The hate in his eyes morphed into shock. He opened his mouth to speak, but no words came.

"On your face!"

Falling to the linoleum, he moaned something unintelligible.

May scooped up Vince's gun. She dropped it into the sink and hung over it, her shoulders shaking.

"You guys okay?" Ruth asked.

"Yeah," Christy managed. She limped over to May and held her. Like she should've done all those years ago.

❧

Harvey helped Christy into one of his cushy office chairs, and she let a moment pass before breaking the news. When she told him Vince was in jail, Harvey immediately barraged her with questions, and she smiled at his concern. Harvey had always been there for her. She'd just been too blind to see it.

It struck her that it had been the same with God. He'd been longing to help and protect her too, but until she took the first step, His hands were tied.

"Thanks for never giving up on me," she said, both to Harvey and in her heart to God.

Harvey cleared his throat.

She wouldn't hold him in suspense any longer. It had been three days since Vince attacked her and May, and she told Harvey all about it. Vince had first been taken to the hospital and treated for his minor gunshot wound, head lacerations, and the second-degree burns on his neck. Yesterday the doctor released him to the county sheriff.

"Needless to say," she concluded several minutes later, "I'm more than relieved."

Harvey whacked his palm against his thigh. "If I were a prosecutor, I'd give that creep one heck of a day in court."

She had to laugh.

"Well," Harvey said, seating himself behind his desk, "shall we move on to a happier note?"

"Gladly."

He peered at her over his reading glasses. "First, I want to make sure this is really what you want."

She took in the paperwork spread across the desktop, almost giddy with excitement over what she was about to do. "Definitely."

"And you understand you won't receive anything else?"

Christy met his caring eyes. "I know what I'm giving up. I want to do this."

He regarded her with a look she couldn't place. When he pulled a pen from his coat pocket and beamed at her, she realized it was approval. Then, with his secretary notarizing, Christy signed everything, including the statement:

I, Christy Williams, do hereby waive my rights as cobeneficiary of the financial portion of the estate of Ms. Edna Williams. It is my wish that my portion of the estate be inherited wholly by my only sibling, May Williams.

Signed,
Christy Williams

Capping the pen, she pictured the look on May's face when she found out the ranch could be saved. May's share alone hadn't been enough to pay what was owed, but the two shares combined covered it all. Harvey had already sent a letter to the bank stating that the full amount was forthcoming. He would let May know later today.

Christy couldn't remember a time in her life when she felt lighter.

Harvey surveyed her from across the desk. "It's wonderful to see you happy."

She was glad he noticed. "May trusted God to take care of her. I'm just so amazed He used me to do it." There was a lot more to share with him about her visit with May, but for the moment she left it at that.

"What are your plans?" Harvey asked.

Christy took up her crutches. "I have to take care of some things back home, but after that, everything's up in the air." Apparently her first lesson was going to be about trusting too. She still had nowhere to live and no job. But she'd seen what God could do. If He could take care of May, He could take care of her too. Surely He wouldn't have brought her this far to throw her out on the street.

"How about a place to stay?"

"Got a room at the Super 8."

Harvey shot her a surprised look. "Well, cancel it. You'll be needing a real home until you get back on your feet." He eyed her cast with an ill-concealed smile. "Literally. And I do believe I saw Betty making up the guest room today."

She smiled. "I'm there."

As Christy drove back to the motel for her suitcase, she reveled in the same peace she'd once envied in May. Somehow in the last couple weeks it had crept into her own heart, and it had nothing to do with her circumstances. Months would pass before she could walk normally again. She had only one credit card that wasn't maxed out. And there was still no promise of anything better in her future than a McJob at minimum wage. But despite all that, she was content. Even though she'd just given up more money than she'd ever dreamed of having, she knew she'd be okay.

Christy glanced at the passenger seat. Tucked in a manila envelope on top of May's Bible were copies of the papers she'd just signed. Smiling to herself, she hoped May was right about Aunt Edna being proud. She gave the car gas as the freeway spread before her like an invitation to a new life.

About the Author

C.J. BEGAN WRITING the story that would become *Thicker than Blood* when she was a fifteen-year-old homeschool student. She has been in the antiquarian bookselling business for over a decade, scouting for stores similar to the one described in *Thicker than Blood* before cofounding her own online bookstore. In 2006 C.J. started the Christian entertainment Web site www.TitleTrakk.com with her sister, Tracy, and has been actively promoting Christian fiction through book reviews and author interviews. She makes her home in Pennsylvania with her family and their menagerie of dogs and cats. Visit her Web site at www.cjdarlington.com.

Discussion Questions

If your book club reads *Thicker than Blood* and is interested in talking with me via speakerphone, please feel free to contact me by e-mail at cj@cjdarlington.com, and I'll do my best to arrange something with you. Thanks for reading, and you can always visit my Web site, www.cjdarlington.com, for more info.

1. Aunt Edna counsels May that God could be bringing Christy to her thoughts for a reason. Do you believe God often leads us through prompts like this? Where during the story do you see God prompting May?

2. How would you describe Christy and Hunter's relationship? Are they just friends or something more? Do you think their relationship will change after the events of the story? In what way?

3. What antiquarian book fact surprised you the most? Have you read any of the books Christy found in Aunt Edna's library?

4. What was your first impression of Vince? When did it change? Are there negative influences in your life that you need to leave behind?

5. Why do you think Christy goes to the funeral only to run away from it early? What is she running from and why?

6. Who was your favorite character in the story? Which one did you most relate to?

7. Talk about the relationship between Christy and Jim. How would you describe it? Why do you think he pushes Christy's buttons, and why does she respond the way she does?

8. Even though May says she forgave her sister years ago, do you think she really did? Why or why not? What causes May to change the way she thinks about Christy?

9. What is your favorite scene in the book? What makes that scene stand out for you?

10. Why do you think Christy has trouble believing God could love her? How did her perceptions about God change throughout the story? How have your ideas about God changed over time?

11. Which character do you think impacted Christy most for the Lord? What people in your life encourage you to grow closer to God?

12. What do you see as the theme of this novel? How does the title *Thicker than Blood* play out in the story?

13. How do you think May will react to Christy's final gesture toward her? What would that scene look like?

have you visited
tyndalefiction.com
lately?

Only there can you find:

↦ books hot off the press

↦ first chapter excerpts

↦ inside scoops on your favorite authors

↦ author interviews

↦ contests

↦ fun facts

↦ and much more!

Sign up for your **free** newsletter!

Visit us today at: **tyndalefiction.com**

Tyndale fiction does more than entertain.

↦ *It touches the heart.*

↦ *It stirs the soul.*

↦ *It changes lives.*

That's why Tyndale is so committed to being first in fiction!

TYNDALE FICTION

CP0021